Begr ι

CW00617610

# IN THE SHADOW OF

# HITLER

*Richard Vaughan Davies*

## RICHARD VAUGHAN DAVIES

Mortu  a  Marsl

Published by Mitford Oak Press

richard@vaughandavies.org
Facebook @RichardVaughanDavieswriter
website https://vaughandavies.org

ISBN: 978 1 999 31560 3

**Acknowledgments**     My grateful thanks are due to Barbara for her loyal support, to Linda O'Donnell and Alexander Vaughan Davies for their editing, to Alan Pollock for guidance, and to Derek Johnson for his technical assistance (and more.) Formatting advice by Dennis Hamley. Cover by Katie Gabriel Allen.

My German teacher at Malvern College, Oskar Konstandt, was my first inspiration, and I dedicate this book to his memory.

**Author's note**     I had Hamburg very much in mind as the setting for this novel, but I have changed place names such as streets to avoid historical confusion. My Austrian geography is equally imaginary, as are the details of the lives of any real people.

I am indebted to Keith Lowe's **"Inferno – the devastation of Hamburg, 1943."**

## Chipping-on-the-Fosse

The sun had already started to warm the flagged patio and the worn steps, burnishing the ancient Cotswold stone to an even deeper gold. The nearby picture postcard villages like Bourton on the Water and Chipping Campden would be full of tourists by now, sucking the scene into their smartphones as if fearful that it might vanish into thin air at any moment.

Apparently startled by the sight of a large jet airliner high above it, a tiny lizard disappeared into a crack in the stones in a flicker of green lightning. The plane had left a long vapour trail, like a child's scrawl on a drawing pad. Two very new Red Admirals fluttered around the lavender, and the big white buddleia was buzzing with flies and hornets. Pigeons cooed their little song to each other, and rooks were wheeling in the tall trees beyond the end of the garden, endlessly quarrelling among their nests. It was a perfect day in rural England.

Adam groaned aloud. Today should be cold and grey, he thought, staring through the old oak windows. There should be rain dripping off the gutters, and a foggy chill in the air. He didn't like this summer morning with its cloudless blue sky. It gave him no pleasure.

An angry buzzing sound drew his gaze upwards. A large bumblebee was scrabbling at one of the lead lined window panes. The creature was maddened, trapped indoors by an invisible barrier. Adam watched it. How could that round substantial body, so handsome in its black and gold livery, lift itself up with just the use of those fragile wings? It had been proven to be aerodynamically impossible. It simply couldn't be done. But the bee was doing it.

Adam reached out to turn the window latch to allow the bee its freedom, but his arthritic hand hadn't the strength for the job. It was the same with walking. His right leg, which several knee operations had made progressively worse, was now completely useless. It had to be dragged everywhere with him like a superfluous item of luggage, 'unwanted on voyage'.

Life wasn't easy when you were in your eighties and permanently at a ninety degree angle to the floor. He was the original L-shaped man. The advance of his disease steadily forced his head ever further down, so that he now viewed everything from a new perspective. This had proved to have some unexpected advantages. He could reach useful dials and switches that had normally required him to go down painfully onto his knees, and he had rediscovered precious books from the lower shelves of his bookcase, previously ignored. The wartime diaries were among them, their associations reviving so many half-buried memories, though his eyesight was now too poor to allow a close study.

He crept towards the bedroom on his Zimmer frame, moving at a tortoise's pace. He knew that he really did look like an old tortoise with his wrinkled neck sticking out ahead of his steeply bowed back. A child had said so, and he had laughed. But by the time he reached his sofa bed he was breathless. With so many aches and pains, everything was an effort. He allowed himself to collapse while he struggled to get his breath.

What time did Erica usually get here? Adam wrinkled his face with the effort of remembering. Things slipped away from his memory so easily. He hoped she would come soon. His mind began to wander, making him dream of the past as he did so often.

He thought of Melancholy Jaques and his Seven Ages of Man... Yes, he had played all the parts, but now he had reached the last scene of all. I was young too once, he thought, raising his chin defiantly. In a world so different from today, I was young.

# 1

*Hamburg, 1946*

"Right. That's more than enough for one day. I'm off. See you tomorrow, Pinkie."

The door opens onto the black moonscape of the ruined street. I am only inches away from dirty snowflakes tearing down the road in great swirling clusters, like dust motes under the broom of an unseen giant.

I'm stiff and tired. There is just so much of man's inhumanity to man that you can take. I have reached that limit, and am ready for home.

Pinkerton looks up at me and through me, running his ink stained fingers distractedly through his thinning hair. He's definitely going bald. He is beginning to get round shouldered too, and some days looks more like a man of sixty than thirty. He has rolled up his shirtsleeves, though the room is warmed only by a one- bar electric fire, and is peering through his wire rimmed glasses at a closely typed document. A pot of ink and a half-drunk mug of coffee stand at his elbow.

"Righty-ho," he says absently. "Oh - better check the doors, will you, Adam? Caretaker's not shown up again. Second time this week."

"It's this 'flu that's going round. Helga's off as well."

My highly efficient secretary, she of the elaborate hairdo and muscular legs, is prone to sudden inexplicable bouts of illness which necessitate her staying at home. They sound life threatening when she reports them, although she always manages to turn up unscathed the next day for work with the briefest of explanations.

"Adam?"

"Pinkie?"

I am not in the mood for a long conversation.

"Can you answer me something? It's important. It's ridiculous, I know, but tell me truthfully – what's your guess of how many camps there were? Concentration camps I mean, obviously. Any idea?"

Pinkie stares at me, pen tapping his teeth. He looks exhausted.

I'm poised awkwardly by the door. I've only popped into his office to say goodnight from a different part of the building where I work. The weather's awful, and I'm freezing just standing here. But I can see that he needs an answer, and attempt to give one.

"Well, I used to just know about the big ones," I say slowly. "Then we realised there were a lot more than we first thought. We're finding more all the time, aren't we? I don't know really, Pinkie. I've only been concerned with the one at Scheiden really."

I shudder suddenly, I suppose because of the hail

rattling at the window. It's getting dark now. The roofless warehouse opposite, with huge gaping holes in its walls, is turning into a grotesque face. It seems to grin at me as it merges into the shadows like a Cheshire cat.

"So…?"

Pinkie prompts me.

"Well – with Poland and so on as well, I suppose… what, fifty, a hundred even? More? Don't tell me – more?"

He puts his pen down and stares out at the wintry scene outside his window.

"I've listed seven hundred now, and there are others coming to light every day. It looks certain there were literally thousands of them. It's quite unbelievable."

"Thousands? Good God Almighty!" I feel as if I've had a blow to the solar plexus. "What? Are you serious?"

Pinkie turns his almost comically worried face to me.

"Okay, I'm not talking about extermination camps, with gas ovens and so, where prisoners only lived a few hours after arrival. There were a certain number of those, I don't know how many yet. I'm talking about KLs, detention camps. They had a staggeringly high death rate too. Do you know what? It seems likely to me that every town in the country of any size at all had one of these located nearby. I'm not exaggerating. Every one. And yet nobody saw a darned thing."

"Yes. Yes, I know."

"And yet we're supposed to work with these people every day."

He was almost shouting. "And treat them like colleagues. I tell you, Adam, sometimes it makes me want to be sick."

I swallow hard. There's a point of view I want to put, and I don't know really why. Perhaps it's because I've learnt surprisingly quickly to regard many German people as my friends and not as my enemies.

"That's unbelievable. But be honest, Pinkie. Would the average Briton be any different, really? We're talking about human nature. We only see what we want to see? Don't we?"

But I've learnt from experience that this is not a popular opinion, and Pinkie isn't in the mood to hear my amateur philosophizing. He cuts me off with a wave of his hand. For my part I don't want an argument either, so I walk over and put my arm round his thin shoulders. I give him a brief hug, conscious that it is a very un-English thing to do.

"Good night, old man. *Illegitimi non carborundum*, or words to that effect."

He manages a weak smile.

"Don't let the bastards grind you down, eh? Well, one can but try."

"That's the spirit. Good night, then. I'm off."

He just grunts, and sits down again to his files.

"Oh, and Pinkie...?"

"What?"

"That's your coffee cup you've just put your pen in."

Pinkie blinks at it myopically.

"Oh, drat. I seem to do that sometimes."

He reaches in his pocket and pulls out a cotton handkerchief to wipe the pen clean.

"Stupid. Makes the very dickens of a mess."

"Pinkie, don't you think it's time you packed it in and went home?"

"Oh, yes, yes. I will in a while. Just got to finish this thing for Foxy."

I had an inspiration.

"Look here, do you fancy a drink? Apparently there's a new bar of sorts opened near where the fish market was. Dancing and so on. Sounds quite interesting."

He bends over his desk again and peers myopically down at his document. "I'd love to, Adam. I would really, but not this evening. Another time perhaps."

"Another time then."

It's a bit difficult to imagine Pinkie dancing the night away. I grin to myself and go out into the night.

It has stopped snowing, but the uneven pavements are slippery as I leave the warmth of the *Kriegskriminalanlage* office behind, hunching my shoulders against the chill. The cold wind they say comes from Russia stings my cheeks as I cut through the remains of the old *Pilsnauerpark* into the darkened side streets and turn off *Feldhausweg* towards home, picking my way carefully through the ruins.

In parts of the city, the whole street system has disappeared. People who were born here and have worked here all their lives can no longer find their bearings. Huge piles of rubble, concrete and collapsed or derelict buildings are the new landmarks to be negotiated, where once stood houses and the shops inhabited by industrious housewives and tired clerks, noisy children and grumbling grandparents. Winding cobbled lanes, with black and white half-timbered medieval houses huddling side by side had survived the Plague and the Black Death, but almost overnight vanished forever. The delicately wrought stained glass windows, soaring roofs, and finely sculpted arches of ancient churches are now just piles of stones and blackened beams.

Broken buildings tower everywhere against the evening sky, mute in their misery. Across the whole city the many canals are still unusable, blocked with debris. Weeds grow rampant in the rubble and I have become grateful for them. Their purple, yellow, blue and scarlet flowers provide a relief to the black, charred landscape of the burnt out cityscape. But their flowers are dying now as winter approaches, and their stems, bending against the hail, are hard to make out in the gloom.

Street lighting exists no more, and the only illumination comes from the eerie glow of bonfires and braziers on the sites of bombed out buildings, where hundreds of the homeless have made shelters in the ruins. Dwellings for entire families, some surprisingly elaborate, are provided by the remains of the buildings and cellars of the houses and shops which line the once elegant streets.

In this part of the city, in some streets only fragments of buildings have survived the last days of the American and British saturation bombing, but even these provide some sort of shelter. I often pass grubby children playing merrily on the piles of rubble, sometimes acting out the actions of the planes and the noise of the bombing.

The aftermath of the holocaust is all around me. In the final days of the endless bombardment the bombing created an enormous firestorm, which sucked out the air and raised the temperature to over a hundred degrees, suffocating to death thousands who until then had thought they had survived. I grit my teeth when I recall that, almost unbelievably, the Allied bombing resumed the following day, seeking to extinguish even such sparks of life that still remained. But the bombers turned away one by one. There was nothing left to destroy.

Yet a kind of miracle has occurred. Slowly, timidly, life has returned, inch by inch, breath by breath. And now, over a year since the war ended, defeat acknowledged, and an armistice signed by the broken survivors, an urban society is re-establishing itself. Food is still scarce, but mass starvation has been overcome, and fuel is becoming easier to get hold of. There is a living to be made by the able bodied, salvaging timber from the thousands of bomb sites and selling it for firewood. The old opencast coal workings near Thorsburg have been reopened too, and coal carts, some of them horse drawn, have begun to appear.

A few trams are running again, and it will not be long before the former highly efficient system will be reinstated. An extraordinarily punctual bus service is already operating in the centre, though I generally prefer to walk.

Now I am passing the perimeter of the Dead City. This is the name the locals give to the old centre, which has been almost totally obliterated. It is cordoned off and out of bounds. The destruction was so devastating here that the authorities have not attempted any restitution apart from cremating some of the corpses to stop the spread of disease, concentrating their efforts on the less heavily bombed areas. Barricades of concrete blocks, decorated with crude skull and crossbones, forbid entry under pain of death, and armed guards patrol the perimeter.

Tens of thousands of putrefying bodies still await burial within this area, and the smell of death lingers here. Its yellow, cloying, sickly odour is fainter now, but it never quite goes away. They say the decontamination teams which work in the Dead City have to use flamethrowers, not just on the decomposing corpses, but on the flies and the maggots which are so thick and bloated that boots slide and slip on them and impede access to the bodies. Huge green flies, as fat as a man's thumb, are of a species never seen before. They still gorge themselves on the newly discovered bodies daily turned up by the diggers.

I have begun to shiver with the cold, although the hail has given way to light stinging rain, and I wrap my army greatcoat more tightly round myself. I pull the collar up round my neck and quicken my pace as much as my stiff leg will allow, in anticipation of a hot meal and a comfortable bed. And there's the cheering prospect of a drop of whisky tonight, I remember.

We are expected to wear uniform at all times, but like many of my colleagues in the services legal department I disobey the rule as far as possible. I've taken to stuffing my officer's peaked hat into my briefcase and pulling on a knitted cap when I walk through the city. Half bricks are all too readily at hand to tempt a starving youth to toss at a member of the occupying forces. French, American, Russian or English, we are all fair game to them. And I can't blame them.

Voices are calling out to me now through the darkness from where a fire is glowing. I stop for a moment, intrigued.

"Hey mister, got any spare change?"

"Any smokes? Beer? Candies?"

And a younger, softer voice.

"Hello, handsome! Give us a kiss then! You want some loving? A quicktime? Just five fags? Mister?"

Then a cackle of laughter from an older woman, and a glimpse in the firelight of a girl's face looking towards me, head tilted, a scarf or shawl tied round her long hair and shoulders. The other woman admonishes her.

"No good, pet! Young fellow like that don't need the likes of you. Better sticking with the married ones!"

The voices are threatening, a rumbling undercurrent of barely repressed violence. It is a chorus from some macabre production of Macbeth, with the witches huddled round their bonfire like wild beasts growling in the background, calling curses on me, the Thane, huddled in my cape after the battle. *How now, you secret, black, and midnight hags! What is't you do?*

*A deed without a name…e'en till destruction sicken.*

I shiver and move on out of hearing range of the jokes and jibes, keeping my head down and trying to ignore my wretched leg.

I'm glad to be home. By one of those unpredictable chances of war, 39 Gottfriedstrasse stands proudly unscathed by the firebombing. It is a handsome house which retains a surprising degree of its former dignity. I suppose it was built by a wealthy merchant, perhaps in the late 1800s, with no expense spared. Its finely proportioned doorway and mullion windows are miraculously intact. A smaller window is set into the mansard roof, from which can be seen a dim glow.

I walk up the worn steps to the front door, conscious of the pain in my leg. Frau Teck comes out from the kitchen as I stand in the dark hallway rubbing my hands together for warmth. She fusses nervously over me like a mother hen, helping me hang up my coat and hat and tut-tutting at how cold my hands are.

"I was worried about you, *Herr Kapitän*," she complains. "You are late, and there are so many bad people about these days. They are like animals in this city. Ach, it was never like this once. It was such a peaceful place once, a place to bring up children."

As far as I know Frau Teck has never had any children, but I let it go. Against her will it seems, her eyes are drawn to my briefcase, and then away again.

"I know I'm late, but we are busier than ever in the office these days," I say soothingly, brushing the wetness off my coat.

"I'm sure you must be."

"Every day more and more evil people are coming out of the woodwork. Terrible crimes were committed by just a few people."

I trot out the official line with little conviction in my voice.

"*Ja!*" she cries. "These criminals must be found, tried, and given the same medicine that they doled out. They are fiends. Fiends! Nothing is too bad for them!" She starts to choke.

"We did not know, *Herr Kapitän*! We had no idea. We knew there were camps – but we thought…" She grabbed my sleeve.

Here we go again, I think. I have to put up with a lot of this from local people, and am finding it increasingly hard to take. Scheiden is one of Pinkie's full-blown death camps which had 'processed' well over 200, 000 victims during the Nazi era, and it is only a few minutes' journey from this house. You must have been able to smell the smoke from the crematoria from here some days. There was talk by the Americans of marching citizens into some of these camps to see the evidence of what went on there with their own eyes, but it has already begun to seem pointless.

"Promise me you will punish them!"

I take her hand gently off my coat, swallow hard, and nod mutely. This is something else I am accustomed to. But the truth – part of the truth at any rate – is becoming clear to me. We are hell bent on prosecuting the guilty, certainly, but only the middle functionaries of the Nazi party system, the typists, clerks, managers, and low ranking officials, or even foreign soldiers conscripted into the German ranks. Meanwhile the real villains are rapidly slipping out of our reach. Argentina is said to be awash with high-ranking ex-Nazis, with more arriving by every ship and aeroplane. But a pretence of justice has to be maintained, even amongst ourselves. The work of prosecution has to be done and be seen to be done.

"Never mind that now," I say soothingly. "I have a little something for you, Frau Teck. Nothing much! But something."

Her lined blue eyes look anxiously into my face, and her bony hands grip mine..

"Some food?"

"Just some beans, a loaf of black bread, a tin of your favourite coffee and a cabbage. A little ham. Oh, and a bottle of something that calls itself whisky."

Her worn face lights up.

"Oh, *Herr Kapitän*, that is marvellous! And the whisky you must share with the *Herr Doktor*! It will do him so much good! I am so much worried about him."

"I'll go up to see him now," I say, smiling down on her. "I'll eat something later. Do you think you could find a couple of your nice glasses for me to take upstairs?"

"Of course!" she cries. "I'll bring them for you now!"

And she bustles off into her part of the house like a mouse scuttling down its hole with a stolen titbit, tail twitching with anticipation.

§

There is a good fire burning in the grate in the attic room where Doctor Ernst Mann lives, studies, and sleeps. A dull but adequate light from a table lamp shines onto his books on the old table where he sits working at a medical history, puffing at his pipe. On the walls are fine engravings and prints, many of his native Austria in earlier days, and some good pieces of bone china. Other books, many on philosophy, line the shelves. The heavy curtains and the sofa smell comfortingly of tobacco smoke, and Schumann's first and only piano concerto is playing on the ancient gramophone.

The doctor quickly clears a space on the table when he sees what I am carrying, wincing slightly as he does so. He is white haired, stiff in his movements, a little bent. For all his seventy odd years he is active enough, though some days he looks a lot older. He seems to have aged again lately. He peers over his glasses at what I am holding, and his face now looks young again.

"Adam! *Mein Gott*, that looks good! Come and try to make yourself comfortable."

I have grown fond of him, perhaps needing a father figure in my life since my own father died in the blood-soaked sands south of El Alamein commanding his regiment. Dr Mann, though, reminds me more of my late grandfather, and has something of the same bookishness about him.

In some ways I prefer the company of older people. The energy of my younger colleagues is liable to get on my nerves. Their indifference, their self-obsession, the certainty of their opinions and judgements, even their optimism can be depressing rather than uplifting.

"It's not real Scotch," I say apologetically. "I mean, it wasn't brewed in Scotland."

No, you didn't brew whisky, did you? That was beer. But we are speaking German, and the distinction is too fine for me to translate. My German is gratifyingly fluent now, although far from perfect.

"I think it comes from Poland."

I hold the glass up to the light.

"It's rather a strange colour, I'm afraid, *Herr Doktor*."

He takes a deep sniff, his old face with its rheumy eyes breaking into a rare smile. There is a melancholy about the old man that rarely leaves him for long. I know little about his past, except that he left his native Austria as a young man, and has served in some capacity in both wars.

He raises his tumbler to me against the firelight, though I have learnt that the Germans do not tend to toast each other. The glasses are pre-war relics from Frau Teck's precious collection, and it is clear that we have been honoured.

"Doesn't smell too bad, though!"

He sips it. "No, not bad at all. *Gesundheit!* Thank you so much. You're very good to an old man, you know."

We grin at each other and sit in comfortable silence for a moment, feeling the liquid work its magic as it goes down our throats. The fire crackles reassuringly as a shower of sleet rattles against the window.

"How was your day?"

I grimace, mumbling some response and avoiding the question, and we speak for a while about the commercial life of the city. Corruption is everywhere, I tell him. The black market is thriving like never before. The authorities seem to have given up on it. But a few food shops have opened up, and there are even clothing and ironmongery stores.

"The shops are reappearing gradually. It's a slow process though."

"What are they like? I wish I could get out to see them, but my hips and this... " He grimaces.

"They're not very nice," I say, smiling. "Not a patch on what they used to be. Not like the old days. The shopkeepers don't seem to have their heart in it somehow."

"You know why?" says the doctor suddenly. "No Jews! We Germans don't know how to sell, to market, to make a show. We're going to miss our Jews."

For a moment I am struck dumb. This

extraordinary remark seems so insensitive coming from such a kindly man, seeming to imply somehow that genocide has been, well, a sort of unfortunate misjudgement. Later on this viewpoint may possibly have become more widely acceptable among the German people, but now it is new to me.

Abruptly the feeling of mild contentment induced by the alcohol is dissipated by a welter of unwelcome memories. I know an officer who had been among the first detachment to enter and occupy Märchenholz in Austria, and the images he related are hard to get out of the mind. The bile rises in my throat as they crowd in against my will. The fairy grottoes they used as torture chambers...The doctor's hand is on my arm.

"I know, captain," he whispers.

"I know, I know. Oh God, how I know. We all have much to learn to forget. You don't need to tell me what you are thinking. Millions dead. Millions and millions. Jews, yes, but gypsies, soldiers, old people, cripples, children too. An entire culture annihilated. Our once proud and civilised nation defeated and the old Europe as we knew it, gone for ever. And all the handiwork of a single madman."

The sleet has turned to rain again now. It is hammering steadily against the windows as a dull background noise in the little room. The old man stares unseeingly into the fire. When he speaks again his voice is so low, I can hardly make out what he is saying.

"And I, Ernst Mann, a simple country doctor... I had it in my power to have prevented it all."

I start to speak. He coughs, and holds his thin hand up to me.

"No – you think I am exaggerating. But I'm not. I only wish I were," he says. He raises his eyes to mine for a moment, and in all my life I have never seen such pain in a man's face. And I have seen plenty.

After a moment I reach out and refresh his glass. The stuff doesn't taste much like whisky, to be truthful, but it is very much better than nothing.

"Do you want to tell me about it, *Herr Doktor*?" I ask gently.

"I don't know."

He takes a sip, then puts the drink down and looks at it with longing for a moment, as if he'd never seen a glass before, pulling at his long earlobe. He gives a long sigh.

"It was my second job after leaving University," he says. "I was still full of youthful aspirations. Young, but not too young."

He gives a hollow chuckle.

"I was going to do such great things. The world – what does your Shakespeare say? – was my oyster. But oysters are damned hard to open for one thing, and if you get a bad one…! Ha! But I digress."

The rain rattles suddenly against the mansards. He clears his throat and shifts in his chair.

"Are you sure you want to listen to all this? Old men can get very tedious, you know."

He is smiling, but looking straight at me with those faded blue eyes, in mute appeal. He has a desperate need to talk, and for my part I want to listen. But something is holding him back.

"If I don't tell somebody, I…" He shakes his head. "When I left medical school I took a position with a practice in Linz. That is where I met Hitler."

I am incredulous.

"What? You knew Hitler?"

"Not well, but yes. He was a patient of mine. He was only a boy then, of course – fourteen or fifteen years old. But there was something about him, even then. I remember the circumstances in which I met him as if it were yesterday, and what I discovered…"

"You discovered something about him?"

"Oh yes. Something that almost nobody else knows."

He shivers a little, and takes a sip of his drink.

"Something that has haunted me, one way or another, for the rest of my life. Let me tell you something about it…"

An hour passes before there is a knock on the door, and I drag myself up into the present day.

"Who's there?" call the doctor. "Is that you, Frau Teck? Come in!"

The door opens and a timid head is thrust into the room.

"Oh, *Herr Doktor*," she gasps. "I am so sorry to disturb you. And you too, *Herr Kapitän*. But I wondered if either of you has eaten anything?"

The head disappears again. As we watch, mesmerised, two plates appeared very slowly through the doorway, each containing small pieces of ham, potatoes, and some cabbage, in a thin gravy, slowly followed by the timid figure of our landlady. A not unappetising smell fills the little room.

The doctor and I grin sheepishly at each other, shifting from our chairs with relief now that the mood is broken. We reach for the plates, and thank Frau Teck with sincerity, brushing away her repeated apologies for disturbing us.

Dr Mann's pale face and the shadows beneath his

eyes show the strain his narrative has been for him. I decide enough is enough for one evening, and when we have finished eating our meal in silence, I put my hand on his shoulder.

"This is an amazing story," I say quietly. "There's a great deal here for me to think about."

He looks at me hesitantly. "You want me to continue?"

"Of course I do," I say. "But not tonight, if you don't mind. I have a difficult day at work ahead of me. Perhaps we may resume another evening?"

"I would like that. You are doing me a great service simply by listening to me," the doctor says. "Good night, my friend. *Schlafen Sie gut.*"

And he presses my hand in farewell.

But it is a long time before I get off to sleep, and even when I do, I sleep fitfully, troubled by vivid dreams.

*Knives, bloodstains, burning buildings, skeletal faces, a young strained face with burning eyes... Then my mother in a fur coat, calm and smiling, a dog jumping up at me demanding a walk, a dark house with empty windows.... Throughout it all a thread is running, in which I have to do find something or someone urgently. It is desperately important, but buildings are crashing and disappearing into dust -filled rubble, and my legs won't move and I can't run...*

*There is a girl with soft arms around me... But she has slid silently away, and I am cold and naked and alone again.*

*Now the more familiar nightmare. I am back on the beach with the sound of shellfire, missiles exploding overhead, the smell of the sea in my nostrils and the taste of vomit and fear in my mouth...*

# 2

*Normandy, June 1944*

It was the morning of my twenty fourth birthday. If there were any justice in the world, I should have been celebrating my graduation from Oxford.

I had very much wanted to read English literature and German, but my father had insisted on my following in his footsteps as a lawyer. Perhaps just a gentleman's degree, announcing to the world you had proved to be neither a perfectly beastly swot, nor yet a drunken wastrel, but a law degree nonetheless and something to celebrate.

A formal party would have been held at my family's seventeenth-century home in Chipping-on-the-Fosse, all mellow golden stone and shaven lawns. The gently weeping willows at the bottom of the long garden would be maintaining their proprietorial watch over the little river Windrush as it burbled merrily along, bustling with brown trout and the occasional snapping pike, midges dancing in the sunlight. I would have been joined by my contemporaries, sons and daughters of solicitors, doctors, land agents and perhaps even the lesser landed gentry of our social circle. The company would have been rowdy and confident, the girls, oh so fetching in their sleeveless dresses showing off summer tans, laughing together as they brushed their hair off their faces, pretending to be unaware of their young figures being shown off as they did it. My mother would have looked worried but still beautiful in her weary way, determined to make the party swing, knowing all too well what Fate might await the young men. She would be fighting back tears as she thought of how proud my father would have been.

But that was all make believe.

Instead, I had still not finished my degree, and on my birthday I was otherwise engaged. To be precise, I was leaning on the deck rail of a very small, very battered ship, retching over the side and wishing myself dead. I had felt sick within minutes of embarking from Portsmouth, but even the need for organising my men during the five-hour voyage across the Channel had not diverted me from my nausea for more than a few minutes.

Now we were actually beached off a nameless French town and were completing the dangerous transfer from the ship onto a flatbed landing craft. Unbelievably the swaying motion of the clumsy craft was even worse than on the ship. The thing lurched clumsily towards the beach like a drunken sailor staggering out of a dockside pub on payday. My overriding preoccupation was to pray to God to please send a friendly bullet to kill me immediately so that the nausea would stop. My prayer wasn't answered, so I staggered towards the rope ladder on the side of the flatbed, pack and rifle impeding my movements. I snarled orders at the men who were clumsily following me, fear alongside the seasickness churning my guts now. One of them swore back at me. In the desperation of the reality, my lofty rank of lieutenant was forgotten, and I pretended not to have heard what he called me.

The flatbed staggered into a setting as nightmarish as anything from a Renaissance artist's imagination. There were literally thousands of men on the wide sandy beach, all surging forward under a blistering hail of machine gun and shellfire from the gun emplacements ahead. As if that weren't enough, dozens of German planes were sweeping overhead and strafing the beach. Even as I watched, two nearly collided with each other. As they hit the various munitions stores on the beach, spurts of sand in enormous explosions shot high into the air.

I looked over the bows of the unwieldy, swaying craft. Three hundred yards away a body of men was clustered round a large Bofors gun which had somehow been dragged ashore. Maybe we should join them, perhaps to help move the gun further inland.

But even as I stared towards them, my eyes narrowed against the spray, they suffered a direct hit. There was a BOOOOM of flame and fire and flying debris. Mangled bodies flew through the air an acrobatic display. When the sand settled, all that were left were body parts, some still writhing. The men had been obliterated before my eyes. There was little left to be seen of them. They might never have been. The big gun lay uselessly on its side. My own troops muttered together at the sight, then fell silent. In every man's mind the same thought was predominant.

*"It could be me next."*

The craft lurched crazily again, still not beached. I

shook my head, blinked and wiped the salt spray away. Oh God, this is the end of me, let it be the end, goodbye, goodbye, let me die now.

I retched emptily for the umpteenth time, at the very moment when the flatbed hit the shore with a bang. It shuddered as if debating whether to float out to sea again, but then settled jerkily onto the sand. All around us the sea was churned up by dozens of vessels, considerable stretches of the water more scarlet than blue. Bodies, some still showing signs of life, bobbed everywhere in the water.

Angrily I wiped the traces of sick from my mouth with the back of my hand and stepped unsteadily off the ladder onto dry land. I was screaming something unintelligible above the noise of the bombardment, blindly waving my men forward.

I stopped for a moment to grin at a white faced boy beside me, clapping an encouraging hand to his shoulder. The young soldier stared back at me like someone in a nightmare, his eyes wild and rolling in his head. He was holding his hands to his chest. He opened his mouth to speak, and then slowly sank to the sand.

I couldn't stop to help him as we surged forward. I looked around for Peter Pullan, my company commander, for orders. Where the hell was he? He was meant to be in charge of this bloody landing. We had had a muttered conversation ten minutes earlier, Peter shaking his head and saying something quite out of character in his quiet voice about the whole thing being a cock-up. But now there was no sign of him.

There was no time to consider this. The noise on the shore was indescribable, and bullets were hissing into the sand round me. Now that my nausea had at last abated, I could think dimly, *Oh, I'm still alive. That's odd. Okay, let's get these men as far up the beach as we can.*

I turned to the man next to him, a squat ugly little miner from the Valleys who grinned back at me. Rogers, that was his name. He had a wonderful tenor voice, didn't he? What was it he sang at the regimental concerts?

*"Hand me down, my silver trom-pet…"* Glorious.

"Rogers! Come on!" I yelled. But as I looked, Rogers' arms and head went one way and his lower half another. Blood, brains, and guts sprayed the air. Rogers and his sublime voice were gone forever.

I ducked away, wiping unspeakable grey matter from my face. Crouched low against the suddenly renewed hail of machine gun fire, I ran, my pack banging against my back. I pounded on and on, in a desperate primeval need to survive, just to get through this hail of death to some kind of safety. I kept ducking stupidly, as if I could avoid the bullets by going under them.

There was a brief, unpredictable lull in the firing, and I felt myself beginning to think again as the noise stopped. I steadied myself, somehow gaining ground uphill. I was panting hard enough to burst my lungs, and I had to stop a few paces further on, doubled up in self preservation.

After a moment I looked round. Some of my men were following just behind me. I ordered them on with a wave of my hand. We reached some sand dunes on upward sloping ground, an area covered with spiny grass, painful to the touch and covered in sea urchins and seaweed, no doubt covered at high tide. We had found by chance a kind of haven, a dip in the ground where in a happier times a family may have taken a picnic, or children kick a ball around on a sunny day at the seaside.

Behind me up the slope came my contingent, or what was left of them. I motioned them to get down, and they needed no encouragement. I realised with a horrible sense of shame that they must have been following me, trusting me as their leader, while in truth I had been blindly fleeing for shelter to save my own skin. I gulped and tried to speak, raising my voice against the barrage on the beach further below them.

"Well done, men!" I croaked, struggling to find the right words of encouragement, too breathless to say any more. "We've got through the worst! Who's the senior NCO here?"

Most of the men were lying flat on their faces gasping for breath, but now they looked around at each other to see who had survived. Out of nowhere a shell landed with a tremendous bang twenty feet away, and we all ducked again.

"Sergeant Lang here, sir," said a voice from the ground. "But I don't know if I'm the senior. And Lieutenant Milne was leading a party just behind us. He should be coming up any minute if they've got through."

"All right, sergeant," I said. "What do you reckon, then?"

"Think we'd better push on up and over this hill, sir," said the sergeant, beginning to crawl over the spiky grass towards me. He was revealed as a long, thin individual, with a permanent expression of wry amusement. Absurdly, I remembered him now from a camp concert in Portsmouth at the barracks, when he'd played a pantomime Dame to great applause.

"We've been lucky, sir. Just come through a gap. I suggest we get the hell out of it, sir. We can get behind the Jerries and shove on into that town while their attention is on the beach."

We both looked down on the scene of unspeakable devastation beneath us. Chance had placed us in a haven of comparative peace, with a birds' eye view of part of the invasion. A hundred and fifty thousand men had landed on those beaches that day, I was to learn much later, the biggest invasion in the history of the world. Nearly seven thousand ships took part. Ten thousand men were to die on the beaches where families played and children swam in peacetime, where the sea was now churning so full of bodies that it had turned scarlet.

And at that particular moment, as the fate of Europe and the course of the greatest war mankind had ever experienced was about to be determined, the ridiculous realisation dawned on me that I was abroad for the first time in my life, and that it was my birthday. I hadn't been shot. I didn't feel sick any more. And the Allied invasion of Europe had finally begun.

# 3

*Hamburg, 1946*

"*Herr Kapitän*! *Herr Kapitän*! It is after seven o'clock already! You said you must be early today, and I thought…"

I push myself up on the thin pillow and run a hand through my hair, groaning softly. That whisky…it must be even worse quality than I had thought. What had I been dreaming? Battle stuff again? The beaches…? No, it's gone.

"*Herr Kapitän*!"

"Yes, very good, Frau Teck!" I call. "Thank you so much. I am awake. Thank you!"

I can hear her footsteps going down the stairs, and heave myself out of bed.

I groan again, this time at the prospect of another day at work. My stomach lurches at the thought, and I make my way to the little bathroom to sit staring at the tiled floor and wonder for the umpteenth time if I am in the right job.

As I walk to the office the sky is dull and grey, half-heartedly squeezing out flakes of snow too mushy and slight to merit the name. The cold air is a reminder that Mother Russia is only a few hundred miles away. Somewhere nearby a child is crying, a monotonous sobbing with no expectation of relief, which goes on and on until I am out of hearing.

I am following a route of my own devising, diverting around some of the worst bomb damage. Many of the streets have not yet been entirely cleared, and some areas are still positively dangerous. There's an overhanging roof on the remains of a butchers' shop that always demands a wide berth, and near there I decide to follow a new track through some bombsites which may afford me a shortcut.

Yellow and purple weeds grow high through the highly polished tiled floors and fragmentary oak staircases of a large house, now exposed to the elements. So late in the season, bees and butterflies are still buzzing round the buddleia which pokes out in profusion from a crack in a wall at first floor level. An old woman is pushing a handcart, piled with miscellaneous salvage - dust caked clothing, a broken broom, sherds of crockery, a cupboard door. I press against a pile of bricks to let her pass. Her face is wild eyed and without hope, and my muttered *Guten Tag* meets with no response.

There is a word for these women now – *Trümmerfrauen*, rubble women. They are the desperate, lonely creatures who search all day through the piles of bricks and beams of collapsed building to find something of value, however insignificant, to sell or barter, in order just to survive. But as the authorities clear more of these sites in its determined reclamation drive, the easy pickings get scarcer. Even the rats that scutter everywhere are not as fat as they were, now that the bodies beneath the rubble are nothing more than bones. They are thinner and more vicious, and very bold.

Round the corner an old man with a mop of white hair has erected a makeshift stall on the steps of a once grand municipal building, which stands roofless, its high windows empty sockets staring out at the sky. On these very steps the mighty once congregated, momentous pronouncements were made by politicians oozing insincerity, as the photographers fought for scoops. Now scratchy grass grows thickly through the cracks and fissures in the stonework.

I smell coffee, or the acorn substitute that mostly passes for it. Three or four people are standing around gratefully drinking the thin liquid, and I stop too, glad of an excuse to delay the day. I drop a few coins into a cardboard box and take the proffered chipped mug with a word of thanks.

One of the customers is a young girl with an intelligent face and big bright eyes, dark hair matted across her forehead. She is pretty enough for me to want to catch her eye and share a moment of comradeship. She drops her head, then raises it again and looks me in the eye, a half smile on her lips. "Hello, soldier boy. Or should I say, sir?"

"Hello?" I say, puzzled now, and look enquiringly at her. I'm sure I've seen her before somewhere, but the question is too banal to frame. The others in the little gathering are watching our encounter with amusement, and I am embarrassed.

The girl is not, and now she's laughing.

"Just a few cigarettes? Quick time?" she mocks. "Remember?"

Now I'm blushing. Of course. It's the girl from the

group that I pass every night, eyes averted.

"Yes," I say. "But we've never – I've never –"

"No! But you've thought about it, haven't you? Fit young man like you? Ach – got a girlfriend already, have you? Or a nice little wifey at home? Shame."

The coffee is so hot it burns my mouth, and I put it down hastily.

"No? Thought not. I can always tell!"

She is dancing in front of me now, pushing her bosom out, enjoying my discomfiture, clasping her long nicotine- stained fingers round her mug of coffee and putting it to her lips seductively.

I am at a loss as to how to respond. This encounter is not of my making. But there is a wistfulness about her, and suddenly I realise, rather to my relief, that she is very young. Her accent is not the rough *Niederdeutsch* I expected, but sounds educated, although she is trying to hide this by slurring her consonants. I suddenly feel more in control of the encounter, and smile back at her.

"Who wouldn't?" I ask, adopting my roguish persona, sipping the hot liquid again but more cautiously this time. "Beautiful young lady like you?"

"Ooh, thank you, kind sir!" she says, dropping me a mock curtsey. Her long coat is dirty and full of holes, but has a tattered real fur collar, and was expensive once. Her wide smile shows off her perfect teeth

"How did you know I was an officer?" I ask. "I always take my cap off."

She laughs.

"Oh, come on. The long coat, the smart shiny boots – you can tell a lot from a man's shoes. The way you walk…"

"My limp, you mean?"

I must sound defensive. She shrugs dismissively.

"Ach, everybody limps round here. You're lucky if you can walk at all. My uncle had a bad leg like that. He used to make a joke about it and called the leg Herr Klumpf. A grumpy old man my uncle had to drag around with him. He told me it made it more bearable."

"I'll have to try it. What happened to him?"

"He... died."

There is a silence as I curse myself for my stupidity in asking the question. But then she laughs.

"No, it's just the way you hold yourself. Confident. But not arrogant, like a fucking Prussian."

She puts her head on one side and surveys me impudently, as if weighing me up. Her eyes are very green, and twinkle as if laughter is never far away. She pronounces her judgment.

"Nothing much wrong with you that a good woman couldn't cure, I'd say."

This is too much for me. I frown and reach for my cigarettes.

"You're very impertinent."

"Ooh, sorry, sir, I'm sure. Forgot my manners. Perhaps you ought to teach me a lesson? Smack my bottom for me?"

She bends away from me, striking her buttocks and laughing.

"Don't be so stupid," I say gruffly, cupping my hands round the match as I turn and light my cigarette. "How old are you anyway, for God's sake?"

This is another mistake.

"Old enough!" she cries. "Got to go. Duty calls! Clients to serve!"

She puts her mug on a cracked window ledge.

"*Auf Wiedersehen, Herr Kapitän.* Come and join my club – male members only – the bigger the better! Satisfaction guaranteed!"

One of the men laughs, while the other customers stare away uneasily.

"Bye, Uli!"

She blows a kiss to the coffee seller, and is gone.

The old man, who has one empty sleeve pinned to his Feldarmee greatcoat above grimy medal ribbons, clumsily collects the empty cups onto a battered tray. A sudden icy breeze makes us both shiver. He looks at me for a moment.

"Sad, *nicht wahr?* Nice girl like that?"

He waits for my reaction, then goes on.

"From a good family, you know. And now – well, as you see."

"Well, who is she?"

"Rose, they call her. Rosa von Schirm und Loewen, to give the girl her full title." He wipes the cups on a cloth so filthy it seems likely to make them dirtier rather than cleaner. "Her family were big landowners. Killed one night in July '44, the lot of them – her little twin brothers, her nanny, the servants…"

He pauses in what he is doing for a moment, and stares into space. Now that he's standing beside me, I can see that I was quite wrong. He's not old at all, maybe no more than forty. But his hair is completely white, and his forehead is scarred and puckered right across.

"The dogs and the horses, yes, and the chickens too. It was just an estate farm really, you know, but the Americans must have thought the Schloss was a military headquarters. The officers used to call in for their eggs, that was all. Wasted a lot of bombs on it that night, the *verfluchtene* Yankees. Got the wrong place again."

*Did you say all? Oh, hell-kite, all? What, all my pretty chickens, and their dam, at one fell swoop?*

My hands have gone clammy, and the wind feels very cold on my face. "And Rose?"

"Oh, she was away at school. She's only young, you see." He shakes his head. "I used to work for the family before the war, on the home farm. Lovely people, they were. Very good to their employees. The Graf paid for my mum to go into hospital, back in '37. When she had cancer. Paid every pfennig."

His eyes are moist and he brushes his forearm across his face.

"And now, to see that poor girl…"

He turns away. I mumble a few platitudes and thank him for the coffee. He looks up at me for a moment, catching my accent.

"Are you American, sir? I didn't mean…"

"No, English," I tell him. For some reason I don't fully understand, many of the Germans seem to dislike us less than they do the Yankees.

"I work round the corner."

I jerk my head, naming the building.

"Ah – war crimes. You're prosecuting those bastards who worked in the camps, aren't you? Good."

He spits out a quid of tobacco. "I hate those scum worse than I hate the Americans. My sister married a Jew before the war. I know what happened to them."

He shudders. A light comes into his eyes, and his mouth twists with emotion.

"I hope you give them hell, sir. Give them the same treatment they dished out to those poor Jews. The English, the Americans – they were just soldiers like us, doing their duty. But those swine in the camps, they were different. Promise me you won't let them get away with what they did!"

I turn my collar up. It's getting colder, and the snowflakes are bigger now, dancing in from the east in spiteful little flurries. The sky is a dirty grey and yellow colour, like a frying pan smeared with dried egg or mustard. I feel empty, without dignity or hope.

"I'll try," I mumble, hating myself. "Well, I must get on."

As the lady says, duty calls, clients to see…

§

Helga is back from her sickbed before the end of the week, and sits hunched, red-nosed, over her typewriter. She doesn't look up. It is going to be one of those days.

"Don't forget van Reen's being brought here this afternoon," she throws over her shoulder. "And you've got that woman tomorrow."

"I hadn't forgotten," I say. "Are you feeling better?"

"No," she says, hammering away at the keyboard as if punishing it for some misdemeanour, perhaps a spelling mistake it persists in reproducing, or a refusal of the roller to move when she is in full flow.

"Need the money, you know? Bills to pay, 'wounded hero' to feed and run errands for day and night? Lazy bastard that he is."

I grunt. Experience tells me the least said the

better, especially when she is in sarcastic vein.

My own desk in my little side office is piled with paperwork, and I begin unenthusiastically scribbling at documents to assist them in their progress from Pending to Out tray as swiftly as possible. Then I pick up the van Reen file to read it through again before the afternoon's meeting, and am transported to a Greek island in the heat of an Aegean summer. We had a family holiday to Rhodes once, when I was a child. I can almost smell the jasmine, heady and intoxicating, but mixed hideously now with the acrid stench of fear.

At two o'clock precisely there is a peremptory knock on the door.

"Come in!"

A corporal named Bletcher, an old adversary of mine, enters with his prisoner in handcuffs in front of him. Bletcher slams to attention, ramrod stiff, and gives me a quivering salute. He is a short man with no neck, a red face and protuberant blue eyes.

"Prisoner van Reen, for interrogation, sir!"

"Yes, thank you, corporal," I say, trying hard to sound as brisk and military as Bletcher. "Take those handcuffs off, please. You can leave the prisoner with me."

I point without expression to a chair and sternly bid him to sit down

"Sir! Sir!" Bletcher protests, his eyes bulging more than ever with outrage. "CO's orders, sir – prisoners under escort to wear restraints at all times!"

"Oh, for Christ's sake. He's hardly likely to… " I begin. Then I recall some of the charges against van Reen, and swallow hard.

"Oh, very well. You're quite right, corporal.

Handcuff one arm to the chair. I don't think he'll get far like that if he tries to escape, do you?"

The order is carried out in silence. Van Reen smiles at us pleasantly when it is done, as if to humour us for our little whims. He looks quite at his ease.

"Fall out, corporal. Get Heidi to make you a cup of coffee. We shall be some time. And ask her if she'd bring me a pot later - and two cups, too, if she would. But not for some time yet."

There is a moment of hesitation to show his disapproval of any such concession to the prisoner, before Bletcher shouts "Two cups? Sah!" He gives van Reen a final glare, executes a noisy about-turn, and marches into the outer office, slamming the door behind him.

If circumstances had been different, van Reen and I would have raised our eyes at each other in mutual relief at his ostentatious departure. As it is I stare down at my file, fumbling through papers, while he smiles at me encouragingly.

Henryk van Reen is a man in his forties, lean, scholarly, with a mild face and a courteous demeanour. He is dressed in the coarse grey uniform of Stattenheim military prison, but one feels he would otherwise be elegantly attired. Since I foolishly let slip to him that I wished I had read English at Oxford instead of Law before being called up, he loses no opportunity to show off his extensive knowledge of English literature. Irritatingly, we seem to have very similar tastes. Now he quotes, smiling faintly.

"Dressed in a little brief authority? *This is a slight, unmeritable man, meet to be sent on errands.*"

This quotation from Julius Caesar often occurs to

me too. The army is full of such persons.

Van Reen has a soft voice, and speaks English and German fluently, as many Dutch do, and no doubt other languages as well. At our earlier, preliminary meeting at the prison we began speaking in German, but it immediately became clear that his knowledge of the language was far more fluent than mine. This put me at a disadvantage that I could well have done without, so we have settled by unspoken agreement on English as our lingua franca.

I clear my throat, ignoring the remark.

"Now, van Reen," I say in my briskest tone, leafing through my file of papers. "We were talking last time about the events of the week beginning 17th of July, 1943, on the island of Sophos. You are aware that you are about to stand trial for a war crime in respect of your actions during that week."

"How many times must I say the same thing, Captain?" he says evenly. "Must I say it yet again?"

"I can say it for you, if you like," I say wearily, leafing through my notes. "Here we are… *I was only doing my duty. A soldier is under orders. If you are in the army, you obey orders. The element of choice is missing. You obey.*' Have I got that right?"

He spreads his hands as far as the cuffs will allow, and sighs.

"What else is there to say?"

"Do you know what I find hard to understand?" I say, pushing my pad aside. "You had been in charge of the occupation of Sophos for several weeks. You had got to know many of its people, probably on a relatively friendly basis. Your regime had not been stricter than was necessary, it seems. And I get the impression that you liked the country and its people.

You even spoke the language?"

"A little."

He turns his head away from me. "It is true that I have always loved Greece, and in particular its islands. I do not speak Greek fluently, no. But it is always helpful to have a rough idea of the grammar, and to have a few phrases to heart. After a few weeks I could hold a basic conversation."

"But you lined up twenty of their menfolk and had them shot on the village square. Is that how you treat people you like?"

He is silent for a long moment, then he turns back to look at me.

"Shall I tell you what it was like, Captain? Would you really like to know? It was the hottest time of the year, and tempers were running high. During the spring I had been able to impose a non-aggressive command of the island, and I encouraged – no, instructed – my men to behave properly in their dealings with the natives. These were mostly men too old for military service, their wives and children and grandchildren, but unfortunately, a few hotheads too."

He starts to raise his hand to gesture, then looks down on it, remembering he is handcuffed to the arm of the chair. He swallows.

"In different times I could have been happy there. There was some very interesting archaeology on Sophos, and the farmers turned up artefacts all the time in their fields. There were the foundations of a harbour wall. There was a theory that Ulysses called there on his epic voyage…"

He leans forward, in pedagogic mode now.

"The pottery was very distinctive. Pre-Mycaenean.

Some of the sherds of decorated ewers were quite exquisite. They were from another coastal village, called Kastoria. The name derives from…"

"Kastro. A castle. Yes, I know. It always suggests a fortified area."

Van Reen leans forward eagerly. There is a new light in his eyes.

"*Ach so, Herr Kapitän.* You are indeed a man of culture. You and I have a lot in common, you know. I have made a close study of the Odyssey. I studied ancient Greek expressly for the purpose, as a matter of fact. I became very intrigued by the so-called legends."

I look down at my pad where I have scribbled 'Kastoria.'

I suddenly come to my senses. This is ridiculous. This man is a cold blooded murderer, and he is lecturing me about archaeology.

"*Van Reen!*"

"You would find it fascinating, I know. We discovered definite indications of occupation dating from ..."

I am livid and don't trouble to conceal it.

"Be quiet! We are discussing the brutal murder of twenty innocent civilians, for which you were responsible. And you want to chat about ancient history. You are trying my patience to the limit."

He shrugs and sits back in his chair.

"War is war. It was no different at the time of the Odyssey. Terrible things happen. I don't need to tell you that, Captain. I was a professional soldier, like you. We soldiers are merely pawns on a gigantic chessboard."

It is something I have often felt myself. I rap my

pen irritably on the desk. "We are talking about the reprisals! Can you give me any feasible reason why they were carried out? A military reason?"

We have left prehistoric Greece, and are back to business.

"Certainly. The village was a hotbed of trouble beneath the calm surface. The island was strategic to our control of that area of the Aegean. I was sent there with a small unit to maintain our command of it, and to eliminate any possibility of insurgency."

He runs his free hand over his lips.

"I was managing to do this without bloodshed. We had quickly established a workable administration, and I was confident that we had matters in hand. Then the progress of the war in the rest of Europe caused feelings to run high in the village. The islanders became restless again. There were some real troublemakers among the young men and I had to take severe measures. Naturally they were not popular. One thing led to another, and one night one of my men was killed."

His face stiffens at the memory.

"Was I supposed to ignore that? I had to act quickly to prevent an uprising. So I selected the men I knew represented the most danger to us, and executed them."

I am making notes, then raise my head.

"Was your action effective?"

He half smiles.

"Very. There was no more trouble. Of course, I will admit, the atmosphere was quite different after that. No more cosy chats in the taverna, or flirting with the women. It was… a difficult period."

"I can well imagine."

"But soon the war moved on. It became clear that the tide was turning against Germany. Very soon we were evacuated to the mainland and over to Italy." He spreads his hands as much as the handcuff will allow, staring down at it again as though he had just noticed it.

"In a strange way I was sorry to leave. But I had, shall we say, blotted my copybook with the village, and…"

"Oh, I'm sure the islanders were devastated to see you go," I say sarcastically. "But perhaps they will welcome you back if you fancy going back there on holiday when things settle down? Maybe renew a few old friendships with the widows and orphans? Perhaps you could do some more research into the travels of Ulysses?"

My sarcasm is greeted with a pained expression, as if a favoured undergraduate had committed some grammatical solecism. Then van Reen scrapes his chair back with a sigh.

"I'm afraid the British are not going to allow me many holidays, are they, Captain? May I ask you something?"

He takes my stony silence for assent.

"What is likely to happen to me, do you think? How many years' imprisonment, for carrying out my orders?"

I am tired of this. I lean forward eagerly. It is my turn now.

"Oh, let's see now. A couple of years in a military gaol, d'you think? A comfy cell and plenty of books to read? Then an early parole for good behaviour? No, I wouldn't comfort myself with that, if I were you. You see, I have a lot more on you in my file, van

Reen. A great deal more. Some of your other crimes make shooting twenty islanders seem very small beer. One in particular concerns another spell in your glorious career, when you were involved in the mass murder of over 300 Russian and Polish prisoners in – let's see, now – Riga, Latvia, in - now, when was it?"

He has gone very still.

"Ah, you didn't know we knew about that, did you? A little matter of a change of name and rank? Well, we do, thanks to some meticulous recordkeeping – a credit to German bureaucracy. Everything, however hush hush, seems to end up being recorded somewhere. It's coming in very useful indeed, I can tell you."

I have been leafing through the file, and now I have come to the relevant pages I put it down and lean back in my chair.

"And the evidence we have here won't cost you a nice spell in prison. Nothing so agreeable, I'm afraid. Oh, no."

Now his face is a shade of yellowy white.

"No need to spell it out, Captain. I'm not a fool."

"Just as long as we understand each other."

"You may assume that we do. What is it you need to know?"

We get down again to detailed work. An hour passes. At the end of it, nothing has changed. He was given orders to assist in executing the prisoners, and had no choice but to carry out those orders on pain of his own court-martial. He gives me the names of his fellow officers, of the general commanding the operation, and of how and where the bodies were buried. It is yet another tale of privation and hunger and misery and murder.

It is all delivered in a disinterested tone of voice, with polite pauses while I write. My head is beginning to swim.

At last there's a knock on the door, and to my relief Helga appears with a tray of coffee and crockery. She's even found some sugar and put a little into a pot. She seems a little flustered, not quite her normal competent self, which I attribute to her indisposition. I motion her to put the tray down on my desk. She hesitates, then goes out, banging the door.

"Very well. We'll leave it there for the moment."

I pour the coffee out slowly. I'm very tempted not to give van Reen any, but his eyes are watching my actions hungrily, like a dog by a dining table. I pass a cup to his free hand and have to get up from behind my desk to do so. I'm damned if I'm going to ask him if he takes sugar, though, like a hostess at a tea party. He can bloody well drink it without.

I light a cigarette, and return to my notes. The coffee is the real thing, a great deal tastier than the poor stuff I had drunk in the street, and I'm very grateful for it. We British are good at looking after ourselves, I reflect. No acorn substitute for us. For some reason the memory of a cheeky smile in a pretty face flashes across my mind for a second, and then is gone.

Van Reen drinks his coffee more slowly than I do. It is probably his first cup for a long time, and he is relishing it. He just falls short of smacking his lips.

The silence is getting on my nerves. I leaf through my notes while Van Reen puts his cup down clumsily on the desk and stares out of the window. The only view is of an empty office block, apparently undamaged apart from its broken windows. The lower walls are covered in graffiti:

*Russians out!*
*Hitler lives.*
*Yanks go home!'*

And a smaller one with a drawing of a heart: *'Gerd loves Mandi.'* Someone has scrawled underneath that one: *'Yes, but Mandi has loved everybody!'*

Outside in the office the typewriter is clattering furiously, then stops. There are raised voices. Van Reen gestures at his empty coffee mug.

"May I have a cigarette?"

"No."

He has opened his mouth to protest, when we are interrupted. The door opens and Helga enters again with just a token knock. She is clearly irate, and not to be lightly dismissed this time. She tugs at her skirt. She can hardly speak for indignation.

"Sir! Sir! That man!"

"Who? Corporal Bletcher?"

"Yes! He is still in my office!"

"Yes, I told him to wait there," I say irritably. "Why?"

She is beside herself.

"He has been filling the room with his smoke, and making improper suggestions to me! To me! I have tried to ignore him. But now, he puts his arm around me and then – ach! – he tries to stick his tongue in my ear! And me with a bad chest!"

She sticks out her well-developed bust, the subject of some admiration in the office. She shudders and strokes her ear as if to decontaminate herself.

"The man is an animal. His behaviour is outrageous! And his breath stinks of tobacco! Could you please ask him to leave my office at once, sir?"

She must be upset to be calling me 'sir', I reflect. It isn't immediately clear whether it is the smoking or the assault on her ear which has offended her most. But this unexpected revelation of Corporal Bletcher as a man capable of making advances to this sturdy, attractive young woman is almost comically incongruous.

"Very well, Helga. Tell the corporal to leave the office and return to pick the prisoner up at – um - five o'clock, please."

"Thank you, sir."

"And, Helga?"

"Yes?"

"Worse things can happen to a woman than that, you know."

There is a short silence in the office. My eyes have fallen onto one of my other files. She starts to speak and then stops, chastened. She glances at van Reen with loathing.

"Yes, sir. I do know that."

She leaves the office and we hear her conveying the message to the corporal in strident terms. I wait until we hear the outer door slam, then I look at van Reen. I pick up my thick file again, and sigh inwardly.

"Now I want to examine your army career before you were sent to Greece. You say in your earlier evidence you were an officer in … "

We resume our trawl through the grim landscape of war- torn Europe.

After a while van Reen begins twisting in his seat.

"If I may interrupt you, sir…" he says.

"What is it now?"

"I'm afraid I urgently need to use the toilet. My prostate, you see - it comes on very suddenly. I'm very sorry about this."

"Oh, for God's sake. All right," I say irritably, rising to escort him, and then stop dead. The man is handcuffed to the heavy chair, and I've sent Corporal Bletcher off with the key. How in the world am I going to get him to a lavatory?

For a moment I have a wild vision of manhandling him and the chair down the corridor, with him still manacled to it. No, we'd never get through the doorway.

Van Reen and I look at each other. He has half risen from his seat, and is waiting politely for me to deal with the problem. There is the faintest hint of a smile on his face. He might almost be enjoying my discomfiture. He seems to have got over the shock of my detailed knowledge of his career all too well. Perhaps he always knew his past would catch him up.

"Sir?"

This is ridiculous. What the hell am I going to do? I can't let him piss on the floor.

He clears his throat.

"Perhaps – a pot?" he says diffidently.

Of course. I glare at him in rebuke. Obviously I would have thought of that myself in another moment. I get up and go into Helga's office. She is at her desk, peering at her face in a hand mirror, and puts it down guiltily.

"Have we a bowl of some sort? A pot? A flower vase? Anything?"

I gesture with my thumb at the prisoner.

"I haven't got the key. He needs to…"

Understanding dawns on her face.

"*Ach, so...* Yes. There is a bucket in the broom cupboard. I will fetch it."

She bustles off, serious faced. I stare out of her window down at a side street. Half the buildings have either disappeared completely, or are merely teetering piles of bricks held together by cement. A young couple are quarrelling fiercely in a doorway. He is shouting furiously at her, but no sound reaches me. They disappear round the corner, still waving their hands.

After an endless delay Helga returns with a stained metal bucket of the sort that is designed to have a mop squeezed out in it.

"Will this serve?"

I take it through to my office and close the door behind me. I hand it to van Reen and go back to my desk, pretending to be engrossed in my files. For some reason I have always found the business of watching another man passing water deeply embarrassing, and am unable to do it myself if observed. In a public toilet I always go into a cubicle if I am to urinate at all.

Clearly van Reen does not share my inhibitions. He has awkwardly unbuttoned his trousers with his one free hand, and proceeds to pee into the bucket. He has a powerful, confident jet, which rings loudly against the metal. I keep my face averted, like a blushing maiden subjected to some form of indecent exposure. I reach for a cigarette and then hesitate, furious with myself for any of a number of reasons.

Now I have a sense of déjà vu.

*I am a small boy again, lonely and frightened, standing at the urinal in the outside toilet block at my prep school. I can see the dirty cream coloured walls, with their scrubbed out graffiti still barely legible. I can feel the cold air, hear the clanking of the pipes, and smell the chunky red blocks of coarse carbolic soap that sit on each basin. I am wearing regulation grey shorts, and my knees are scratched and caked in dried mud after a damp game of football, a game I loathe to this day.*

*A red-headed boy with a chalky white spotty face named Thomas, big for his age, is challenging me to pee in front of him, making caustic observations.*

*Come on. Let's have a look what you've got! Don't be a weed. Ha ha, call that a willy? Let's see it in action! Come on, sissy! Want me to warm it up for you?*

*Hard as I strain, in my terror I cannot summon up a single drop. Thomas stares at me for a long moment, then shrugs and walks away. I am not yet ready for him. He will come to me next year, when my body has developed and I shall be worthy of his further attention. Young as I am, I understand that very well.*

"Sir. Sir?"

Van Reen has finished, and is holding the bucket out to me like a child apologetically offering a dubious gift. I take the bucket from him. The urine is bright yellow and steam is arising from it. The bucket is surprisingly heavy.

I open the door but barge hard against Helga, who must have been poised on the threshold to await my signal to enter the room. To our mutual horror a portion of the contents of the bucket spills over her, drenching her neat grey skirt. She utters a stifled exclamation and recoils across the room. I gasp out an apology, dump the bucket on the floor, and retreat back into my own office, wiping my hands on my trousers and blushing furiously. This is a nightmare.

I hear a strange choking sound, and look up hurriedly. Van Reen is purple in the face, and I think for a moment that he has had a fit. Thoughts of cyanide suicide pills flash through my mind, but are gone in an instant. It is now obvious that he is merely helpless with mirth, sitting bent double in his chair with tears of laughter streaming down his cheeks.

I want to scream at him to be silent, and indeed open my mouth to do so.

"The expression on her face! I thought she was going to explode!" he moans.

I stare at him in fury. After the revelations from the doctor, the hideous details that are emerging from van Reen's interrogation, and the after-effects of last night's whisky, my nerves are bad. I think for one dreadful moment that hysterical laughter is going to sweep over me as well.

Then the memory of the woman I am to interview again tomorrow, the so-called Monster of Märchenholz, including one particular practice she enjoyed perpetrating on pregnant women prisoners, comes into my mind unbidden. I am not looking forward to tomorrow. Nor am I enjoying today. Any urge to laugh completely disappears completely.

"Shut up!" I rap at van Reen. "Be quiet or I'll see you put in solitary for a month!"

After a moment my obvious fury overcomes his mirth, and his face stiffens into his usual haughty expression.

"I do apologize, sir," he says, wiping his eyes with his free hand. "But her skirt was completely soaked…"

He is nearly off again, but then regains his composure. I clear my throat and pick up the file. It is becoming increasingly clear to me that I am not cut out for this work.

"I shall put this hysteria down to the effects of the horror of what you have been telling me," I say sternly. "Now we will continue…"

He nods, his expression now as serious as mine, and straightens in his seat. He resumes his normal demeanour as solemnly as an actor leaving the Green Room where the cast have been carousing, to go back on stage. As we pick up the narrative, we return to contemplation of this man's past actions. I take a deep breath, and light a cigarette.

"Now the exact numbers of prisoners who died, and their disposal…"

Much later I glance at my watch. I had heard indications from the outer office that Bletcher had returned. It's nearly five o'clock and I'm hungry. Visions of food pass before my eyes. I also need some fresh air, gulps of it. To say that I've had enough of van Reen and his affairs would be an understatement.

I call to Helga to tell the corporal that our interview is concluded. She makes no reply, but Bletcher stamps into the room and comes noisily to a halt. A strong odour of urine wafts in from behind him, and I can see Helga hunched awkwardly over her desk, typing furiously.

"You may escort the prisoner back to prison, corporal."

"Sah!"

"And next time leave me the key to the handcuffs."

"Sah!"

Was that a smirk on his podgy porcine face? I

ignore it. He transfers one of the handcuffs from the chair to his own wrist.

"That is all for now, van Reen. We shall resume on Monday."

Van Reen bows his head courteously.

"I look forward to it, sir."

The incongruous pair leave together, Bletcher attempting a full military manoeuvre with stamping feet and stiff torso, while van Reen ambles alongside him with an amiable smile on his face like the innocent participant in a pantomime. It is a scene from a farce, but I cannot raise a smile. The door closes behind them.

I work for another hour, then wearily store my files away. As I walk home, I remember how I met Thomas again in very different circumstances.

# 4

*Caen, Normandy, June 1944*

Some time after we had landed – it could have been an hour, it could have been ten for all I could tell – I had twenty or so men strung out along the street behind me. There was now another officer with me, Paddy Milne, who was just junior to me. He'd dropped back to attend to little Philips who had collapsed onto the pavement, half conscious after a flesh wound that was getting worse. Philips had been looking bad for a while, and I'd kept half an eye on him. I'd had no orders, and I was so tired my brain had stopped working. All I could think of doing was to press on blindly into the city without any very clear objective, and attempt to eliminate enemy resistance as we came across it.

William the Conqueror's once noble city, with its lovely medieval castle and ancient University, was being fiercely defended against an English enemy, and not for the first time in its history. Now Caen's precarious security was in the hands of a crack German Panzer brigade, the 21st. They had been taken by surprise by the Allied invasion, and seemed almost as disorganised as we were, though with more excuse. The fighting was sporadic, unpredictable by either side, but it was clearly vital to the Germans that they should hold the city for as long as possible. The Allied task was to take it.

We had come to an area with narrow cobbled streets and old, crouched houses, often half-timbered. Some had been badly damaged by shellfire, and many of the window panes were cracked or missing. There was little sign of the inhabitants. It was rumoured that the Germans had ordered and expedited a civilian evacuation of the city, whether for humanitarian reasons or simply to clear the arena for fighting, I never discovered.

I raised my arm to signal a halt and turned to speak to Lang, who was walking rapidly up behind me.

"Everyone all right, sergeant?"

"Yes, sir. Well, no sir – that's to say…"

"Where's Lieutenant Milne?"

Lang was panting slightly. He looked as exhausted as I felt and his normally immaculate uniform was smeared with dirt.

"Copped it, sir," he said indistinctly.

"What?"

"Dead, sir," he said, more loudly this time. "Took a direct hit two streets back. Sniper. Don't know about Philips – we had to leave him."

He hesitated a moment. He knew Milne and I had been friends. "I'm very sorry, sir."

Now I was the only officer. And I'll have no-one to play chess with. I shook my head to clear it. Paddy and I used to play for money to give the game some bite. Then we'd get too drunk to play properly, and just sit and laugh. I owed him thirty bob. And – and his wife had just had a baby.

*Why, this is hell, nor are we out of it.*

I had to bunch my fists to stop them trembling. I saw the sergeant eyeing me, and he started to speak. As he approached, the first of a series of sudden loud crashes made us both jump, drowning out his words. Milne's death was forgotten, his very memory dashed into non- existence. The explosions came from some distance away, where an orange glow had begun to spread on the skyline. We stared out towards it, then I pulled out of my tunic pocket the crumpled map of the city that had been supplied with the original briefing orders. It looked as if the bombardment was in the area of the railway station, an obvious target. There were more booms and rattles of gunfire, and then were still.

A large plume of black smoke began slowly to smudge the perfect blue of the sky. In the silence I could hear the twitter of sparrows from a bush growing up a wall of an old house. A child's pram lay upended on the pathway in front of it. A broken doll had been flung out, its skull cracked, and flies buzzed around it. The bushes had small bright scarlet flowers among the thorns, like drops of blood. It *was* blood. I suddenly averted my gaze.

Small bees were buzzing busily round the bush in the sunshine, oblivious to the movement around them. Feathery spiders' webs silhouetted their fragile delicacy against the light. Nature continued on her stately course, aloof and unabated, while our human world crashed around us.

I pulled my eyes away with an effort. I wiped my

throbbing head with an oil-stained handkerchief, where a deep graze had begun to bleed again.

"Looks like the station. We'd better go and see if we can help."

"Sir."

"And, Lang. You're second in command of the company now."

"Sir."

Lang showed no pleasure at his sudden promotion, but stood waiting stolidly for further orders. He was a calm sort of man, and I'd already learnt to rely on him. I showed him the map and we discussed it briefly.

"Right. Do a quick roll call if you can. Then get the men ready to move off. Carry on."

"Sir!"

I stuffed my handkerchief into my pocket and pored over the map again before putting it away. The bombardment in the distance suddenly redoubled in intensity. Our obvious duty was to head towards it.

Just as I reached this conclusion a loud rumbling noise made me stiffen and I raised my head. I could hardly believe my eyes. Slowly round the corner, in a scene out of a comic film, trundled a German half-track infantry carrier, clanking along like some aged dinosaur. Five or six men were crowded into it above the caterpillar wheel, all of them heavily armed. The half-track had a large gun mounted amidships behind the two front wheels, which was rocking about precariously. The whole ensemble looked like a military version of the Keystone Cops.

We scattered immediately like frightened rabbits, raising our guns. I was armed with only a pistol and couldn't get it out of its canvas holster quickly enough. I had a moment of panic while I scrabbled at the flap.

Then I realised that the troops were not Germans, but were from our own regiment, though a different division. They must have captured the tank from the enemy. We all arrived with relief at this conclusion at the same instant.

"All right, Sergeant," I called to Lang, straightening up. "As you were!"

The officer seated in front by the driver smirked. He gave an order, and the vehicle came to a noisy halt beside us. I saw he wore the crowns of a major, and saluted. He glared at me without bothering to return the salute properly.

" 'Hell you lot doing here? You in charge?" he barked.

"Yes, sir."

"Shit yourself, eh? Thought we were Jerries?"

"Just for a moment."

He laughed. "Lucky for you we're not."

He didn't move from his seat. He offered no explanation as to how he came to be commanding a German vehicle, and I didn't ask. The fortunes of war ebb and flow in unpredictable ways, as any soldier quickly learns.

"What are your orders?"

"None, sir." I gestured towards the station area in the distance. "But there's a hell of a racket going on over there by the station, and we were going to head towards it."

"Seems like a bloody stupid idea to me. I reckon we'd all be better off just pressing on to the far side of town and leaving them to it."

He thought a moment, scowling and pulling at his

chin with a plump freckled hand. He was an ugly, red-haired man, with little piggy eyes that darted this way and that. A line of sweat ran above his fleshy upper lip. Although he seemed vaguely familiar, I couldn't place him. Probably I'd met him on some regimental occasion or other.

"Any of your men qualified drivers?"

He jerked his thumb at the man beside him. "This fool hasn't a clue how to drive this fucking thing. It'd be a damn sight quicker to walk."

The man blanched but said nothing.

"Excuse me, sir," said Lang. "Edwards would know. That right, Edwards?"

One of my men came forward hesitantly and saluted. He was a stocky, fair-haired Welshman, a good steady type.

"Well?"

"I do know a bit about these, sir. It's an old M3, like. Us and the Jerries both use them. They're buggers to drive though, isn't it?"

He stepped towards the vehicle and peered at the controls.

"Well now. You might want to move that lever over for a start, like. That gearbox is a tricky enough sod without that." He grinned. "It might help if you took the bloody handbrake off as well."

The men in the back of the truck began to laugh and offer comments about their driver's ability, with liberal references to tractors and sheep shagging. There was a cacophony of bawdy laughter. The wretched driver squirmed.

"Shut up, all of you!" shouted the major and turned to the driver. "You – out!" He pointed to Edwards. "And you get in and take over. And let's get a fucking move on."

Edwards looked enquiringly at me. The wound throbbed in my forehead, and it was then that I realised where I'd known the major before.

"Hang on!" I said. "This man is under my command. You can't just take him over like that."

"Oh, is that what you think?"

As he spoke there were more heavy booms in the distance, and then after a pause a huge explosion. We all stiffened. The sky lit up with a red-and-yellow light against black clouds, like an ominous dawn before a thunderstorm. The sound of gunfire intensified.

"Edwards stays with me!" I yelled. "Sergeant - get the men formed up." I pointed to a narrow street.

"We'll go that way. Single file, ten yard intervals. Head towards the station. All right, let's go!"

The major's face had turned bright red.

"How dare you disobey my orders!" he shouted. "What's your name, Lieutenant? I can have you..."

At that moment his driver, who had been fiddling with the controls and had clearly been inspired by Edwards' observations, must have suddenly let out the clutch. Whether or not this was intentional, I couldn't tell. The vehicle shot smartly forward, nearly dislodging its passengers, and began roaring up the main street at a fair speed. I saw the major's mouth open and shut like a dying fish, but the monstrous ugly contraption quickly disappeared round a corner out of our sight, making a terrific racket, its huge gun swaying perilously. As it vanished we could see someone frantically clambering onto the back of the truck while his comrades hauled him in.

An unseen voice called out "All aboard! Any more for the Skylark?" Loud laughter rang out and the tension was broken. I began to breathe more normally. Some sort of order was returning and we were ready for action again.

"You did the right thing there, sir, if you don't mind me saying so," said Lang, shifting his rifle up onto his shoulder, and indicating their places to a couple of stragglers. "Come on you lot, move your arses!"

"What a cheek," I said feelingly. "Who was that officer, d'you know?"

"Major Thomas, sir," said Long. "Came across him in training camp. A right… "

As he spoke, there was a whistling sound over our heads, louder and louder till it felt as if our ears were bursting. We ran for shelter, but the shell passed over us and out of sight. A second volley followed. Almost immediately there was a tremendous explosion a couple of streets away, followed by another. Lang and I looked at each other.

"You men stay here!" I yelled. "Wait for my orders."

Lang and I ran round the corner following the route of the major's party. We didn't have to go far. It was a scene of carnage. The half -track had taken a direct hit from one of the shells. It was lying on its side, with its occupants spilled out of it like limp rag dolls. As we approached Lang put his hand on my arm to stop me. Oil was pouring out of its ruptured tank, and the gun was on its back pointing upwards at a grotesque angle. Flames were beginning to lick along pools of spilt oil.

"Might go up any second, sir! Keep well back, for Christ's sake."

The words were hardly out of his mouth when the

remains of the truck exploded with a huge whooshing noise. The blast of hot air blew us to the ground. Metal shot over our heads and rattled against the walls of the houses.

A hideous screaming noise was coming from somewhere. I screwed up my eyes and stared round, and it was a little time before I realised there was a man trapped in a plane tree near the half- track ten feet above the pavement. He must have been propelled up there by the blast and been impaled on one of the broken branches. It was a grotesque scene out of Hieronymus Bosch. As I gazed helplessly upwards, he fell silent. Two men, who had survived the impact, were slowly standing up. One was a corporal, and I recognised the other as the driver. He was half kneeling on the pavement, moaning and holding his back.

I took a quick tour round the remains of the vehicle which was now burning steadily, but there was no sign of life. The occupants must have all been killed by the blast. Then I heard a groan from a figure on the ground some way from the truck, and saw the crowns on the epaulettes. It was Thomas all right. That red hair and the thick lips...

He was lying by the side of the road looking up at me, his cap at a stupid angle. He seemed to be trying to speak. One of his legs had been blown clean off. Below his knees there was nothing much left but white bone showing through crimson and grey pulp and khaki rags. A boot was lying separately with most of the bottom part of his leg still in it, and the gutter was rapidly filling with dark red blood.

I knelt beside him, pulling out my water flask and putting it to his lips.

"Here, Thomas," I said gently. "Have a sip of this."

He stared at me and his mouth moved, but no words came out, and the water dribbled down his chin. Part of his jaw had collapsed, and his face was a mess. His eyes never left mine, and he was paler than ever. As I knelt beside him I felt Time swerve and stop.

Was this pathetic lump of flesh really the same Thomas who had made my life a misery in my second year at school? The swaggering bully, the school lout, who had held my head down the lavatory basin and pulled the chain, while he and his cronies yelped with laughter? And then who took me into one of the cubicles… What, this dribbling fragment that was gripping my hand, lips drawn back over uneven teeth, breath coming in gasps? Was this really him? *Where be your jibes now? Your flashes of merriment, that were wont to set the table on a roar? What, quite chop fallen?*

I put the stopper back in the flask, and thought, the little boy that I was once is getting his revenge. This should feel good. But I felt nothing at that moment, and I feel nothing now.

"Try and hold on," I said. "We'll get you some help."

But he choked suddenly, and blood began to gush in a steady stream from his mouth. His eyes fixed on mine again in an expression of mild astonishment before clouding over. His head lolled, and he was dead.

After a minute I pulled his ID disc off the chain round his neck as standing orders dictated, and slipped it into my pocket. My trousers were soaked in his blood. I stood up and moved away, and looked round at the scene, trying to re-orientate myself.

"What's your name?" I said to the stocky corporal.

"Jones, J. P, sir," he replied.

"And the wounded man?" I asked, indicating the vehicle.

"Oh, that's Jones, R. W., sir. Got a shell fragment in the arse, like. Don't worry about him, sir. He's the major's batman. Wasn't much use before, and he'll be no bloody use at all now."

"Very well, Jones. We'll have to leave them here. We'll head towards the firing and try and find out what's going on."

"Sir."

He didn't move.

"What shall I do with the major's body, sir?"

"For Christ's sake leave it where it is and let's get on," I said shortly. "I'll write to his family"

"What will you say, sir?" he asked. "You didn't even know him, like. He'd been with us since… "

"Oh, I knew him, all right," I said shortly, cutting him off. I stared towards the black smoke filling the sky. The bombardment had increased again and now I could hear the rattle of small arms. If our troops were trying to capture the station they could no doubt do with our backup.

"He wasn't an easy man, sir." He sniffed.

"Tell you the truth, he could be a bastard, but…" he gestured towards the legless corpse. "I remember once when Bill Pritchard and I…."

"All right. That's enough."

Jones J. P. was obviously the garrulous type, and not even battle conditions could stem his flow. Nerves were making him babble. I turned away and looked around.

"Lang!" I called. "Nothing much more we can do here. Let's get moving again."

"Sir!"

"Let's look sharp."

And so we left the destroyed half- track and the bits of bodies on the road and the figure in the tree and the blood and oil mixing in the gutters and the remains of Major Thomas, and moved on through the town, each thinking our own thoughts.

# 5

*Hamburg, 1946.*

It is now a regular ritual for me to go to the old man's room and perhaps share our simple meal together, after which the doctor likes to talk. For the moment he is silent to concentrate on each mouthful, though what the meat is, neither of us inquires. The possibilities are not appetising.

It is clear that he is not going to find any peace until he's told the whole tale, and normally I am happy to be his confidant. I am keenly interested to hear more of the tale of the young Hitler. Tonight however I am not much inclined towards further revelations from anybody. We eat our meat pie together without speaking, although as usual the doctor's ancient gramophone is playing in the background. I am being treated to the Mozart clarinet concerto. Its sweetness fills the little room and transports each of us to our different memories.

When the record has come to an end the doctor puts his knife and fork down and stares out of the window. It is rare that he finishes what is on his plate, however modest the portions. He has developed a cough that racks his whole body. His face is hollower than ever, the lines deep by the side of his mouth. I have learned not to tire him out by staying with him too late, but I am like the Wedding Guest – there is no escaping the skinny hand or glittering eye of the Ancient Mariner.

"Are you all right, *Herr Doktor*?"

Dr Mann gestures impatiently.

"Of course. Just a touch of this winter 'flu they talk about. It's nothing. And I would very much appreciate it if you would call me Ernst? I think our friendship has advanced beyond the formal? Well, I hope so."

"Thank you, Ernst. And of course you know I am Adam."

I am moved by his old-fashioned courtesy, and nod my head as graciously as seems appropriate. I tiptoe over to the gramophone and replace the arm in the cradle.

The doctor smiles.

"Now where was I?"

"You were telling me about young Adolph."

"Ah yes," says Ernst, looking around for his pipe and tobacco, and then composing himself. The cough has become so severe that it is impossible for him to continue smoking his beloved pipe, but he doesn't want me to know that. He sighs.

"I should tell you some more of what I know about young Adolph after his father's untimely death."

He sees me stir and cross my legs, and looks at me anxiously.

"But only if you want me to continue? An old man's recollections... But I think it is perhaps important."

"Please do go on."

"Well, I saw him only rarely after that, but I met his sister sometimes, and my friend Fritz kept me informed as far as he could. I could not shake off a morbid interest in the young man's fate, God help me. It was somehow as if I had an inkling..."

He shakes his head.

"Did he stay on long at school?"

"No, not long. As I expected, once his father's influence had ceased and his mother was settled with a small pension, he left school. The authorities seemed happy enough to see him go, and I doubt if there was much effort made to persuade him to continue with his studies. In any case, his private reading had taken him well beyond the somewhat narrow confines of the school curriculum."

The doctor coughs again, putting his hand to his side, closing his eyes with a grimace of pain. Then he continues.

"I saw him once or twice when he called in at the surgery for something or other for his mother. She was very ill. She had breast cancer, I believe. Bloch was treating her. But she died later, well after his father. I know he was very badly affected by her death. Bloch told me once he'd never seen anyone so cut up. But Adolph wasn't my patient, and if our paths crossed occasionally we never acknowledged each other. I had made my decision not to pursue the matter of his father's death. But I could never get the manner of it out of my mind.

It has got much darker, but neither of us has

moved to turn up the lighting. If this tale is true – and I have absolutely no reason to doubt it – I have an obligation to make it known to the authorities. But I need to consider this more carefully. The doctor is speaking again.

"And of course the boy was a beast!"

He is almost hissing now. "*Ach*, Adam, I was so stupid, so cowardly. Can you imagine? I could have had him charged, arrested, maybe imprisoned. It would at least have stopped his career! Millions, yes, millions of people have died because of my timidity, my cowardice!"

He beats his hand on his head, his face twisted with grief. "Can you imagine how it feels to hug that knowledge to myself for all these years?

I am impatient now.

"Ernst! Stop it – you're talking like a fool! We are all corks floating down a river. Sometimes we enter rapids, sometimes shallows. We negotiate our way as well as we can, that's all. None of us knows what may result if we turn left instead of right, talk to one girl and not another, miss an appointment or a train. It's not your fault!"

Ernst shakes his head wordlessly, staring at the carpet. He is inconsolable. I have an inspiration.

"You know the story of Gustav Prinzip, the assassin of the Archduke Ferdinand? He had a poor sense of direction, apparently. He couldn't find the route the Archduke's procession was taking in Sarajevo on that fateful day. He had actually given up on his assassination plan and was going home, when he lost his way again and came upon the procession purely by chance. It was then that he took out his revolver and fired the shot that reverberated round the world, the spark that ignited the first world war. Ten million people died because he had taken a wrong turning."

"I had not heard that story."

"Yes, well. You know what I believe?" I ask. "You didn't make any decision, Ernst. It is all chance. What happened is what happened."

The doctor looks at me with a new respect and chuckles briefly. "You believe that, Adam? We shall make a philosopher of you yet."

I reach across and put my hand on his knee. He looks at me with his pale blue watery eyes, but for a moment seems a little comforted.

"Quite a story," I say. "A lot to think about. And now, goodnight. You should sleep well now that you have unburdened yourself. And believe me, you have nothing to reproach yourself with. Nothing."

The old man says nothing. He just smiles at me and raises one hand weakly in farewell as I leave the room and tiptoe to bed.

§

*Hamburg, 1946*

Repetition of horror does not make it any easier to bear. I have waded through more files, more accounts of self- justification from half a dozen people whose affairs are my concern and whose future may depend on my activities, I tidy my desk and prepare to leave. I am sickened by what I read, day after day, and I need fresh air.

The other lawyers have all gone home to their

wives, children, briefs, or lovers, and of course to ponder on their fee bills and bonuses. I say goodnight to Helga, who is still sulky and disinclined to catch my eye, and go down to the basement to see my friend Gustav in the kitchens, a visit that has become part of my routine. He is a fat, solemn young man, prematurely bald, with an unexpectedly wicked sense of humour. His jokes are delivered deadpan, and it has taken me some time to learn to appreciate them through his thick Bavarian accent.

He wipes his greasy hands on his already greasier apron, reaching into the pocket for his cigarettes.

"So what is it tonight, Herr Kapitän?" he enquires slyly. "Another bottle of something special? You have a side line going on the market, perhaps? Or a very thirsty little French girl friend?"

It is a standing joke with him that I am a notorious black marketeer with a string of mistresses, which it is useless for me to attempt to deny. In fact both activities are far more applicable to him than to me.

"Ah, you may be right there," I say, tapping the side of my nose and dropping effortlessly into my role of man-about-town. I have the illusion of having several different personae at my disposal, to be produced according to the person I am speaking to. Does everyone do this? Or – moment of panicky introspection – is it just me?

"But she's getting a little tired of brandy. Have you perhaps anything else more... suitable for a lady?"

I deliver this with an attempt at a leer, like a customer buying contraceptives from under the counter in a barbers' shop.

His face lights up. "Now, as it happens, I just

might have."

He beckons me furtively into the gloom of the vast kitchens that run under the building. They are much older than the uninspiring offices at street level would suggest, and these cellars, with their low ceilings, arched corridors and battered stone floors may be a remnant of the sixteenth century city.

They were in constant use as air raid shelters during the last months of the war, when the bombardment went on day and night without remission. A firestorm could suck all the air out of a shelter, no matter how deep. The occupants would start bleeding from the ears, nose and eyes, and then be rapidly asphyxiated. Perhaps it happened here too. The ancient walls are still decorated with stern official notices forbidding smoking, urinating, or discussing military affairs, tangible mementoes of the very recent past.

The dark crannies and vaults are damp with despair and dread. I shiver and shake my head to dismiss these thoughts.

Gustav whispers, "I do have a case of pink champagne. Very high quality, liberated from the cellars of a Belgian aristocrat. I could perhaps let you have a bottle at, let me see... you are paying in dollars, of course, *Herr Kapitän*?"

He shows me the case, hidden under some damp sacking in the corner of the stockroom. I pick a bottle out. It is cheap *faux* champagne in an over- elaborate packaging, with a garish label. This shows dancing girls at the Folies Bergeres in a poor depiction of the famous Toulouse Lautrec poster. Still, it is alcohol, and probably pretty strong at that. And there is nothing much else on offer.

"Gustav," I whisper, my lips close to his sweaty ear. Now I am being an expert negotiator, a spiv in the current London jargon. "That is not champagne, my friend, that is fizzy cat's piss from a moggy with a bladder infection. Nobody in their right mind would give you more than a handful of Reichsmarks for the lot. But I'm going to take three bottles and give you a dollar, because the war has affected my brain. I shall expect a dozen of your finest and fruitiest Frankfurters thrown in, though. With a jar of real Senf as well, of course."

Good German mustard is scarce too.

I pull the greenbacks from my wallet. His greedy little eyes shine and he holds them up to the dim light by the doorway.

"*Echt* American dollars?" he asks, turning them over and over, pretending he knows what watermarks to look for.

"Of course. But look sharp before I change my mind."

We are both a little young to remember it, but we know very well that not so long ago, twenty four billion Reichsmarks were needed to buy a kilo of butter. Such things stick in the mind. Even today you would need a week's wages, say two hundred Reichsmarks.

I know – he does not – that the Reichsmark is shortly to be replaced by the Deutschmark, and that the banknotes are already being secretly printed in America. But the smart currency of the moment is the dollar, even better than the ubiquitous packet of cigarettes. I've been acquiring dollars from pals at the Officers' Club, well-heeled Americans who chuck their money around. The exchange rate for German currency is still all over the place, and dollars are the only sure bet. But for the average German citizen they are hard to get hold of.

The greenbacks disappear into Gustav's grasp and are instantly lost to sight beneath his apron. They will buy him a good night out on the town if he knows where to go – and he does. And now so do I.

§

After the usual delights of my day at the office, I set off into the night like a thief, with my swag in a canvas bag and a song in my heart. There is a full moon, and the streets are as bright as daylight. The moon throws her silver beams onto the bare ruined choirs of the Santa *Margarethekirchen* round the corner, rising slowly through the sightless eye of one of the great Gothic windows. The snow crunches beneath my feet, and a baby rat scuttles into a broken drain not a yard away from me. But my heart is as light as the silver sky. I'm going to have sex tonight and little else much matters. And I don't much care who I'm going to have it with.

I am making for the dark street where the voices accost me. There is a rabbit warren of alleyways running behind the *Königstrasse*, where Rose and her fellow conspirators seem to have made their base, though I've felt no wish to investigate it until now.

Tonight the full moon emboldens me, and I step out as jauntily as Herr Klumpf will allow, past teetering ruins and rows of houses and shops with more gaps in them than an old woman's set of rotting teeth. Whole streets are still blocked in places by mountains of rubble, where the bombweeds grew profusely in the summer months, and amazingly, now in winter too. Well beaten paths have begun to form around the mounds of broken bricks, and on these you have to watch your step.

There are still a few people about, a mother fussing with a child, a bearded muttering man with a tubercular cough pulling a cart, office workers hurrying home with coat collars turned up against the stinging snow. Clouds are obscuring the moon now, and there is little illumination.

A man on a bicycle comes past me from behind without warning and makes me jump. A few paces further on, a sudden yelp and strident yapping reveal two scrawny dogs quarrelling over a soil covered bone. Often these bones are recognisably human, parts of the many thousands of undiscovered bodies still buried in the ruined city. I don't look too closely, but hurry on. It has got noticeably colder since I left the office, and the snow on the road is beginning to freeze hard.

My confidence is a fragile flower, and begins to wilt as I approach my destination. It is with a kind of relief that I hear a soft voice calling from the shadows.

"Well, look who it is! The handsome young Englander. *Guten Abend, mein Herr!*"

Tonight is different. I stop instead of hurrying past. I am in the market for whoever it is she is offering. I look towards where the voice is coming from, and at that moment the clouds move away from the moon. Instantly it is as bright as day.

A figure in a hat and a long fur coat is standing in a doorway, watching me. Her smile is devilish. She is smoking, and the moonlight reflects a pretty bangle shining on her wrist. From a distance she looks extraordinarily elegant, like an advertising poster for an exotic brand of cigarette. Snow has settled on the shoulders of her coat, and her breath leaves little puffs of mist in the cold air.

"Hello," I say.

"Hello indeed!"

I try to think of something witty, but my mind has gone blank. "Aren't you cold standing there?" I say.

"Oh, I get warmed up every now and then!" she cries. "When some kind man takes pity on me... How about you, *Herr Kapitän*? Aren't you cold too?"

I shake my head.

"Not rushing away? Aha! Tonight is perhaps the night? There is something I can do for you perhaps?"

She is teasing me. I stand very still, feeling the weight of my bag dragging on my arm.

"Well, now," I say. My voice has gone a bit squeaky, and I am conscious of my heart beating. "It all depends on what you have to offer."

Her laugh rings out, tinkling like a bell. The first owl of the evening has begun to hoot softly from the grotesquely twisted silhouette of a tall roofless warehouse further down the street.

"Oh, well, that's no problem. Which way does your fancy lie, kind sir? Are you a bully who's missing his bullwhip, or a gallant knight, seeking a night of true romance? We cater for all tastes here, you know."

She has come up to me and raises a hand to the lapel of my greatcoat, then blows smoke in my face. "What's it to be then? Speak!"

I take her hand in mine and pull it down to my side. Close to, you can see the black shadows under her eyes and the darns in her grubby clothes. Her eyes are very green and her face is pale.

"You look tired," I say. "And cold, and maybe hungry."

Her mood has changed, and I see the vulnerability in her young eyes.

"All that and more," she says quietly. "All that and more."

The bag has become heavy and I put it down on the ground. The bottles chink a little.

"What have you got there then?" she demands. "Ooh – some treats perhaps? Something nice for little Rose?"

"Depends if little Rose likes champagne." I say. "And frankfurters with real mustard. And onions. Oh, and afterwards, some chocolates…" Christmas Eve.

"Ooh, ooh…" she cries. Then her face falls. "But perhaps you have only enough for one. My friends, you see… we share, you understand. It is the only way to survive. Ooh, come and meet them!" She grabs my arm and dragging me into the shadowy lanes behind the ruined doorway. "You'll like them when you get to know them, really you will! Now… "

She stops and wags her finger at me in mock ferocious fashion. "But don't be put off by appearances. They're all right, I promise you."

"I can't wait to meet them," I say truthfully, and am urged on into the narrow cobbled alleyway. In for a penny, in for a pound, as my mother used to say. But she is not someone I want to think about at this moment.

After a minute or two, a little path leads us down the side of a large roofless house of handsome proportions. We pick our way carefully in the gathering gloom. Round the back we enter the remains of an enclosed cobbled courtyard, ghostly under the moon. Greenhouses, their panes shattered, stand against one wall. A battered stone lion lies at an angle in a corner of the yard, staring resentfully towards where plants have run wild in a flower bed. One patch though has been cultivated and is well tended and stocked with herbs. I can identify some of them – basil, lovage, and mint, sturdy rosemary, fenugreek and comfrey, thyme and sage. I stoop to sniff at the lavender, squeezing it between my fingers.

Rose has stopped to watch me, her eyes bright.

"You like herbs? We grow them for food, and for medicine. You would be surprised what a good larder we have here."

"So I see. Are you the gardener round here?"

"Oh yes. I've always loved flowers. Even the ones people call weeds. They are my favourites, really."

I smile and quote. "'A weed is a plant whose virtues have not yet been discovered.' Isn't that right?"

She laughs delightedly. "Yes – and I'll tell you another one! 'A weed is only a flower growing in the wrong place.' Isn't that lovely? Do you know who said that? A wonderful man, an American negro called George Washington Carver."

The moonlight catches her face and she looks like a beautiful child, innocent of all the wicked ways of the world.

"Why so?"

She does a little twirl, raising the hems of her long skirt under her coat. "Because that's what they call us! Here we are all fireweeds! You know, rosebay – *Feuerkraut* – the fireweed that flourishes here in the ruins! Haven't you noticed all the beautiful weeds that sprang up everywhere this year? Some of them had never been seen before. And they were completely out of season."

"Yes, they're lovely. I've often wondered at them. But I don't know their names."

"Some are cannabis plants. Yummy yummy! And a terrific painkiller," she giggles. "The others are mostly rosebay willow herb. The purple and yellow ones. Did you know, they too are medicine? They are really good for tummy aches? And they make a good mouthwash too. But without a fire or a disaster they would never flower. Their seeds hide away unseen, waiting, waiting for the bombs, as if they knew…"

She gestures, opening her arms wide.

"And then when catastrophe strikes, they miraculously appear and bring beauty and health to a place of despair! Isn't that just amazing? Like me, you see! I'm a Fireweed!"

I feel an unbearable pity for this brave girl and for a moment I can hardly breathe. Then she grabs my arm.

"Come on and meet my friends. The other Fireweeds!"

"What is this place? It must have been a fine house once. This was the walled garden? Do you live here?"

"Oh, yes. Now. This is just one of the houses my family used to own." She says it dismissively. "We used it sometimes for entertaining when we were staying in the city. It was what we called *das Löwenhaus*, the Lion House. Because of the statues, I suppose. And now? It is my only home. The only thing left. So much destroyed."

"That's awful."

"No!" she cries. "Not awful! What did we need all that for, the houses, the servants, the estates? All I need is a warm place, somewhere to eat, to sleep – and to entertain my clients, of course."

Her face has become serious. She opens the door and I follow her cautiously inside into a hallway, with a staircase leading up from it. She hesitates for a split second, then leads me into the room off to the left. It is the kitchen, with dressers, sink basins and a cooking stove in the corner, and a large battered oak table in the middle of the room. On the walls hang saucepans and cooking implements, with huge bunches of herbs on hooks in the ceiling, giving the place a fragrant, rustic smell. Oil lamps light the room, casting yellow pools of light like spilt gold paint. A good fire in the iron stove makes the room comfortably warm.

Two women are busy at the stove. One is tall, angular, and bespectacled. She is in her forties, I would judge, and is clearly in charge. She glances around and nods unsmilingly at me. A stocky younger woman is timidly helping her, too intent on her task to bother with newcomers.

At the table where papers are spread out sits a big man, busy writing something. He has a mop of tangled hair and a beard to match, and is smoking an evil looking pipe. He doesn't look up from his work.

Rose claps her hands for attention.

"Look who I've found!" she cries. "An English officer and gentleman! Let me introduce - " She stops and looks puzzled. "Do you know, I don't even know your name? How silly of me."

I clear my throat. "Adam. My name is Adam."

"This big bad bear is Max. And this is Dagmar,

who keeps us in order. Oh, and that's Elena slaving away over there."

The big man flicks his eyes over me without much interest, and indicates the inner door with a jerk of his head.

"Well, don't hang around, Rosa. What are you doing in here? Get your business done and then we can eat."

Dagmar makes a "hah!" noise and shrugs one shoulder. "There's nothing in this pot to get too excited about, I can tell you that."

She turns to Rose.

"Never mind dragging in some damned Englishman to crow over our misery – did you get any food? We can't live on nettle soup, you know."

"Take you what you came for, Englander, then give the girl some money and go," growls Max.

"No, give her the money first, for Christ's sake!" says Dagmar, suddenly exploding into life and banging the table. "Don't you know the bloody rules yet? You remember those Americans the other day!"

She is clearly the madame of this establishment.

"Look, I…" I stammer foolishly, feeling more awkward than I'd ever done in my life. "I just wanted to…"

Rose is still holding me by the hand, and now she hauls me out of the room.

"We know what you want!" she yells. "Well, come and get it then!"

§

I find myself following her upstairs, still carrying my bag like a doctor visiting a sick patient. Halfway up the stairs she stops and looks back, winking at me as if to ask me to forgive her bit of playacting. She flings open the bedroom door.

"Well, here we are! Make yourself comfortable."

The room contains a large bed covered with a huge quilted eiderdown, once a fine piece of embroidery but now stained and faded. Propped up among enormous pillows is a battered teddy bear with one eye missing. Long velvet curtains reach the floor, and the wallpaper, of a soft delicate green and gold design, is peeling away in parts.

To my relief there is no sign of what I presume to be the room's main function. No whips adorn the walls, nor do fancy frilly undergarments line the clothes rail. The few pictures on the walls are distinctly uninspiring, and feature mostly solemn black and white scenes of a vanished Germany. Whatever I have vaguely imagined a brothel should look like, this is not it.

Rose stands looking at me for a moment with a smile on her face, then takes her coat off and lays it on a Louis XIV spindle legged chair, nearly toppling it over. She holds her hand out for my greatcoat, and I take it off and give it her. She is standing very close to me. I can see she is trembling a little, perhaps with cold.

"You know, I…I'm not really…."

"Oh, shut up!" she says. "For God's sake get undressed. I'll be back in a minute." She opens a side door and disappears. A minute later I can hear water running.

Well, this is it, I think, and start unlacing my boots. When I've finished removing everything but my underpants, I sit rather primly on the bed and wonder what to do next. Memories of my previous bedroom experiences, none of them the occasion of much satisfaction to either party, flutter unhelpfully into my mind.

Ah! Inspiration strikes! I take one of the bottles of so-called champagne out of the bag. I start unpeeling the silver foil and wire around the neck and look round for some receptacles.

At that moment the bathroom door opens and Rose comes out. She is wrapped in a long pink towel. Her feet, arms, and shoulders are bare, and her long dark hair has been quickly combed. She stands quite still and we just look at each other. I am quite sure I have never seen anything more beautiful in my life.

She sees the bottle and sums up the situation. "Champagne! *Fantastisch!* But wait. Glasses!" She opens an armoire on the wall and brings out two magnificent crystal glasses, darkened with age but glinting like jewels in the light from the oil lamp on the dresser. "My great grandfather's, I believe."

She breathes on them carefully, looking up at me mischievously as she polishes them on her towel. As she does so a fold falls away and one of her breasts is exposed, its erect nipple as pink as the towel. Seeing this she giggles, and with a shrug lets the towel drop. She advances towards me with a glass in either hand. Then she stands in front of me as naked as the day she was born, waiting for me to pour the champagne.

As I gaze at her young body, with its patch of pubic hair forming a perfect heart shape below her smooth stomach, I twist the bottleneck nervously in my hand. Then to my horror the cork shoots out without warning and rockets across the room, startling us both. It hits a gilt ormolu mirror on the wall by the bed and bounces onto the floor. A spray of fizzy liquid spurts over Rose's exquisite bosom. She hoots with laughter, and after a moment I join in.

"My God!" she gurgles. You must learn better self-control, Adam. We call that early pearly! But I never saw it happen quite so early in the proceedings!"

I pretend to apologise. "I must have got over excited. You must forgive me."

"But such style! *Ah, les Anglais – quelle finesse!* But yes, that's good champagne – you'd better taste some, *Herr Kapitän.* Don't want to waste any, do we?"

She cups her hands under her breasts, and offers them to me with her head tilted and a wide smile across her face. My heart is pounding so hard I think for a second that I am going to faint. Then I lean forward and take her nipple between my lips, sucking it gently into my mouth. She takes the bottle gently from me and sets it down on a little table. She reaches behind me and runs her finger slowly down my spine. We sink down together onto the bed.

§

Max and Dagmar are at the table when we get downstairs, picking morosely at some greenish concoction. Max jerks his fork at Rose.

"You took your time! I hope you charged him extra. Now sit down and eat your meal."

"I think you should see what the captain has brought us," says Rose. "Then you might not be so rude. Look!"

She spills the contents of my bag onto the table. "Real frankfurters! Some bacon. Potatoes. And good bread. And even some chocolate for afterwards. And see – a bottle of champagne! Now what do you say, you grumpy old bear?"

"Hmm," says Max, impressed despite himself. "Prewar mustard, too. Where do you get such things from, *Herr Kapitän*?"

Dagmar has got quickly to her feet.

"Never mind where he gets them from – let's eat them, you fool."

She whips the food off to her cooking place and starts making her selection from her range of jars full of herbs, presumably from the garden. Max picks up the bottle and inspects it in the lamplight.

"Doesn't look much like good champagne to me," he grumbles.

"Cheap rubbish, I should say," I admit.

"It's actually very nice!" cries Rose. "Isn't it, Adam? We've had a bottle already, upstairs. But that means you won't want any then, Max?"

"Have you just?"

Max pulls the cork out with his massive fist and pours the pale fizzy liquid out into a mug. We wait while he swigs it. He screws his face up.

"As I thought. Disgusting. I'd rather have some decent lager, any day. But better than that damn firewater we've been drinking, I suppose."

He pours himself some more.

"I agree with you," I say. "It's cats' piss. But it's alcoholic. And it's free. It is my little gift for you. So drink up, please."

I make as if to leave, but Rose puts a hand on my arm.

"Where do you think you're going?" she cries. "You're going to stay and eat with us. Isn't he, Max?"

Max looks at me for the first time. He would be a fat man if food were plentiful. As it is, he's just big. He has unkempt hair, with pale blue eyes that *'have seen things no man should be asked to see, and done such bitter business that the day would quake to look on.'*

We look at each other for a long moment, and miraculously some kind of mutual respect emerges. Little more than a year ago we would have been obliged on pain of death to kill each other on sight. Now we are just two men struggling in our different ways to make sense of the world.

He makes his mind up.

"Oh, sit down. We could do with some new company. Rosa – get some glasses. And don't forget one for the chef. *Mein Gott,* those sausages smell good!"

They do indeed, as Dagmar fries them with onions and spinach and some other nameless herbs. Soon we are tucking in and chatting easily enough. We avoid discussing the war itself. It is a potential minefield, best avoided. We speak of how the damage clearance is proceeding, sometimes astonishingly fast, other times inexplicably bogged down in bureaucracy, of the dangerous state of the streets, the insensitivity of the foreign tourists who come from abroad to gape at our misery, the emergence of Bolshevism.

Rose sits beside me, and after a while I feel her hand move onto my thigh under the table and give a gentle squeeze. We smile at each other in perfect understanding. The world is good. It couldn't be better. Everything is perfect. Now even this cheap champagne tastes likes the finest pre-war *Moet et Chandon.* It seems to be of a higher alcohol proof than I had thought, for we are all grinning at each other inanely. Even Dagmar has relaxed her grim expression into one of reluctant resignation. It is curiously unnerving.

The front door bangs, and a young man comes into the room. He is skinny, with closely cropped hair and a badly scarred face. All conversation ceases. He glances at the company, and goes over to the stove.

"Kaspar!" calls Max. "Have you eaten? So sit down and meet our new friend. And no more politics, for the love of God. Elena – have we finished all the sausages? Get another plate for Kaspar."

The newcomer shakes his head, grabs some bread and one sausage out of the pan, and goes out without a word. The tension he brought with him is broken, and the remaining sausages are served by the dumpy girl.

"Adam – more amber nectar? Rosa – drink up! *Ach, nein!*" Max raises his arms towards the ceiling. "*Scheisse!* The damned bottle is empty!"

"Just one moment, please."

I reach into my bag again like a conjuror, all eyes on me, and produce the remaining bottle with an exaggerated flourish. "Ladies and gentlemen - fortunately I took the precaution of bringing a third, just in case the disgusting nature of the vintage happened to become less repulsive after the other two bottles."

"My God!" roars Max, seizing it in his mighty fist. "This is a man after my own heart."

He makes a mock bow to Rose, who just looks at him expressionlessly. "Rosa – I think you are to be congratulated. Do you know something? I feel our luck is finally on the turn. Elena? What about some of that *Apfeltorte?*"

The conversation starts up again, more loudly now, as the snow drifts past the windows and the logs glow brightly in the stove. Max is on noisy form, sometimes banging the table. Once or twice we hear the front door open and footsteps going up the stairs, a girl's strained laugh or a man's deeper voice. We have finished our meal now. Rose has stopped contributing to the gathering, and once I see Max staring hard at her as if conveying an unspoken message.

One of the oil lamps gutters and goes out, leaving some of the room in darkness. A shadow has fallen across the table. It is clear I am in danger of outstaying my welcome. I am about to get to my feet when Rose scrapes back her chair and stands up.

"That was very nice," she says indistinctly, her hand to her mouth. "But I am neglecting my duties."

She rushes out of the room and we hear her running up the stairs. I look questioningly at Max, stupidly slow to get the point. It is Dagmar who speaks.

"She must work, you know," she says harshly. "She has to get out and find customers. One customer an evening will not keep us fed for long, even if he does bring sausages with him!"

"You mean she's going out on a night like this?" I say incredulously.

"Of course! Customers are leaving the bars now. She must be out there to catch them. The other girls will have been at work for hours already. There is a rota, an arrangement…"

I open my mouth to speak again, but then Rose comes back into the kitchen with her coat on. She refuses to look at me but mutters something to the others, and suddenly she has left the room. I hear her talking to another girl in the hallway. There is an icy draught as the front door opens and shuts.

I rush upstairs and get my coat and balaclava, and go to follow her. I am leaving I suddenly remember something, and thrust my hand into my trouser pocket, bringing out a fistful of Reichsmarks which I leave on the table.

"Sorry. Nearly forgot. Give this to Rose."

The others stare at the money in silence, perhaps mentally calculating its value. Then Max raises his head and calls out, "Leave her tonight, my friend! Let her go. You will only upset her. She has her work to do."

I stop with my hand on the door knob.

"But perhaps next time we will be able to feed you ourselves. There is something coming up this weekend…"

He stops.

I take the hint and nod my farewell.

# 6

*Hamburg, 1946*

Too much pressure, too much paperwork, and the only time to do it undisturbed is when everyone else has gone home from the office. Coffee and a plate of salami and coarse bread have kept me going, but now I'm ready to go.

Naturally my route through the ruined streets meanders off course slightly to take me past the *Löwenhaus*, and of course I decide to call in for ten minutes, to say hello to the gang. Some chat, a little banter, a glass of wine, a kiss from the girls, before I face Frau Teck's worried face? Where's the harm in that?

But when I get to the Lion House, the place is as quiet as the grave. Dagmar is alone in the kitchen. For once she isn't working on paperwork or at the sink, but is sitting moodily at the table, smoking. After hesitating a moment I sit down beside her, dumping my bag on the table. She scarcely glances at it.

In fact this evening my canvas bag contains nothing more than the odd shaped bottle and a box of fat Cuban cigars, which have materialised in Gustav's maw from God knows where. For most of the afternoon I have been looking forward to smoking one as a reward for my long hard slog at my desk.

Now I open the wooden box, and the delicate aroma of Havana tobacco is intoxicating. I take a wooden handled knife off the table and carefully cut the end of one of the cigars into a V shaped indentation. Then I lift the cigar to my nose and sniff it appreciatively, rolling it between my fingers. Not too dry, not too moist. Perfect.

I say a silent prayer of thanks to Gustav and his mysterious ways, and strike a match. I breathe in deeply. I am not normally an inhaler, or indeed a heavy smoker at all, but sometimes... aaah... life isn't too bad, after all. I lean back in the hard chair and half close my eyes. I sense that Dagmar is watching me dully, taking little interest in the proceedings. Her mind is elsewhere.

"Where's everybody tonight?" I ask after a while, sitting up and tipping the long fine ash into a dirty saucer.

She shrugs. "The girls are out working. Don't know about the men. There's some flap on as usual."

I pull out the grey glass bottle of colourless liquid, which describes itself on its fancy white label as Bols Genever. A quick sniff does indeed detect a gin-like flavour, and I pour us each a large slug into a couple of chipped wine glasses. I put one in front of Dagmar, but she hardly acknowledges it.

Degas' painting *L'Absinthe* comes suddenly into my mind: the sad prostitute in her jaunty white headwear sitting before a glass of greenish liquor, a woman contemplating a bleak future, lost in thought, her shoulders slumped: one of the world's great paintings. Imagine that woman's astonishment if she had been told that her despair was to be immortalised by the great artist, to become one day an object of veneration for millions of art lovers yet unborn. Perhaps that weird knowledge would have offered her comfort in her misery.

"*Was gibt's dir denn,* Dagmar?" I ask kindly.

"Nothing. I'm good."

But she takes a sip of the gin, blinks a little, and then takes another, deeper draught, looking up at me as if seeing me for the first time.

"But tell me, Tommy. Have you any idea what it was like here during the *Feuersturm*? Really any idea?"

"Well," I say. "Um – some idea, I suppose. I know the statistics. Thousands of people – tens of thousands – killed… It must have been unbelievable…"

"Unbelievable, yes. I think that is the word."

"I don't know much really," I admitted. "Nobody seems to talk much about it."

"Talk about it? What is there to tell? The world we knew came to an end. That is all there is to tell."

We sit silently. The kettle is burbling quietly on the hob. Dagmar gets up abruptly and takes it off, then she sits down again.

"*Ja.* My life finished that day when… my little boy was taken from me. Now I just exist. Running a brothel. Pah! Who would have thought it!"

She wipes a hand across her face and squeezes her cheeks, eyes tightly shut, as if trying to block out her memories. I say nothing. After a few moments she shakes her head and stares into my face.

"Little Emil would have been six today," she says finally. "Perhaps that is why I am – like this."

"I'm so sorry."

It is totally inadequate, but I don't know what else to say. "So very sorry."

"Ach, listen to me. I think I'm the only one? I'm one of thousands of mothers who lost a child during those terrible days. When our old city vanished under the firestorm."

"It was a terrible time," I say stupidly.

"Yes. It was. Did you know you British bombed us by day for thirty days, and the Americans bombed us by night? So there was no relief, hardly a minute, when we could gather ourselves together?"

Her voice has risen.

"Do you know – can you have any idea – what it is like to be bombed day and night? When the darkness brings no rest? When the daylight brings only fresh horror, with no chance to try to recoup? Never stopping, on and on, bombs raining down on you, day in, day out, night in, night out? Can you imagine what that is like?"

There is nothing for it. My brief mood of contentment has passed, and someone else's pain has taken its place. I pour us out some more gin, trying to forget that gin, like absinthe, is itself a depressant.

"You don't have to talk about it if you don't want to," I say gently.

The floodgates have opened, and it all has to pour out. Outside it is very dark, but there is still no sign of the others. She talks dully, her eyes sightless. All I can do for her is to listen. I seem to do a lot of that, these days. At work and at home. Perhaps I have found my role in life, letting people talk.

*It was July, and very hot. My little boy was getting too big to carry. Bernd would have lifted him onto his broad shoulders like a feather. But he had been killed in the early days of the war, in Sudetenland. Ja, they gave him a medal posthumously, and I still had a good job as a teacher, but that didn't help me carry Emil down the blazing street. Yet somehow I found the strength. Our road had been lucky until then, and it had been just possible to stay where we were. But when the firestorm was approaching, I took him in my arms and we ran.*

*We didn't know where we were running to. There were a lot of people on the road, in cars, on bicycles, just running. You couldn't stand up against the fire winds, and the smoke was everywhere. We were bent double, but we hurried on. The heat was unbelievable. They say that in the centre it reached over 800 degrees centigrade… People had their eyes burnt by the heat, and went blind.*

*My sister was with us, but she dropped behind. Then a car was hit and went up in flames. She must have been right by it. I looked back and saw that her hair had caught fire, and then her clothes. Her screams were terrible. She fell to her knees, screaming, screaming.*

*There was nothing we could do for her, because then another bomb dropped nearby with a terrible sound – it was a phosphorus bomb – and flung us to the ground. When we got up again there was no sign of her. I never saw her again. She was my only sister.*

*Most of the people with us had disappeared into the smoke and chaos. Some others were screaming in agony. The phosphorus was designed to cling to human skin. Designed! Can you imagine that?*

She is sobbing now, her words coming brokenly.

*The only thing I could think to do was get to the canals. We'll jump into the water! We will be safe in the water!*

*At last a canal, full of sunken boats and debris. I jumped in when we got to the bank. I pulled in Emil with me. Other people were doing the same thing. For a moment it was a relief from the searing heat.*

Dagmar reaches for a cigarette, but her hands are shaking too much, and I light it for her. Dagmar might – must – have been pretty too once, I suddenly think. Not easy to believe when looking at her bony face now.

She takes a deep drag and blows the smoke out of her lungs as if she is trying to drive something out of her brain. But now she has started, she won't stop.

*But not for long. Do you know that water can burn? Do you know that? No? Well, it did that night. There was a layer of oil, you see – and maybe some other chemicals – on the canal from all the barges that had sunk. In parts, the water was ablaze. But still we waded in. We had no choice. It was either that, or be burned to death.*

*I kept pushing Emil's head in and out of the water to protect him from the searing heat, and ducking mine in too. Bombs were still falling, but some way away now. He was screaming all the time – Mutti! Mutti! – and choking with the filthy water. All around us buildings were blazing. Then we could hear still more aeroplanes in the darkness above us, and then still more. It was never going to stop. Never.*

She takes another long drink of the gin, which seems to steady her. Then she goes on, mumbling sometimes so that I can hardly hear her. My cigar has gone out, but I can't bring myself to strike a match to relight it. I lay it carefully in the ashtray to save for later. I wish she would be quiet, but clearly there is no hope of that.

*The bombs rained down. They never stopped. It was hard to believe there was still anywhere here worth bombing. Or anybody. But still they came.*

100

She looks up at me, her face bemused for a moment.

*They weren't aiming to destroy the actual buildings, you know. Knocking out doors and windows was enough just to spread the fires. Destroying whole buildings created firebreaks, and the damned English didn't want that. Ach, no, they didn't want that for us! That might have given us a chance…*

She shakes her head.

*Bombs were falling near us all the time, but somehow missing us. Then a house by the canal suddenly disappeared in an explosion, raining debris onto us. We ducked, but a woman who had been muttering to me was struck on the head by something, and vanished under the water. One moment she was there, the next she was gone.*

Dagmar is crying openly now. Then after a while she composes herself and goes on. I say nothing. I just hope it is doing her good to talk, because it certainly isn't cheering me. She is an educated woman, but she has lapsed into the local dialect which I don't always understand. She is surprisingly graphic, and I wonder what she taught. I have underrated her. I do that with people a lot.

*I stayed in the water holding Emil until I couldn't stand the cold any more and my arms wouldn't work…. .I don't know which was worse, the cold or the terrifying heat. I wanted to die, but I had to look after Emil. I kept talking to him, but he had long ago stopped answering.*

*Sometimes I wanted just to sink below the surface, and go, both of us. But there was this old man with a lined face and white hair who kept talking to us, saying stupid things, and singing too. We screamed at him to shut up. But while he was there we kept going somehow, and we even sang with him. Sometimes songs from the First War.*

*'Ich hatt' ein' Kameraden, ein bess'ren findst du nit…'*

She hums it tunelessly. She is lost in a world so dark that I cannot penetrate it. Then she continues.

*The man was wearing the striped pyjama- like outfit of a concentration camp prisoner, so filthy it was hardly recognisable. He must have been one of the many who were forced to clear away dangerous obstacles and defuse unexploded bombs. They worked under close guard, and were barred from the air raid shelters even when the bombs were falling, poor devils. But he must have broken away and joined us.*

*Finally, the bombing became less frequent, then it stopped altogether. It was morning, and the bomb crews had finally gone, their work done. The daytime bombers had not yet arrived, but soon they would come. It was slowly getting lighter, though we couldn't see the sun through the smoke. I was still clutching Emil, but he had been silent for so long. I knew in my heart that he was dead. But I was so nearly dead myself, that in a way it hardly mattered.*

*We all climbed out of the water, and a little group of us started walking off blindly. Someone, the old man I think, said to head for the park. I just stumbled along, with Emil in my arms. His face was empty now. He looked so peaceful.*

*I couldn't walk and carry him any more, and after a while I fell against a wall. The others waited for me in silence. When I felt a little stronger I got up and laid Emil on a patch of ground. After a while I just said goodbye to him. I didn't know what else to do. The old man covered him with some bricks, and said some words over him that I didn't recognise. Then he took my arm. I could see a number tattooed onto his skinny wrist.*

*"Let me say something to you, please. You are a handsome young woman," he said. "It doesn't seem possible to you now, but one day you will marry again and have more children - when all this horror finally becomes just a memory, a bad dream. Believe me, I know what I am talking about. I had a*

*family too, myself – once."*

*I knew that he was wrong about me having more children, but I said nothing. Then he gently moved me on.*

*We could still hear bombing, but it must have moved away. We walked a long way through the ruined streets, sometimes startled by falling debris. Blackened bodies were everywhere. After a while you stopped noticing them. I didn't care about anything any more. I just stumbled along.*

*The old man seemed to be leading us somewhere, but it was hard to tell where we were. The streets we had known all our lives were just… well, nothing. There were scattered clues - a broken church, the name board from a shop, a battered street sign… The buildings I had known all my life could not even be called buildings any more.*

*I was so tired, I was just numb. But the man wouldn't give up. "Nearly there now," he said. Then we turned a corner, and he stopped abruptly.*

*"No! No! Oh my God, no!" he muttered.*

*We had come to where the great department store Klingmanns stood, a place so grand I had rarely dared to enter it, let alone buy anything. It had dominated the street. But there was little of its former grandeur left. It must have suffered a direct hit. Its fine arched windows were empty sockets, and of its five floors, two had collapsed completely. It had been famous for its roof garden, where ladies could take afternoon tea when they had done their shopping. But now it had no roof at all.*

*After staring at it, the old man drew a deep breath. Then he led us carefully through the rubble to a place we could get in and go down to the store basement. I didn't know how he knew the way, but he led his little band down the long stairs into a vast underground area. It was full of long shelves, still partly filled with boxes which had held stock for the store.*

*The place was suffocating. I could hardly breathe. We couldn't see anything at first. But as my eyes got used to the darkness, I realised it was already inhabited. There must have been fifty or so people down there, men, women, children. Some babies. There was little conversation. They looked at us without interest. Nobody said a word to us.*

*"Why are there no lights?" I whispered.*

*"There is not enough oxygen," said the old man. "The matches won't strike. The fires are so big, they have sucked out the air."*

*He was gazing around him, as if unable to believe his surroundings. We could hear that outside the bombardment had started again, and a new wave of aircraft was coming over. Was there anything left to destroy? How they must hate us, I thought.*

*"You know Klingmanns? You worked here?" I asked, not caring if he answered.*

*"Know it? Oh, yes, I know it." He smiled at me then. "My grandfather founded it, you see. He came from Russia with nothing. After the pogroms."*

*I didn't know what to say. "My name is Marcus Klingmann," he said. "So, yes, I know it."*

*"I'm sorry, sir," I said, quite abashed. "I...I didn't know."*

*He lifted his shoulders in a hopeless gesture. He looked so old, I thought.*

*"What is there to know, my dear?" he said. "I had wealth, yes, and some status once, I suppose. Now, I have nothing."*

*He shrugged his shoulders. "My family are all gone. So now there is no point in me being alive. None at all. Just look around you."*

*He spread his hands. I didn't know what to say.*

*"What are we going to do, sir?" I whispered.*

*He looked at me and said, "Do? We are going to stay here. Stay here and wait to die. Why not, already?"*

Dagmar is silent for a long time, staring into space.

"But *you* didn't die," I say.

She shakes her head numbly.

"No, I didn't die. Many did. We were down there for what seemed like forever, but perhaps only three or four days. Most of us lived, I don't know how. But others went, of thirst, of hunger, of exhaustion, of fear. There was almost nothing to eat or drink, although some of the men went out from time to time when there seemed to be a lull, and brought back what they could, which was almost nothing. The babies cried incessantly, but the older children were mostly silent. The old man - he did die, yes, on the third day I think. I wasn't near him. I didn't find out for a while.

It meant nothing to me then. Now, I think he was a hero. I would like to have thanked him for what he did for us. But ..."

She raises her hands, fingers stretched out, then drops them again.

"When we thought the bombing had finally stopped, we went out into the streets. We wandered around like zombies. It was like looking at the craters of the moon. We kept waiting for the planes to come back. But, it was over, for a while. So slowly we began to exist again. If you could call it existence."

She looks at me then as if realizing something for the first time.

"You! You British! And the damned Americans. Why did you do it? The war was nearly over. Did you have to kill thousands of women and children? Wasn't it enough that we were defeated in battle?"

"The war was not over, Dagmar. Everything still hung in the balance. War is war. It is terrible. We have to leave it at that."

Enough is enough, I think. There's just so much I can take. Of guilt, of sorrow, of pity, of rage. It wasn't the British who had started the war, or carried out the first air raids on cities. You can blame Hitler for what happened, not us. We were bombed too. Nearly a thousand people died in Coventry alone, I've been told. It wasn't me who bombed this place, for God's sake... No, just some of my school friends, and my service colleagues, and... Oh, shut up.

Dagmar is reading my mind.

"Do you know how many people died here in that month?"

"Thousands, I know," I mumble.

"Yes, thousands. Twenty, thirty, forty thousand, they are saying now. But we can never count them, there are so many. My son is just one of them."

Perhaps suddenly eight hundred casualties in Coventry doesn't sound so many, terrible though the event was. Oh, it's lives that matter, not numbers.

"Dagmar, that is a terrible story. I'm so very, very sorry."

There is a long silence. Then I rise to my feet, my chair scraping on the tiled floor. She catches my sleeve.

"You know, you're not such a bad fellow for an Englander. There's a little mutton stew left, if that will do? And some potatoes?"

But I am not hungry, and suddenly I have had enough of death and horror. I gabble something, and go out into the street, pulling my coat on. Dagmar stares after me, then turns silently back to the kitchen, her white face a mess of tears.

# 7

The sky is unusually dark as I arrive at the Lion House the next day, and black storm clouds are massing behind the ruined buildings. They have an ominous yellowy tinge to them. I hear the first rumbles of thunder some way away.

I have fallen into the routine of calling two or three nights a week at the Lion House on my way home from work. The house fulfils my basic needs – male companionship and political conversation, a total distraction from my work, meals and drink with the food which I am happy to supply from my comparatively princely salary, and sex. But most of all of course, the latter.

Until now, my sex life has been, to say the least, inadequate. At my boarding school we were forbidden even to talk to girls, even if there had been any available apart from frightened little serving maids, or the starchy school matrons in charge of our medical needs. The inevitable consequence was a society where the prettiest boys or most athletic sportsmen were adored and lusted after.

Once I left school and went into the army, my own gender ceased to have any appeal. But I hardly met any girls. Some of the other officers had girlfriends or even fiancées at home, and photographs were proudly shown and daring exploits confided. The men would go into the town near the barracks and find plenty of outlets for their lust, but such activity was not encouraged for the officers.

In this post war city things are very different, and it is said to be no harder to find a willing woman than to buy a cup of coffee. But until now, and more from shyness than for any other reason, I have practised abstinence while devoting myself to my work.

Now however, perhaps as an antidote to my daily fare of horrors, the sexual release since I have come to know Rose and the Lion House is like pumping the life blood back into a corpse. And Rose of course is only one of a dozen girls who work in this establishment under Max's harsh command. Her best friend is Leonie, who I have not so far taken to bed. Then there is Marta, so dark she might be Indian, naughty little Gaby, haughty Beate, giggling Katya...all ruled over by the humourless Dagmar, who misses nothing and watches every Mark.

They are all available to me for the price of a few drinks, and, young, callow and war damaged as I am, I take full advantage of my position, like a schoolboy given the key to the tuck shop. Yes, Rose is my favourite, and I know in my heart that she is worth more than the rest of the harem put together. But my greed presently supersedes my capacity for romance, or for any consideration of her feelings.

It is not all unalloyed pleasure, of course. Apart from the ever present worry of being infected with venereal disease, it is curiously distasteful after a month or so to know these girls only carnally. Some of the encounters are unsatisfactory to say the least. Quite often the girl will show all too clearly how demeaning and unpleasant it is for her to earn her living like this, and will break down in tears. They have all got dreadful stories to tell of hardship and bereavement, and some are clearly exhausted. Nor are all their clients as undemanding and well- mannered as I am.

The sex is fun, terrific even, but I am slowly coming to realise that it isn't everything. Nothing is achieved without a price to be paid, and not one that a handful of notes will satisfy. Gradually I want these other girls less and less, and to see Rose more and more. And not just in her bedroom.

She comes upstairs with me as soon as I arrive, diverting me from the kitchen where I can hear male voices. I raise my eyebrows.

"Oh, they're just plotting dark deeds as usual. Come to bed."

She grips my arm. She is tense, and her eyes are brighter than usual in a white face. Outside we hear the thunder much closer, and the occasional flash of lighting illuminates the room. The atmosphere is heavy, and dulls the senses. We undress quickly, but the preliminaries are abandoned by mutual consent, and quite soon I take her roughly. She gasps once, but makes no complaint.

Now she is sitting up very straight against the pillow, refusing a cigarette because of a headache. She too is unnaturally spiky tonight. Neither of us has experienced much satisfaction from our hurried concourse. My leg is hurting, and I rub it hard. It sometimes helps a little. A loud clap of thunder makes us jump.

"So, what's the matter with you this evening, Adam?" she enquires suddenly. "Are you getting tired of your little Röslein already? Too many quick times?"

She is mocking me.

"Place a bit sordid for your Lordship? Not what you are used to?"

She chews her lower lip and picks at a fingernail. I take her hand gently to stop her.

"It's not you, my love," I say wearily. "Just had a hell of a day, that's all. And now you're going to get dressed and go out and have sex with a lot of other men. Jolly good."

She doesn't rise to this bait, but turns her head to look at me. The rain has come at last and is rattling hard against the window. Puddles are already starting to form on the wasteland outside the house.

"Do you want to tell me about your day, Adam? I'm not in a hurry to go out. There won't be any business about while this storm is on."

Now that the storm has broken, some of our tension has gone with it and I want to talk.

"All right then. My job today has been to spend several hours listening to a man named Henker who spent most of the war murdering people."

I light another cigarette. It is the last one in the packet, and I have forgotten to buy any more from the store.

"Oh, Adam."

"He told me how tiring it was to deal with hundreds of wailing Jews, as he put it, and how slowly the gas chambers worked when they were overheated. He said he and his fellow soldiers were underpaid and overworked, and that no-one gave them any credit for their efforts. They had targets to meet, he said, and if they fell short they would be severely reprimanded. He was exhausted when he got home in the evenings, and his wife wasn't very understanding either."

And neither was I. But the nature of my job means that I have had to listen to a great deal more of this kind of thing, and now some of it is pouring out of me, in a nonstop flow, a toxic catharsis like vomiting after a bad meal. All the time I've been speaking, Rose has been holding my hand, occasionally shuddering, but saying little. Now she gives me a kiss on the cheek and gets out of bed. She stares out of the window.

"I've got to go out now. The rain has eased off."

"What do I do, Rose? How can I listen to this stuff and keep my sanity?"

She shrugged, stepping daintily into her lacy panties. She has been deeply sympathetic, but now her mood changes.

"You deal with it, that's all. 'This stuff' happened. It isn't happening any more. So leave it behind you at the office."

This isn't the reaction I wanted, and my temper snaps.

"It's all right for you to say that! I can't just leave it behind at the office! Do you know, I'm sick to death of hearing this poison day after day, can't you understand that?! I'm sick of my job, this city, this nightmare bomb-scape. Come away with me, Rose. Let's get out of here before we're infected with the corruption."

She flares up suddenly in return, pulling her coat over her dress. "You're sick of your job, yes? Are you so tired too of your warm office, and your sexy secretary and your food and your booze and your free fags? How would you like to do what I do? Pull your pants down every night for a lot of filthy, smelly, drunken animals? Do you fancy that, eh?"

"You can get out too. We can escape together, before we both go mad."

"We? Who's we? You can go, Adam. Go back to sleepy England with your church bells and your sheep in the fields. I belong here. This city is my home. I've got to stay and help my countrymen recover from this nightmare."

"What? By sleeping with Russians? How is that going to help? Yes, come back to England with me!"

She laughs in my face. "What nonsense is this? Have you read your own laws? You could be shot for being in this room with me, let alone for taking me back to the *Cots – volds* with you. Be your age, Adam. This is life. It's grim and it's earnest. And there's no easy way out."

She slams the door behind her and is gone.

I lie on the bed for a long time, smoking and staring at the wall. She is right. The anti-frat laws have in fact fallen into disuse, by dint of nobody in authority having the heart or will to enforce them. Nonetheless for a British officer to marry a German girl would be what Foxy might term as a very big hurdle indeed to jump.

Suddenly I hear footsteps on the stairs and a man's deep voice, slurring his words. I leap out of bed and am starting to put my trousers on when the door opens.

One of the girls of the house comes in, arm in arm with a man in a navy greatcoat. She is a thin, pale redhead with skinny legs, whose name I forget, if I ever knew it. They stare at me in surprise.

"Sorry!" I call. "Sorry! Just leaving."

After a moment they decide to ignore me. The man smells strongly of drink, and is mauling the thin girl, pushing her up against the wall. She is protesting half -heartedly, but he is too strong for her. I heave on the rest of my clothes in a panic, and leave the room, still apologising in an idiotically English sort of way.

As I stumble past the kitchen I hear raised voices and what sounds like a fist banging on the table. I hesitate, curious to know what is going on. I hear Max's voice shouting

"I tell you it is too risky! How many times must I say it?"

My better judgment prevails, and I go out into the night. It is still damp everywhere, but the rain has stopped. For once it isn't snowing either. The storm has passed.

Tomorrow I shall go up to see the old doctor again. My little bag of goodies will be appreciated by Frau Teck, whom I have shamefully neglected lately. But tonight I am too tired.

# 8

"So you decided to take no further action. I can understand that. What did Adolph do after that, anyway?"

I'm tired now. I reach for my cigarettes, then as Ernst coughs again I change my mind and put them away.

"What we expected him to do. He discharged himself early from the *Realschule* and took himself off to the bright lights of Vienna, to the Academy of Art and fame and fortune as an artist."

He takes a sip of brandy to ease the bout of coughing. Then he laughs shortly.

"Or so he thought. He got a terrible shock when he got there though. The Academy wouldn't accepr him. Said his work wasn't up to standard. Ha! It must have been a bitter blow to someone so certain of himself and his abilities."

"How did he take it?" I ask absently, trying hard to focus. But it's no good. After my meal, and with the alcohol, my mind has begun to wander. This story of long ago is all very well, but it is I who am the young man now, and my head is full of my own affairs, battling that stream of consciousness that floods back in at the least excuse. What someone said today, how Rose looked at me yesterday when I left, the pain in my leg if I sit still too long – stretch it out now! – what am I doing tomorrow… and always there is the pulse of sex, the need, the expectation, the urgency.

But one particular face and pair of bare arms and pair of lips and pair of hands and pair of breasts fill my thoughts … why does the human body consist of so many pairs? Is it because we need to pair up, in order to feel fulfilled, satisfied? Why does the name Rose sound so right for her? What is she doing at this moment, I wonder? No, better by far not to let my mind wander there.

I quickly shake these thoughts away. I have missed some account of young Adolph's adventures in Vienna, and pull my attention back. I've had my fill of listening to people's war stories. But someone once told me a good lawyer must be a good listener, and I aspire to be both.

Ernst senses my distraction, and stirs irritably in his chair for a moment, looking hard at me. Had I actually dropped off to sleep? But he is intent on his own memories, which are too bitter and vivid for him to consider the concerns of his audience. He cannot contain them and must let them out. I am as good an audience as any, young and inattentive though I am.

I pour us both some more brandy. This is much better stuff than the so-called whisky we had drunk before. It had no right to call itself whisky. But what's in a name? *That which we call a Rose by any other name would smell as sweet!*

Stop it! I tell myself sternly. Get your mind off that girl and listen to what the poor old man is saying.

"Well, as you might expect, Adolph didn't take his rejection well. I knew people who were acquainted with him at the time. People like…"

Ernst catches my eye.

"But I am wandering. Adolph ranted and raged for nearly an hour, we are told. Made a complete fool of himself. He even called on the Academy President at his office and abused him in front of his staff. Told them they were a lot of fossilised bureaucrats, and that the whole place ought to be pulled down!"

He smiles at the thought.

"He got nowhere, of course. In the end he had to swallow his pride and go off to look for work."

I get up and stand by the dying fire. The logs are rather damp, and the fire hisses and crackles. Outside the window the snow is still falling thickly, although it is almost too warm enough in the little room.

Ernst has paused, lost in recollection.

"Hmm. Do you know something, Adam? Something that has just occurred to me. When I come to think of it, the Academy President was Jewish. D'you think perhaps a little drop of poison was injected then into an already infected mind?. I remember his antagonism towards little Wittgenstein at school. The Jews were very prominent in Vienna at that time, and some of them – not all, by any means – were making themselves very unpopular with their shows of wealth. Flaunting their fur coats and expensive motorcars in front of starving people. Foolish indeed. But what a terrible price they were to pay for a bit of vanity."

He runs a finger round the rim of his glass

meditatively, shakes his head sadly, and takes a sip.

"Whatever the truth of it, I suppose we shall never know everything. I imagine Adolph had burnt his boats by then, and there was no way he was coming back to Linz. So he hung around Vienna, pretending to be an artist, and doing odd jobs. Fritz said he'd heard from a colleague who'd seen him there that at one time that he was literally begging on the streets."

"Imagine that. Hitler, begging his bread. Begging in the streets of Vienna," I say, more to show that I am attending than for any other reason. "It is a vivid image."

"It is indeed."

He shakes his head.

I push the stopper in the bottle firmly and put it on a side table as a hint that we have had enough.

"When Austria-Hungary declared war on Serbia – and then immediately on France – it must have been a godsend to Adolph. The chance of some activity. And when Britain declared war on Germany, the whole insane farce was launched."

That's enough. I stand up. I am going to leave before we have to fight the whole of the Great War. Herr Klumpf is complaining loudly by this time, and my eyes are closing. Ernst does not appear to notice my yawn.

"The war offered him an escape route from failure and penury, of course. He joined up in the Army very early in…"

"Good night, Ernst," I say firmly with a broad smile, scooping up the bottle and trying to shake his hand and open the door at the same time. "Sorry to be rude, but save it, please. Tell me tomorrow. No – not tomorrow. There is some meeting I have to attend after work, at the office. End of week briefing, you know the sort of thing."

"Ach, but…" He stops.

"I'm sorry, Adam, you must find me very boring."

"I'm not bored," I assure him. "Just very tired. Good night, old friend. And try to sleep."

§

I am pleasantly surprised to find Ernst up and dressed, and apparently waiting for me when I return from work. He is standing in the hallway talking to Frau Teck, and they break off when I come in.

"Ah, *Herr Kapitän!*" says Frau Teck cheerily. "If you are not too exhausted from your day at the office, we wondered if you would like to accompany Dr Mann on a little stroll? It is really important that he doesn't stay cooped up in my attic all the time."

"Yes, fresh air and exercise!" cries the doctor. "How often have I given that advice to my own patients, but have forgotten to take it myself!"

He is wearing an ancient dark green velour overcoat, belted and double breasted, with a scarf at his throat, and a felt hat with a feather in the band. He looks quite the dandy he must have been once.

"I should be delighted! You must be feeling much better," I say, putting my briefcase down by the coat stand and taking his arm. "You look very distinguished, sir. Very Austrian, I think."

He laughs, pleased with the compliment. "Yes, sometimes people forget I am not *echt deutsch*, you know? Shall we take the air?"

"Why not?"

"Wait!" Frau Teck goes scurrying off into her

room and reappears a moment later with a fine Alpenstock, a handsome knobbly wooden stick with a steel tip and a carved handle.

"This belonged to my late husband. He was very proud of it. He brought it back from one of his military operations, and said there was quite a story attached. But when I asked him to tell me about it, he told me I would prefer not hear it. But please accept it as my gift, *Herr Doktor.*"

There is a moment's awkward silence, which the doctor breaks by doffing his hat and bowing as he accepts the stick, saying only that he is deeply honoured. I can't help glancing at it for any sign of bloodstains, but it is clean and well-polished, evidence of a gory history long since disappeared.

It proves a useful support as we walk slowly through the dirty snow and puddles of the ruined streetscape. The doctor looks pale and strained with the effort, but his eyes are bright with interest as he inspects the small indications of rebuilding all around us.

One house has lost its front wall, with the ghost of a living room appearing incongruously behind it. The tattered wallpaper is still hanging, and part of a fireplace is still blackened with soot. At another house little remains but steps leading down to a cellar, already fiercely overgrown with weeds and vegetation.

A skinny rat pokes its head out to inspect us as we pass before it scampers back down its hole. On the other side of the road is a shop selling a selection of oddments, from clothes to prams, kettles, furniture, and a battered-bicycle. A child has emerged with his mother, and they are smiling over some purchase that the little boy is holding tightly to his chest.

Although it is early evening, a team of men are still working at shifting piles of masonry. A whole building has been cleared away, ready for a new one to take its place. A covered cart stands alongside, but I instinctively look away. Remains of bodies are still being discovered every day, and they are not a pretty sight. They are taken away to be meticulously dissected and listed, along with any hints of identity, in the thorough manner endemic to the Germans.

"It is good to see life returning," says the doctor. "The human spirit is indeed indomitable."

It would seem so, I agree, as I steer him to the left and away from the working party.

"No, not down that street, sir. It is still in a very dangerous condition. There are several buildings there which look as they might collapse at any time."

He steps delicately over a smashed paving stone.

"It is going to take a long time to rebuild this city. But I know the German people. They will not remain defeated for long."

For a while we walk on in silence. Then I remember something he had said.

"You were going to give me a little gossip about Hitler? Something that might amuse me?"

He glances at me with a smile. "Well, I am not sure. But I wonder. Did you know that our Führer had a great weakness for English aristocratic ladies? Well, one in particular caught his eye, and they had a long romance. Someone who should know told me official diaries show that they had been out to dinner together over a hundred times. So it was no casual flirtation."

I am intrigued. This is news indeed.

"Who was she?"

"She was Unity Mitford, one of the six daughters of an English milord, a great admirer of Germany and particularly of Hitler. Her middle name was Valkyrie. That would have appealed to a lover of Wagner like Hitler."

He smiles thinly. "Obviously the whole thing was kept as quiet as possible. But this is the scandalous part. Apparently she became pregnant, and to make a bad situation worse, this was just before England declared war on Germany."

"What? When she was pregnant with Hitler's child? My God! What then?"

We stop at a point where the roadway is still blocked with rubble, and then must retrace our steps to try to find another way round. Finally defeated, we turn back, with me taking the doctor's arm.

"They say she tried to kill herself with a pearl handled revolver. Shot herself in the head. But she failed to die. Those little pistols are ladies' guns, more for show than anything."

"Still, a bullet in the brain…?"

He shrugs. "I've seen it happen before. There are men walking around today with half a dozen chunks of metal in their bodies, seemingly none the worse for it. The human body is very resilient, you know."

A curious tale, I say. "Is there a reason you think I might be especially interested?"

"The thing is that I rather think the woman came from your part of England. What is your home town called again?"

"Chipping-on-the-Fosse. You may have heard of it?"

He shakes his head.

"I don't think so."

I am relieved. My beautiful little country town is the incongruous location of one of the aerodromes that the bomber raids flew from, bound for this city among others. This is not a fact I feel it would be judicious to broadcast.

"I have a strange feeling that is where this lady came from, but I may be wrong. I know it was a hall somewhere in the middle of England. Does the story mean anything to you?"

"No, nothing. But what happened to her?"

He stops again to get his breath. I can hear his lungs crackling with the effort. "After her bungled effort with the revolver, Hitler had her shipped back to England through Switzerland just after the war began. In a private plane at the dead of night, I heard. Quite a romantic tale. And that should have been the end of it."

"But...?"

"But according to my informant, the baby was duly born. The mother threw the poor thing out of her bedroom window in the Hall, hoping to kill it. It suffered a permanent head injury, but it did not die. Someone – a servant, perhaps, bore it off to safety."

This tale has caught my imagination now.

"*What?* Do you mean Hitler has a surviving child? In my own town, by the sound of it?"

"It would seem so. I have heard that Unity Mitford is still alive, but with the mental age of a ten year old."

He was overcome by coughing.

"The child was presumably put out to foster parents. I have no means of knowing. You must remember that this is all very much a third hand account of something that was deeply confidential. Things get exaggerated. But...as far as I know, it is true. And it hardly matters now. Just think - Hitler's child might be growing up somewhere in England. Perhaps even identifiable by a mark on its head. Hitler's shadow! There's a good story for you?"

We laugh together.

"Where do you get these tales, Ernst?"

"Oh, I had a very old friend who told me the story. His name was Fritz, and we knew each other well when we were young men."

"In the place where Hitler came from?"

"Yes, that's right. In fact, Fritz taught the boy for a while, and he followed the fortunes of the Führer thereafter on a personal level, if you see what I mean. He reached quite a high rank, and met Hitler more than once in Munich in the years leading up to the invasion of the Sudetenland, and again even during the war."

The doctor shakes his head and sighs.

"Dear Fritz. His wife Magda was alone in their home when the Russians invaded. She was never seen again."

He falls silent. He is getting tired now, and we walk more slowly. Two little boys rush by, laughing at some game, and he smiles at their infectious enthusiasm. The children of the bombing are far more cheerful than their parents, I always notice. The thought offers a faint ray of hope

At our house he pauses in the hallway, and I help him off with his overcoat, putting the stick into the umbrella stand.

"My mind constantly goes back to the years before the war. Before both wars, in fact. A weakness of age, I suppose. Good night, Adam, and thank you." He shakes my hand, and slowly climbs upstairs.

§

I call round as usual, and find Rose alone in the kitchen. "Ah," she says, without looking up from the sideboard where she is soaking some herbs. "The handsome Englander. Which horse from your stable will you ride tonight? You may have to make do with me, I'm afraid. Everybody else seems to be otherwise engaged."

I sit down heavily at the table and light a cigarette.

"Rose? May I talk to you? Just talk?"

"Oh, talk, is it?" she says, glancing back at me from her task with a tight smile on her face, brushing her long hair back with a bare forearm. She looks pale and unhappy, I think, and not her usual merry self.

"What's the matter with you, then? Can't have run out of money, surely. Got the clap, have we? A bit sore in the business area?"

"No, it's not that. Thank God. Do you think I could have a beer? I haven't brought anything tonight."

"Sure, help yourself. So what's the problem?"

She finishes what she is doing and comes over to join me.

"Rose, do you despise me going with these other girls too? Am I behaving like a moron? I'm making a fool of myself, aren't I?"

She laughs, tossing her head back.

"Of course you're not. You're doing what any young man in your position would do. Grab it while it's there, why don't you! The male is designed by the Creator to scatter his seed as widely as possible to propagate the species. The female's job is to attract a suitable mate, and tie him down. *C'est la condition humaine, mon ami.*"

She swigs some of my beer, wiping the froth of her full lips with a long delicate finger. Even when she's tense and tired as she clearly is now, she's very beautiful. My heart lurches. What a lecherous, selfish fool I am. Quite odious.

"Yes, no wonder you're having a good time while you can. I don't blame you at all. Marriage to some boring little English girl and loads of kids is all that waits for you back home. And you'll soon have had enough of this battered, beaten, buggered up country. Enjoy yourself while you can, I say. Nothing lasts for ever."

"I feel bad about it, now," I say quietly, staring into my chipped beer mug. "I've behaved like an animal these last few weeks. Now I've had enough. Do you know what the problem is?"

"What?"

"It's you."

My voice is rising.

"I'm having all this senseless sex, and all I can think about is you. Just you."

"Me?" she screeches. 'Well, come on then. Room's free. Sure you haven't got crabs? I'll have to check, you know."

She grabs me by the wrist to drag me to the door, face set. I've never seen her like this. She's always been so sweet. I shake her hand off.

"No, Rose. Not like that. I want to take you out for a meal, look after you…I worry about you. You look so tired. Come out somewhere with me, Rose. Not for sex. Just to talk, walk, get to know each other…"

To my utter surprise her face screws up and I can see she is nearly crying. .

"Oh, for Christ's sake piss off and leave me alone! Anyway, I've got to work. And now my face is a mess, thanks to you."

She pulls a coat on from the back of the door and rushes out into the street, leaving me pouring out another large drink and thinking for the umpteenth time how little I understand about life and what a complete fool I am. From now on I am only going to have Rose. I shall say no to all the others, and if she isn't available, I shall wait until she is. I square my shoulders. I'm going to go out and find her, and tell her so.

§

Outside in the street a half moon has disappeared behind banks of dark cloud. Snow flurries sting my face mercilessly. Rose is not in her doorway. I search around the nearby streets, peering down alleyways. I'm bent over against the driving sleet, pulling my coat collar up round my face for some protection.

Secretly I know it's useless, but I keep on for searching for her, holding back a dull pain that threatens to turn into naked panic if I permit it. Sometimes I call her name. Rose. Rosie. Rosa! *Röslein!* But there is no reply. Passers-by look at me furtively and hurry on.

A shrieking choking sound scares me for a moment, and I stop, staring about me like a man beset by ghosts. What the devil was that? Then the sly shade of an urban fox flickers against a pile of bricks, his eyes gleaming yellow as he glances contemptuously at me. With a swish of his brush he is gone, and I am once more alone.

Riding high in the cloudy sky, the moon reappears, grandly aloof  as if to mock my efforts. The bare streets, with their potholes and piles of timber and masonry testifying to so much death and destruction, are bathed in a harsh silvery light. I stand and stare up at her – Selene, the beautiful pitiless moon goddess, notorious in mythology for her promiscuity and countless love affairs. Has she a message for me? No, she gazes down expressionlessly on me, just another foolish mortal among the millions. Then the clouds return, blacker now, and she disappears from my view.

The roadways are treacherous with snow, and I am careful where I put my feet. Herr Klumpf is hurting so much I want to tear him off and throw him into the shadows. It is very dark when I get home.

I look out of my bedroom window at the snowflakes, falling, falling, as they dance their mad gavotte against the glass, dashing themselves to wet pulp like hapless infantrymen under machine gun fire on Omaha beach. When will those images be still?

# 9

*Normandy, June 1944.*

An hour after we left the wreckage of the half-track, we had still not reached the station. Many of the streets were blocked by various obstructions, and we were occasionally opposed from different quarters, more or less ineffectively. My idea was still to get through to reinforce the troops besieging the station by whatever route we could find.

Lang had stayed beside me. We entered a small street, and were moving up it in single file, alert and crouching as we went. Then a sudden hail of machine gun fire scattered us like frightened rabbits. The noise was as frightening as the bullets rattling off the cobbles. It was coming from the windows of a house on the corner in front of us.

We crouched behind abandoned vehicles, trying to return fire without getting our heads shot off. I looked round. Two of my men were dead, their corpses sprawled awkwardly across the roadway. Another man was holding his arm and moaning softly.

We couldn't stay here like this for long. I tried to think of a coherent strategy, and failed. My brain had frozen again.

"We'll have to get rid of those buggers, sir," said Lang.

He displayed an icy calm that I envied, and seemed unmoved by the prospect of imminent death.

"Yes," I said.

"Let me take three or four men round the back of the house, that way..."

He gestured towards a narrow alley. "Looks like there's a bit of rising ground. If you'll try and keep their attention directed down here, sir?"

I nodded dumbly, only too glad of his initiative.

"Then when it's all clear for you to advance, I'll blow this whistle, and you can move up? But carefully, sir. All right?"

He tapped the whistle that had materialized on a cord round his neck, and, taking advantage of a brief lull in the firing, disappeared up the alley with his men. I could have sworn he was enjoying it. There wasn't much doubt who was in command of this operation. And it wasn't me.

The remainder of us carried on firing sporadically towards the snipers. I suddenly remembered my house-clearing drill, in which hand grenades played an important part. But for whatever reason, we had no grenades. Too late to wonder why not. I reloaded my pistol, and breathed a prayer to the gods of war, if for some bizarre reason they happened to be on our side and not the enemy's.

A couple of minutes later there was a long rattle of fire from a different direction. Then another exchange of fire, and then a long pause, after which no further bullets came our way. The enemy clearly had had their attention diverted by Lang's attack from the rear. I held my breath. Almost immediately came the shrill urgent sound of Lang's whistle, three long blasts, repeated once. That was the signal to move.

"Go, go, go!" I screamed. We rose from our positions and charged up the little street, firing from the hip as we ran. We burst in through the splintered front door of the little house. The body of an old man lay in the hallway, and we leapt over it. I ordered the downstairs rooms checked, and pounded up the stairs yelling like a maniac as specified in the training manuals.

I kicked open a bedroom door with my pistol in my hand, and took the scene in at a glance. Two men in field grey were lying unconscious or dead by the broken windows that looked into the street. Machine guns lay abandoned on the floor. Another man lay motionless further away. Crouching in the corner was a young German, broken spectacles on his nose and an expression of terror on his face. His uniform seemed too big for him. He was holding his hands up and gabbling something.

Downstairs I could hear my men slamming doors as they scanned each room for occupants. Our orders were to shoot the enemy on sight and take no prisoners, as we had no resources to spare on guarding them, and I had impressed this on the platoon more than once during the day.

The young German saw my finger tighten on the trigger, and burst into a further babble, of which I could only make out *"Nein! Nein! Bitte! Ich bin nur...!"*

I was quite unable to move for a moment, while willing my finger to squeeze the trigger. The boy was so young, so white faced….for one absurd moment I had a clear image of his mother getting the news of his death. It was so detailed that I could make out her apron and see the kitchen behind her. There was a telegram in her hand. I could even smell the food cooking, and see the anxious face of a small child looking up at her mother as she read the message.

Then a movement from the figure on the floor distracted me from my paralysis. The other German, his tunic stained red, was awkwardly raising a small pistol and pointing it towards me, and as I turned I saw the flame from its barrel as the gun went off. There was a terrific blow to my leg as if someone had taken a hammer to it. At the same time and without warning, from behind me came a rattle of firing, deafeningly loud in the confined space. Both the man on the floor and the bespectacled German boy disappeared in a fountain of blood and brains and entrails. A machine gun fired at close range does horrible things to a human body.

I was hurled against a wall and was lying on my back, the whole scene blurring before my eyes. The pain in my leg was indescribable. I was dimly aware of Lang – where had he appeared from? – throwing down his machine gun and leaning over me with an expression of real concern on his face.

"All right, sir," he said. "Don't try to move. I'll be with you in a minute."

The room was full of men now, Lang issuing rapid orders as my consciousness ebbed and flowed.

"That's one of ours dead and three wounded, including the officer," I heard him say. "Bring the other two wounded up here. The rest of you, get ready to move on and out. I'm just going to take a look at the lieutenant."

I opened my mouth to ask the names of the casualties, but no words came. Lang was kneeling beside me examining my leg, his face impassive. The only sign that he might be affected by what had just happened was a twitch in one eye. I was lying with my leg crooked in front of me, aware of blood pouring from the wound and forming a pool on the floorboards.

"I was going to shoot him," I whispered. "I was going to shoot him when you fired…"

But I don't think Lang could hear me.

"Try and keep still, sir," he said. "I'm just going to cut away the trousers round the wound so that I can see what's happening."

A pocket knife had appeared in his hand as if from nowhere.

"Nobby! Find me some clean cloth and a bowl of water from somewhere. Quick as you can. Try that bedroom."

He peered at the wound and then clasped his hands tightly round my leg. I was gasping with pain, but he spoke to me quietly. "You'll be all right, sir. I think the bullet's gone skimmed your calf, but it's hit your knee. You've been lucky. If it had hit a major artery, you'd be dead by now. You're bleeding a lot, but we can stop that."

The man was a miracle worker. Was he a doctor as well? He must have read the question in my eyes, because he smiled and said, "I used to run the weekly First Aid training unit back at base, sir. Learnt a lot that way."

He straightened up his long gangling frame as a man brought a bedsheet and a battered tin chamber pot full of water. Lang cut the sheet into strips and bound the leg deftly.

"There we are, sir. Sheet's not too clean but it will have to do. But don't try and move before the bleeding has stopped. And keep your leg propped up."

He looked around for something to put under my foot and found an empty ammunition box.

"With a bit of luck you'll be all right for a bit now."

I was able to speak more clearly at last, but very hoarsely and with an effort.

"Well done, sergeant. Bloody good job all round. What about the other two? Are they badly wounded?"

"They're all right, sir. Looking after each other. They're not fit to move very far, though."

"Leave us and get on towards the bombardment."

Lang leant forward to make out what I was saying, and I had a sudden thought. "I had a map – where's it gone? I had it here?"

"It's here, sir. Keep calm. I've got it."

He extracted it carefully from my tunic pocket and studied it briefly, ready to rally his little troop.

"Right, sir. Sorry to have to leave you and the others here, but there's no choice. I reckon you'll get picked up by our mob. There's plenty more coming up off the beaches by the sound of the shelling. And Jerry won't be hanging around in this part of town. But you've still got your pistol...?"

I nodded, then I heard the men clattering off downstairs. A couple of them muttered, "Good luck, sir," as they went. At the doorway Lang stopped, and threw me a final salute. He accompanied it with what looked suspiciously like a wink, and for some strange reason this cheered me. Then they were gone, leaving our three silent figures lying uncomfortably on the floor of the little room, each of us staring into space.

Large black flies were already buzzing round the bloody remains of the four dead German soldiers, which covered a surprisingly wide area of the room. My two men started talking quietly to each other. The blood seemed to have stopped flowing onto the floorboards beneath me. It was very hot and stuffy in the little room, and I closed my eyes.

I'm sure it's bad form for an NCO to wink at an officer. There must be something in Army Regulations about it, I thought, and I found myself smiling. Lang was an extraordinarily able man. I must remember to recommend him for a decoration when… when…

Much later I drifted back into consciousness. The two privates were shouting at someone. One of the German soldiers who had been manning the machine guns, a large red- faced young man with cropped fair hair, was showing unexpected signs of life. I had assumed they were all dead.

*"Wasser! Bitte, hilfe mir! Wasser!"*

It was a long drawn out groan.

"What's 'e sayin'? Vassa?"

"Water. Wants water."

*"Wasser! Um Gottes Willen, Wasser!"*

"Fucking Kraut. Leave him. Let 'im get his own fucking water."

I opened my eyes and tried to speak. But no words would come. Lang must have given me some sort of strong dope to kill the pain, and I drifted off again.

Day had passed into evening when I next surfaced. The men were still propped up against the wall, and one of them looked at me curiously. His trousers were blackened where he had peed his pants, and the stench of urine and faeces was strong in the air.

"Are you okay, sir? You was makin' funny noises. We couldn't do nuffin' for you, like."

"I'm all right."

The German soldier was finally dead, though his eyes were still staring upwards. His face was twisted into a rictus of pain, and his arm was outstretched, but there was no sign that he'd had the water he craved. I stared at the two privates and started to speak, but turned my head away.

One of them was barely conscious anyway. Time passed slowly as darkness fell. The other private and I occasionally exchanged a word. But we had withdrawn into ourselves, clinging insecurely onto life, total extinction beckoning hour after dark hour.

It was after dawn when we heard a tremendous banging on the door below, followed by the sound of boots hammering upstairs. In all probability these were our own troops from a second invasion wave, advancing through the city and carrying out house clearance operations as they came. We looked at each other blearily in the half light, knowing we were virtually unable to defend ourselves.

Then came an English voice, high pitched and shrill with tension.

"Anyone in there? Come on, who's there? Identify yourselves!"

A grey tide of relief flooded over me.

"British," I croaked, as loudly as I could, and named the regiment. The door was forced abruptly open, and a young officer, hatless, pistol in hand, burst in and stared at the scene. There were other men behind him. Their trousers were covered in mud, sand or blood, and they all looked in the last stages of exhaustion. The lieutenant was pointing the gun straight at me, a wild look in his eyes.

"Hands up! Or I'll shoot!"

"For Christ's sake stop waving that fucking thing about before you do yourself an injury!" I said. "What the hell have you fellows been doing? Rock paddling?"

There was a frozen silence. Then suddenly the tension was broken and the room was full of excited chatter. Someone knelt by me to examine my wound. "This officer needs a stretcher, sir. Nasty wound."

It was going to be all right. I had copped a Blighty, and was on my way home. With luck I might even finish my degree course. The war was free to move on to its next phase without my further assistance.

# 10

A busy period in the office keeps my mind focused on the gruesome subject matter that is grist to my daily mill. The next batch of war crime trials is scheduled shortly, and the pressure to complete our cases is intensifying. I spend the day wading through figures and testimonials. So much anguish, so much despair. And the misery hasn't stopped since peace was declared and the gates to the camps opened. There are millions of 'displaced persons' (DPs in the jargon) all over Europe, still imprisoned or desperately marching and dying in their hundreds of starvation and exhaustion every day. I pick up Henkel's testimony again, telling of the events of the days after the Americans got to the camp.

In one instance the newly released inmates had strapped an SS guard to the steel gurney of a crematorium. They slid him into the oven, turned on the heat and then slowly brought him back out. They beat him again, and put him back in again and again until his burned body was just a corpse. It was a mistake for Henkel to have smiled as he told me this story.

"I did nothing to stop it, you see sir, because I was too scared they would give me the same treatment. Does that make me an accomplice to murder? I hardly think so."

I sigh and make yet another note on my pad. There is a knock on my door.

"Sir?"

Helga puts her head in, after her customary token tap on my door with her stubby bejewelled hand. She is careful not to damage her newly painted fingernails. It is a relief to raise my head from my paperwork and look at her.

She has spruced herself up lately, with some different lipstick, a more elaborate hairstyle and a smart new outfit. Tittle tattle among the minor clergy of the legal hierarchy suggests that the challenge of caring for her bad-tempered crippled husband has led her to seek consolation elsewhere.

"You look very smart, Helga, if I may say so," I say, tilting my head on one side and smiling in my best impersonation of a sophisticated man about town. "Nice frock!"

She frowns and looks down at her dress as if she has never noticed it before, as women do, and blushes prettily.

"Ach, zis zing?" she says. "It is just – well, zank you."

There is an embarrassed pause while she decides whether to say anything more, a faraway look in her eye. Lately she has taken to speaking English to me, which may or may not be significant.

"You knocked?" I prompt her, meaning You

scraped the door lightly with your knuckles?

"Ach so. The *Herr Oberst* wishes to see you if you have a moment to spare, said he. But I think perhaps it an order is."

I snap a folder shut, glad of the break. I wish she would stick to German – she is easier to understand that way.

"Thank you, Helga. I'll go and see him at once. Any idea what it's about?"

*"Gar keine."*

She adjusts some unseen underclothing and tittups back to her desk on what look like new high heeled shoes. Her bottom has taken on a pronounced wiggle, which puts a smile on my face as I make my way upstairs to the rarefied heights of the senior legal administrators' fiefdom.

It is my turn to knock on a door.

Colonel Fox-Martin, the senior legal officer in overall control of our department, is a small sandy haired man with a permanently worried look on his face. I sometimes think he's in the wrong job and knows it, but all the same he's a shrewd lawyer for whom I have a lot of respect.

He pushes away some files and pulls out of his uniform pocket a silver cigarette case decorated with a horse's head. The ashtray on his desk is horseshoe shaped, and old copies of the Racing Post can be seen among the law books on his shelf.

"Ah, Adam. Thanks for comin' so promptly, what? Take a pew, take a pew. Cigarette?"

"Thank you, sir."

"Everything goin' all right? Up to scratch for next month's tribunal and so on?"

He has a staccato delivery which reminds me of a

certain Maxim machine gun I once tried unsuccessfully to silence in Normandy. It isn't an agreeable memory.

"Oh yes, all fine, sir," I lie, blotting out a list of unfinished tasks from my mind. "One or two things to sort out still, of course, but – no, no, it's all going fine."

The colonel may or may not have swallowed this, but he's got other things on his mind.

"Right you are then. Keep me in touch. Let me have an up-to-date summary of exactly where you've got to on each job, won't you? By tomorrow lunchtime, shall we say? What?"

I cough on my cigarette. "Well, sir, there's already the daily record sheet and…"

"No, not that stuff," he barks. "I want a proper update from you. Real opinions, d'you see? Personal impressions of these people. Gut reactions. You know the sort of thing, Adam. Don't want bald legalistic claptrap. I'm not your Daddy doing conveyances for sheep farmers in the Cotswolds. This is high politics. Tinder dry and tryin' to avoid sparks. Got me?" I nod.

"This fellow van Reen of yours. Tell me now – what do you make of him?'

I inhale my cigarette. It is a better make than I am used to, a Passing Cloud, formed in an elliptical rather than cylindrical shape and presented in an attractive pink packet. The colonel must get them sent in specially from England.

"Well, to be frank, sir," I say, "Sounds odd, but we get on pretty well. A bit too well sometimes, if I'm honest. He's very well read, and he's got – well, a sympathetic manner. But he's a cold-hearted bastard underneath. Shot twenty hostages on that Greek island. And he was an officer in a regiment which bumped off hundreds of prisoners. He'll hang, of course."

The colonel drums his fingers on his desk.

"Well, that's the sort of case I want to talk to you about. Professional army officer, followin' orders, what? Jury might see his point of view, let the bugger off? Doncha think? Then we've spent thousands of pounds prosecutin' him, all for nothing."

"You're going to let him go free?" I say incredulously. "Walk away without a stain on his character?"

"Useful man apparently. Knows a lot about the top brass. Oh, we'll find some charge to lock him up for a year or two. But let's move on. Who else have you got?"

"Well, there's the Monster of Märchenholz, the camp near Linz? She had a Rottweiler she'd set on the sick prisoners. The Bitch's bitch, the prisoners called it. She should hang for sure. Bloody slowly if possible."

"Oh, agreed, agreed. Ghastly woman. Who else?"

"There's Henkel, a senior guard in Scheiden here . He's a nasty piece of work. Lots of witnesses to his little tricks. A born sadist."

"Yes, he'll hang. But you'd better understand my position, Adam. The budget's bein' cut, we're movin' on. We've got post war Germany to plan. And if we lock up all the bad guys, well, quite frankly – we'll have no-one left to run the bloody country."

The colonel gets up and goes over to the window, looking across at what was once a large clothing store. Most of the huge building is roofless, and parts have disappeared altogether. But a section of the ground floor has recently reopened and boasts a lighted window display, which is already attracting attention from a few pedestrians. The blackened ruins on either side give the window the appearance of a stage set.

"There's all these nuclear scientists, for a start. The Yanks are shipping them off to the States in droves, no questions asked. That's completely out of my control. Not to mention the head honchos in the Nazi party, Hitler's cronies, and a lot of underlings. Half of them have got out to South America, and the other half won't be here much longer. Good riddance, is the official view I'm getting. Saves us the cost and embarrassment of hundreds of trials."

This is too much like what Max has been saying for my liking. And I had told him it was rubbish.

"That's beyond my remit, sir. But people like van Reen – it sticks in my craw. What if he does get acquitted? I've a hunch there's a lot more he can tell me first. We're... well, we're on the same wavelength, if you know what I mean, sir. Doesn't mean I'd mind seeing him going to the gallows though."

"All right," he says, without turning round. "Keep on with getting what you can out of him. But there's some rum stuff goin' on with the politicians, I can tell you. Turnin' a blind eye, that's the new watchword."

He comes back to his desk and sits down again.

"Can't pretend I like it, what? But there it is. Your work is important, make no mistake about it, and if some of these fellows get off, the powers that be won't exactly rap your knuckles, d'you see. Let sleepin' dogs lie, don't you know. Get my drift?"

I've got his drift. Keep hammering the small fry, poor little sods, but let the big fish off the hook. And whatever I feel about the morality of the matter, I have to admit it'll make my job a lot easier. And I suppose that's good news.

I get up to leave, but Fox-Martin hasn't finished yet. He waves me to sit down again.

"Before you go, Adam – another thing. Bit delicate, what?" He lights another cigarette. "How can I put it? Rumour has it you're doin' your bit for Anglo-German relations? And that's putting' it mildly, get my drift? Gettin' a bit too pally with some of the local *Fräuleins*, what? To say the least, eh?"

I feel myself flushing. How the hell does the old fox know about Rose?

"Now look here sir – with due respect, my private life's my own affair, isn't it? The war is over, I'm reliably informed."

"It may be over, Adam, but you know damn well the anti-fraternisation orders haven't been repealed. It's only a few months ago we weren't even allowed to talk to German children if they were starving in the streets."

"For God's sake, sir!"

I am getting worked up, and hear my voice rising. "That was just damn silly, and nobody took any notice. The Yanks have dropped it because every other GI is shagging a German girl, and there's damn all Ike can do about it."

"I know, Adam, and not just the GIs, is it? We've had some of our own men applying for leave to marry a *Fräulein*, and they're being turned down. Last thing we want at the moment is one of our own officers, especially in the legal department, disobeying orders."

"Nobody's said anything about marriage."

"But there is someone?"

"Yes," I say, speaking more quietly now. I wonder again how he knows. But people talk.

"There is someone I'm – fond of. It's all happened very suddenly. You know how it is."

Fox-Martin smiles, and for a moment I see the ghost of a younger self. "Yes, Adam, I do know how it is. I've not completely forgotten what it's like to be young and foolish. Take it easy, that's all. Don't do anything rash. And if things develop – come and see me."

He stubs his cigarette out, and glances at his watch. "I'll be honest with you, Adam. If you did think of marrying a *Fräulein*, you'd have to consider your career prospects very carefully. Especially with the job you do. Our masters don't want to be seen as bein' any softer on the Jerries than they are already. *Verb sap?* Word to the wise, what?"

The interview is over.

§

Of course I am soon back at the garden gate. I had planned to go straight home tonight after another wearing day, but my footsteps had a mind of their own, and I have followed them. If Dagmar is on her own again, I shall make an excuse and leave. Last time I left her what was left in the gin bottle and went home. Coward as I am, I can't face a repeat performance. And if Rose isn't free, I shall go home.

"Well, Tommy? What have you brought for us tonight?"

It is Leonie, one of the other girls who work from the *Lion House*. She has long tangled blonde hair and olive skin, and a grimy street urchin look that lends her a kind of animal earthiness. Till now we have been on speaking terms, but no more. She is standing in the doorway from the garden, effectively barring my way.

"Hello, Leonie," I say. "How are you this evening?"

"Are you looking for Rose again? Always Rose?"

Closer to her, I can smell cheap perfume, so heady I catch my breath. She looks at me insolently and then slowly runs a long dirty finger nail down my neck and under my chin.

"She is not the only girl here, you know, *Herr Kapitän*. But then you know that very well now. We are all missing you. We're all yours for the price of a tin of beans, *nicht wahr?*"

I am holding my trademark bag of provisions, and instinctively draw it over my groin like a shield.

"Is Rose here?"

She shakes her head and her long mane swishes across her back.

"Busy tonight, I'm afraid. Out on an assignment. Ivans, Russkies, call them what you will. Animals, the lot of them."

She spits and curls her lip, and shivers a little. She is standing very close to me now.

"She won't be back till late. And then she'll be very tired, I think. Too tired perhaps to look after even you, Tommy." She smiles.

It is a horrible image, Rose returning late at night exhausted from God knows what activities with a bunch of Russian officers to find me still hanging around here.

I hesitate. I'm cold and tense after another long day at work interrogating an old man who regularly drove a train delivering Jewish prisoners to one of the camps, packed in like cattle. He knew and saw nothing, of course. Drove it home again empty and slept like a baby, no doubt. God blast his soul. I sigh and bravely hold up my bag.

I sit like a child turning up at a party with a present, fearful of being turned away. Leonie shrugs. Rose would have shown delight and made a joke. Leonie is more interested in earning some money. She pouts her in a parody of a seductive moue. When she comes closer I can smell her almost feline odour, like a cat on heat. She slips her hand coaxingly under my arm.

"Tell you what, Tommy. You'd better come upstairs with me for a while, or Max will dock my earnings if he finds out you're getting free hospitality. I need to earn some money. Then I'll cook you a meal. Max is out at the moment and there's only Dagmar and Kaspar here. What do you say?"

How weak we men are, how easily driven by our primitive instincts, how close to the animal. She takes my bag roughly from me and bangs it down on the kitchen table. Then against my will I find my eyes fixed on her swaying bottom as she walks up the stairs, looking backwards down at me. I do not appear to be in control of my own body. Perhaps my mind is too weary to make sensible decisions. The tilting movement of a young woman's buttocks in a tight skirt is a wondrous thing for a young man to behold. I fight with my conscience for all of five seconds.

Then I follow her upstairs as if pulled by an invisible cord, my mouth dry with anticipation. The place is a brothel after all, I say to myself unconvincingly. I'm not really doing anything wrong.

It's just a trade transaction. It's as easy as that. Rose isn't available, so...

Leonie is sitting on the bed, taking her shoes off. She looks at me teasingly through half closed eyes.

"We don't have to do anything, you know, Tommy," she says. "Just give me some money so that I can account to that bitch Dagmar. We can just sit here for half an hour and talk as long as ..."

But I am close enough to her again now to smell her animal scent, and her hand runs slowly up the inside of my leg till it reaches the top of my thigh.

"Well, I don't know..." I start to say thickly. "No, don't... Leonie... Leonie... We shouldn't...."

And my arms go round her.

Leonie's lovemaking is different from Rose's, wilder, more primitive. There is none of the tenderness Rose and I share, no little smiles or affectionate stroking. Leonie and I are like two mating animals in the jungle. She has a beautiful body. We make the beast with two backs, the bed squeaking and groaning along with us like a third participant.

Finally at the height of our passion she rakes my back painfully with her dirty red nails. We gasp together. We are locked in a sweaty union, which leaves us both lying back on the pillow, spent and exhausted.

I stop panting, and almost immediately feel the familiar self- disgust as my breathing returns to normal. What has happened to my good resolution? How pathetically weak I am. I sit up, reaching down onto the floor for my trousers.

I pull out the packet of cigarettes in the pocket. Leonie has already slipped out of bed and is splashing herself cursorily from a basin in the corner.

Her room is darker and shabbier than Rose's, cluttered and messy. Pinups from magazines, mostly American, decorate the walls. They are presumably intended to put clients into a suitably excited frame of mind, but in fact they are endearingly unerotic to my eyes. They portray over-developed young females looking uncomfortable.

Leonie watches me as she bends her lean brown body, twisting a grimy towel between her legs and under her arms. Her long hair falls over her face.

"It's not my own room, you know," she calls from under her mane. "We all share the rooms. Except Her Ladyship of course – she has her own."

There is a sour note of distaste in her voice.

"Yes, I have gathered that. How does she manage it?"

"I suppose… it was her own bedroom as a child, and she's just sort of hung onto it."

As she shrugs she lets the towel slip off her onto the floor. She kicks it into a corner with a long brown leg. Then she comes back to the bed and reaches a cigarette from my pack, holding it up for me to light. She blows a smoke ring.

"Well, *Herr Kapitän*. How do I compare with your little *Röslein* ? Better? Worse?"

"You've scratched me," I complain, running my hand awkwardly behind my back and wincing. There is blood on the pillow. "Ouch! Do you always do that?"

She growls at me and makes pretend stabbing gestures with curled fingers. "Always! I am a tigress! *Rruuhhh!*"

Then she frowns and adopts a shocked expression.

"*Mein Gott* – but what will poor little Rose say?

How will you explain the marks of my fingernails, Tommy? You are being unfaithful to her!"

The thought has already occurred to me.

"Did you do that on purpose?" I ask sharply, narrowing my eyes against the cigarette smoke. "You did. You little bitch!"

There is an ugly side to this woman. But I can't help smiling as well, and now my mood has changed again. Suddenly I am looking down on the scene, seeing myself as the very devil of a chap. Quite the Lothario, lying on soiled sheets sexually satisfied, with this attractive creature naked beside me. I contemplate the thought of Rose being jealous of us as we lie here in *the rank sweat of an enseamed bed, stew'd in corruption, honeying and making love over the nasty sty.* The thought is exciting.

We sit together on the bed in companionable silence, enjoying our cigarettes. After a while she stubs hers out and nuzzles closer to me, her head on my shoulder.

"You really like Rose, I think, Tommy?"

"Yes, I do," I tell her. "I do."

And I really do. But sometimes I feel unreasonable fury against her welling up inside me. Why can't she quit this dreadful way of life and devote herself to me? The answer to that is of course quite simple. We haven't long met, we don't really know each other, she is deeply involved with this cabal at the *Löwenhaus*, I can't invite her back to Frau Teck's. And I don't truly know if this is love I feel for her, or just lust.

I say something of this to Leonie, who listens intently. I look her in the eyes. Closer to, her neck is wrinkly. She is older than Rose, and God knows what she has gone through in the last few years. I see her suddenly as a human being, and not just as a desirable amalgam of breasts and lips and thighs, an object for my lust. I feel shame again at my selfishness.

"May I ask you honestly, Leonie – what do you think of her? You are her friend. And... what do I mean to her? Anything?"

She thinks for a moment.

"Rose is a lovely person. Much nicer than me. And really well educated. And – *mein Gott* – her family tree! Do you know she is a Countess, descended from princes? *Wirklich*. This is not a lie."

She wrinkles her nose.

"And yet now she is just a whore. Like me. She is fiery, yes, daring. Foolish, often. And also I worry she is in danger of falling into Max's way nof thinking."

"Communism?"

"A kind of communism, I suppose. It is fashionable suddenly. But that does not seem to be the most important thing for them. Revenge is what they want. I myself am not interested., but they frighten me sometimes with their talk. And Rose is so young..."

She shrugs, and breaks off.

"Adam," she says quietly into my shoulder. "I am jealous of her. I admit it. She has so much more than I have. I'm pretty, yes, I hope. Or at least I used to be. But she is beautiful. And so young. Much younger than me, you know. And I am uneducated, just ... a street girl. But her, you know..."

She couldn't be crying, could she? No, but her face has stiffened.

"Yes, I have feelings too. And like all the girls here – I dream. I dream that one day one of these men will see me as a human being, not as a sex object, and love me, and take me away with him. Of course that is what Rose wants too. What we all want. And then along comes a man like you. Sensitive. Innocent. Intelligent. Safe."

As she speaks, she strokes the top of my thigh with her long fingers, drawing her nails down my leg and then back up. A shiver runs down my spine, and she smiles.

"Ah, ready for more. The old Adam, indeed. You seem to be well named."

She tilts her head and looks up at me. Her green eyes are wet.

"Good looking. Rich too, I expect! And yes – I am jealous. So don't ask me! I'm the wrong person to ask. And by the way, don't forget to pay me!"

Now she's jumping off the bed too and scrambling into her clothes. I pull on my trousers and reach into the back pocket for a handful of Reichsmarks. The notes disappear mysteriously somewhere about her person, like a conjuring trick. I hear myself sigh and realise I am hungry.

"Come on then," I say. "I'm starving! Let's see if someone will cook this bloody fish!"

Leonie is staring at her face in the bedside mirror and shows no enthusiasm at this prospect. Business concluded, it seems she is already regretting her confidences to me. She tilts her head and reaches for her lipstick as I leave the room.

# 11

Downstairs Max has returned from whatever nefarious mission he has been on. He is sitting at the kitchen table talking animatedly to Kaspar and another man, a stocky tough looking type with a red beard and the look of a Van Gogh self-portrait. I am not given his name, so Vincent will do for me. He wears a Wehrmacht combat jacket over civilian trousers, with faded marks showing where the badges of rank have been removed.

The air is already thick with cigarette smoke, and empty beer bottles litter the table. The men glance up at me as I come in, and the conversation stops. Then Max jerks his thumb at me and tells the others, "This is Adam – *der Englander*. But you are one of us at heart, Adam? A true revolutionary? You want to overturn the established order, *nicht wahr*?"

He laughs hoarsely and gestures to me to pull up a chair. Dagmar is at her place by the stove, with little Elena in attendance, and the fish is already being cooked, along with some ham and mounds of vegetables, pickles, and cabbage. There is a good smell of herbs and spices. Leonie comes in and goes briskly over to help her.

"Adam is our catering supplier," explains Max, grinning. "He supplements our poor efforts with what he steals from the other British lawyers – isn't that right, Tommy?"

"Is that so?" asks Vincent sharply. "You have access to food supplies?"

"No, not really," I say. I lean across the table to shake hands with each man in the continental manner. Kaspar's hand feels strange in mine, and I realise he is short of a couple of fingers. Vincent just grunts.

"I just keep one of the cooks sweet and buy his leftovers. We do each other favours from time to time."

"Where is it you work?" asks Vincent, staring at me.

I tell him. He is still suspicious of me, and with reason, I have to admit. I am not keen to be seen as complicit with this quasi-communist cell, and if it weren't that the food smells so good, I would slip away now. In fact I am rehearsing how best to make my escape, when Leonie puts a steaming plate of food down in front of me. She looks at me coyly under her lashes, and says, "I think our benefactor should be served first, don't you, Max? To keep his strength up? Where would we be without him?"

She giggles. She is playing the coquette, a role she slips into readily, easing her blouse down on one side as if unconsciously, to reveal a shapely shoulder. Max roars with laughter.

"Yes, not only does he bring our food, but he also fucks all the girls!" he shouts. "He is becoming one of our best customers, it seems. First little Rose, and then some others, now Leonie too? Is no girl safe from you? You'd better look out, Dagmar. He'll be after you next!"

I am furious to feel myself blushing. The others all laugh, and Dagmar makes a sour face and bangs away at the oven more noisily than ever.

"I've had better men than him for breakfast in my time," she throws over her shoulder. "Decent Germans, too, not English…"

She uses a word of contempt that perhaps fortunately I don't recognise. If I had imagined that her previous confidences had established some form of empathy between us, I have been deceiving myself.

"Dagmar! The English are not our enemy now!" Max calls. He is serious. "We have new challenges to deal with."

Dagmar's silence is eloquent. There is a moment of embarrassment in the room, in which I share, then all at once the meal is served and we are all tucking in. Max munches away noisily, then puts his cutlery down and takes a long pull at his beer.

"You see, Adam," he says. "We have a new order of things. Our country has been destroyed by the fucking Nazis. Our city is a heap of ruins. Our families are dead. Hitler, Himmler and his gang have brought us to our knees. Our great culture has been annihilated. The once proud name of Germany stinks across the globe. The concentration camps alone – the Jews – millions tortured to death, gassed, burnt, starved…"

There is a stir. Kaspar has been listening to all this in silence, but now his glass has tipped over, spilling beer across the table. He twitches and starts nervously, his mouth working, unsure what to do.

Little Elena is quick off the mark and gets a cloth to wipe the table.

Max opens his mouth to continue his lecture, but apparently decides against it. Kaspar stares round at us all. His face is white and his lips are working. He is trying to say something. Then he pushes his plate aside, and stands up and leaves the table.

"Sorry, Kaspar. Sorry," says Max. "Sit down, for God's sake."

But Kaspar has gone.

Leonie glares at Max.

"Poor Kaspar. When I think what he was like before…"

Max holds his hand up to silence her and goes on as if nothing has happened.

"The swine who did this to Germany must be hunted down. We must restore the good name of this country. You British – and the damned Yankees – are going to let them get away with it. Isn't that right, Adam? You're just catching the sprats, and letting the sharks get away untouched?"

"No, that's not true… I begin angrily, but Max brushes me away, waving his fork.

"You know damn well it's true. The Americans are hungry for our scientists, and they don't want to disturb the bureaucrats who run this country, in spite of all the barbarity those little bastards turned a blind eye to. The top Nazis have already scuttled away to South America. So they will all get away with their vile actions, unless a few people like us act to see that justice is meted out."

"But if we  get rid of all the middle people, the infrastructure of the country will crash. At the moment all the social services are running amazingly smoothly, aren't they?" I say.

"Yes, they are. German efficiency is a wonderful thing, thank God."

"Okay, we are only picking out a few minnows," I say. "But pretty well every bureaucrat is – was – a member of the Nazi party. So any one of them can be sacked and arrested at any time, and it's my opinion that's the way it's heading. Then where will you be?"

Max spreads his hands.

"It's a mess. I agree. But it's the real bad bastards I want. The torturers, the sadists."

I shrugged. "How do you tell the dyed-in -the wool Nazis from the people who just went along for the ride? That's something I could do with knowing. But there's no way of telling. I'll be honest with you – it worries the hell out of me sometimes."

"Anyway, our bad apples… if you English are not going to get them, someone must. And that's where we come in."

He jerks his head at Vincent.

"That's right," agrees Vincent. "Some of us do something about it, don't we, Max? Is there any more beer, for fuck's sake?"

He is already a little drunk. He turns to Leonie, who has sat down between us. He puts his arm round her. She looks at him with distaste.

"Come on, *Liebchen*, get me another beer, will you? I think I've earned that much this evening?"

I notice suddenly that there are dark brown stains on his tunic and that his hand is bruised and bloodied. He runs it down her spine to the hollow in her back. She pushes him roughly away and fetches some more bottles of lager from the sideboard.

"Yes, we've settled a couple of scores tonight, eh,

Max?" Vincent continues, drinking straight from the bottle and brushing a hairy arm across his mouth, his eyes on Leonie's face. She turns away quickly, but his hand is on her arm.

"Those *Scheissenhausen* had it coming to them. Did you see the fat one's face, Max? He didn't expect that, did he? Ach, what a noise he made! Screaming like a stuck pig!"

His face is flushed and he laughs, showing a couple of missing teeth. Max leans forward, then thinks better of whatever he is going to say and sits back again.

"Yes, you did well. But we are talking to our English friend here about politics. He doesn't want to hear about our little games by the canal. We are looking at the big picture. What will happen to Germany now? Will we do the bidding of the Yankees, become a 49th State? Join in their worship of the God of Mammon? Or look eastwards towards Communism, and its glorious ideology, 'where every man is equal and the class system is no more?'" He rolls his eyes in mock admiration.

Silence falls as we solemnly contemplate this enormous paradox. I wonder who is going to respond first. I for one can think of nothing sensible to say, knowing I am well out of my depth. Anything I contribute is certain to be irrelevant at best and offensive at worst, so for once I have the sense to stay silent. The men continue their argument, Vincent holding Leonie's arm the whole time. She glances quickly at me in mute appeal, but I look away.

§

My mind turns again to Rose, as a subject far more relevant to me than Germany's choice between capitalism and communism. I reach for another cigarette, and at this very moment the front door bangs and Rose comes in. She is with another girl, a pretty little blonde named Angela with lovely long hair. They both look white faced and exhausted.

Rose glances quickly over to me without acknowledgement, then at Dagmar, and then at Leonie.

"Is there any wine?" she asks. Her tone is listless.

"No. But aren't you hungry?" says Dagmar. "There's some fish left. And some pickled gherkins. And Sauerkraut."

Rose shakes her head. "No, nothing. I'm going to bed."

She starts for the door. Angela is at the stove very slowly spooning some food onto a plate. I can see now she has a bruise across her jaw and is trying to keep her hand in front of her face to hide it. Nobody mentions it.

"Rose! Hello!" I call out foolishly, like a host at a cocktail party greeting a late arrival. "Come and sit down and talk to us. Max was just saying…"

"I'm very tired, all right?" she says. "If there's no wine left…"

I remember suddenly the two bottles of Riesling, unopened. I reach for my bag and pull them out. Vincent's eyes are on them.

"Here," I say. "Take a glass up with you."

I get up, my chair dragging noisily across the tiled floor. I find a corkscrew by the basin and clumsily open the bottle. Now I feel a sort of panic rising in me. God Almighty, this is an awful scene. Rose is so sweet, so vulnerable, and has been subjected with the other girl to who knows what tonight. I'm sitting here eating a good meal with two men who seem likely to have spent the afternoon murdering people, and I've just had passionate sex with Rose's best friend. I've had two steins of strong Bavarian lager in rapid succession, and it's gone straight to my head.

"Adam?"

With an effort I pull myself back to the present, and look up to see Rose staring at me. She looks so wan, so tired, and yet so beautiful that my heart aches. I have one of those moments when I seem to be looking down on us all, a kind of out-of-body sensation.

I am young, I am at the threshold of life. I have seen and done things – dreadful things – that will stay with me all my life. Meanwhile, back at home in Gloucestershire, my mother will have kept my bedroom as it always was while I was away at boarding school. My sister will be visiting her at the weekend, with her nice husband who is Something in the City and her little baby, my niece. My father... well, he lies lost forever in the sands of Egypt. And I am in this room looking at Rose, my future, and my love. I twist the corkscrew viciously.

I am suddenly completely and utterly certain that I love this girl, totally, passionately, and beyond any doubt. For ever and ever. The knowledge takes my breath away and the universe seems to suspend its course. I have been struck by a *coup de foudre*.

I pour some Riesling into a glass, and take it across the room to Rose.

Everything has gone completely still. Then into the silence I hear myself say, "There you are, Rose, *mein*

*Liebchen.*" And slowly I hand the glass to her.

She just looks at me with her steady level gaze, and finally says, "Thank you." She gazes down at the glass, and takes a long, slow sip. Then she issues a shuddering sigh.

We all wait for her verdict, except Vincent, who is sucking his bruised knuckles and then reaching greedily for the pieces of ham that are left. Leonie has finally escaped his grasp and is sitting down across the table from him.

"That's really lovely," Rose says finally. "Absolutely delicious. In fact it's the nicest wine I've ever drunk."

She is speaking very clearly and precisely, like someone in a trance. She raises her glass to me. "Thank you, Adam. And now, if you'll all excuse me, I really am going to bed."

When she's left the room I find myself looking across at Leonie. I am lost, totally lacking the ability to make any decision at all. She is staring at me with a strange look on her face. The men have started talking loudly together again. Elena has gathered up the plates and borne them off to the sink.

"There's some currant pudding," Dagmar calls in her gruff voice. "And help yourselves to coffee. I'm not a bloody waitress. And it's only acorn. Unless our English lover boy has been to Brazil lately?"

Leonie gets up and comes over to me. "I should give her ten minutes, then go up to her, if I were you, Adam," she says quietly. "And be very, very gentle with her."

I pour her a glass of wine as well, and put it in her hand.

"Will she know about us, you know, tonight?" I

ask her quietly. I say it very nervously. She laughs.

"Of course she'll know. She's a woman. That doesn't matter, you fool. We are whores! This is a brothel, not a French salon! Here you get honesty. This is real life, Adam. Embrace it!"

Max and Vincent are beginning to shout at each other.

"We can't kill them all, you fool!" Max is saying. "We've got to look to the future. First we must rebuild Germany – starting with this city!"

Vincent is shaking his head. "The city can wait. These swine will not. Starting with… Let's look at that list again."

Their heads are together. They have forgotten us. Max has a stubby finger going down the paper. We are in the conspirators' scene in Julius Caesar.

*These many, then, shall die; their names are pricked.*

*He shall not live; look, with a spot I damn him!*

I shake my head in disbelief. Then I smile at Leonie and hug her shoulder.

"Thanks for tonight," I whisper. "It was terrific."

"You paid, didn't you? You got what you paid for, *nicht wahr?*" she says sharply. Rose would have given both men a kiss and begged them to stop quarrelling, but Leonie is indifferent to their quarrel. She draws her chair up between the two of them and reaches for the wine bottle.

Nobody notices me leave the room.

# 12

*Hamburg, 1947*

I still think about marriage, and the realities of my job in the War Crimes operation. There is an irony at the heart of it that I am deeply reluctant to reveal. But it is time I came clean to someone, and that someone must be Rose. She has a very understanding nature, that girl, and a damn shrewd insight into human behaviour. Time I talked to her properly about both the topics the C.O. raised a few days ago.

Lost in my thoughts on my journey home, I have not paid attention to my surroundings. I have gone a little off track and am a street or two away from my normal route, consciously or subconsciously avoiding my usual encounter. But as I turn a corner to change direction I see a figure sitting on a heap of bricks by the side of the road. A woman, cigarette in hand, is crying quietly.

For a moment I don't recognise her and peer at her through the driving snow. Then I am brought up short.

"Rose! It's you. I nearly didn't recognize you."

She looks up with blank eyes.

"What's the matter? You're crying. What are you doing here?"

I sit down beside her and put my arm round her, smoothing her hair with my hand. Then I reach in my pocket and pull out a clean folded handkerchief. "Here – blow your nose, and tell me all about it." Two passers-by, huddled in thin coats against the cold, look incuriously at us for a moment and then hurry on. A woman in tears is too commonplace a sight to merit a second glance.

Rose shakes her head mutely but takes the handkerchief. Her lip is puffing up, and there are fresh ugly marks on her throat. She sees me staring and puts up her hand to her neck.

"Come on, what happened?"

"Ach, it is nothing. Oh, well, it is just everything," she says, and starts to cry again. "First I've had a row with the others – I'm not pulling my weight, who do I think I am, why do I.... "

"Bring an Englishman to dinner?" I prompt.

She shrugs. 'Well, that, maybe. But now tonight, there's this Polish guy. Even Karina won't have him again, so I must." She starts to shake. "Ach, Adam, I know men, I know what they want, I know how to please them I think – but this man, he is an animal. *Ein Untermensch*. I can't tell you…"

She chokes. The tears are flowing again. "Now Max is threatening to throw me out, and…"

I stand up. "Right. Enough is enough. This is going to stop. Now. And if you've been thrown out, that's fine. We've got the evening to ourselves."

"Have we?"

"Yes, we have. I'll sort Max out. But first we're

going to go and get something to eat. A proper meal in a nice restaurant! How do you fancy that?"

The ghost of a smile returns to her face. "Are there still such things?"

"Oh yes. You know there are. One or two, anyway, and more every day. There's a French couple apparently who've just opened a little place near the cathedral. Black market of course – hush hush stuff. But I heard from someone in the office it's really good. Hey – they've got French wine too!"

"But – won't it be very expensive?" she says, wrinkling her nose and opening her blue eyes very wide.

"Pah! A mere bagatelle to a man in my position! I've had a promotion at work – well, I think I have. I'm going to tell you all about it. Then you'll know my guilty secret."

"Oh, how exciting!" she cries, springing to her feet. The tears are forgotten and the young Rose has returned, like a flower springing up after the rain.

"I love secrets! But Adam – I can't go to a smart restaurant looking like this. I need a dress, and some lipstick, and to do my hair…" She touched her head.

"Fine. We'll go back to your place first and you can see to it."

She catches my arm. "No, Adam, we can't! Max was so angry. And Kaspar. And Leonie – they all hate me. They've told me not to show my face there again, or they'll…"

"Nonsense. I'll talk to them. Anyway, I'm not taking you to dinner until you've done your face. I've got my reputation to think of, you know."

"Beast!" she cries. "Well, you'll have to protect me.

Adam – I'm serious. There are things going on there that you …you don't know about."

We've arrived at the house. She hangs on tightly to me and we go in together through the garden and in the back door. She looks genuinely scared. Max is sitting at the table surrounded by documents again. He looks up and glares at Rose.

"I thought I told you to get out!"

"Yes, but…"

"Look," I interrupt. "This is my fault, Max. Can you and I have a chat while Rose sorts herself out?"

He sighs, then nods. Rose slips quietly upstairs

"This can't carry on," he says curtly. "She isn't pulling her weight. The other girls are complaining… and I've got a job to do. You know?"

"I don't know, and I don't want to. How you live and what your politics are, that's your own business, and the less I know the better. Can I sit down?" He hesitates, then indicates a chair and moves some papers. He pulls a battered pipe out of his pocket.

"Can I ask your advice, Max?"

There are few people who don't like being asked for advice. Max says nothing, stuffing strong smelling black tobacco into the bowl with his thumb.

"I like Rose, Max. I like her very much. And this world isn't for her. I know she's got into communism – I know how you all feel about how society has betrayed you. And I respect your views. Really I do. But Rose – she's too young and – well, innocent for all that cloak and dagger stuff. Surely you know that."

Max bangs the table with his fist. I have gone too far.

"Rosa, innocent? Hah! You want to 'take her away from all this? You think you are in a movie in *Holly-*

*vood?*' he sneers. "She is the whore with the heart of gold that the dashing young officer comes to rescue in the last reel?"

"I know it must seem like that to you. And – yes. I suppose that's exactly what it's about. I've left my white charger tied up outside, but otherwise…"

He gives a short sharp laugh, and puts a match to his pipe, drawing hard to make the tobacco catch.

"I'll tell you something, Adam. Man to man. That sweet innocent little girl you're going to rescue is a damn tough cookie, you know that? I could tell you some stories… She's as hard as nails and as cunning as a vixen. Don't be fooled by a pretty face and wide eyes. They've led many a man to damnation. That and a slippery pair of thighs."

His pipe is drawing well now. I come close to losing my temper.

"She's damn well got to be hard!" I shout. "What other choice has she got if she's to survive? A D.P. camp? An army brothel? She's got guts, that's what she's got. And, yes I am indeed going to take her away from all this. That's precisely what I'm going to do."

"Oh yes? What the hell are you going to do to with her then? Take her to your lodgings and see if your landlady will do you a special deal for two? Take her home to present her to Mummy and Daddy in England and say, see what I found on a bombsite in Germany, isn't she cute? Be your age, man!"

He pulls his paperwork back towards him.

"You want my advice? Shag her whenever you want, and leave the money by the bed afterwards. Just don't get involved with things you don't understand, that's all! Or you might get yourself hurt. Terminally. Get me?"

He stretches his neck out and runs a finger across his throat.

I've heard enough. I stand up and open the door.

Rose is standing silently outside in the hallway. I don't know how much she has heard.

She is wearing a midnight blue pure silk dress of a very simple but expensive cut, and her arms are bare. Silver jewellery adorns her bosom and wrists, and she has tied a wispy chiffon scarf round her neck to hide the bruises. She has combed her hair and let it hang loose down her back. Round her shoulders is a stole that looks to me like a mink. Her coat hangs over one arm.

She stands in the hallway with one hand taking her weight against the wall and the other hand on her hip, crossing her elegant ankles. It is a pose from a fashion shot. Her head is tilted to one side, and she has the mischievous glint in her eye I have come to recognise.

"Will I do?" she says.

Max and I are both speechless. Then he looks at me, and shrugs his shoulders. The ghost of a smile on his face shows through the unkempt beard. I just gaze at her. She looks a million dollars.

"You look a million dollars," I say.

She dips her head prettily. "Thank you, kind sir. Will you be taking me to dinner now?"

I look at Max. "She'll be coming back here, all right? Until we can sort something out."

"Maybe. We'll see," he says grudgingly.

"Max!"

"Well, I have to hand it to you, you make a good-looking pair," he says gruffly. "Get off with you both and have fun. But you know something?"

He leans back in his chair and stares at Rose, who

looks levelly back. "You're no longer my responsibility, got it? I've been like a goddamned father to you, but it looks like you belong to soldier boy now. Clear your things out tomorrow. And anything you heard here in this house stays in this house. Got it?" His face is grim now. "Because if I find out that…"

"You won't," she cuts in. She darts quickly over to him and kisses the top of his head. "Tomorrow I'll start looking for a proper job. And Max – thank you for everything."

Max grunts, and turns away dismissively. My temper rises.

"Anyway, you can't chuck her out. This is her house, remember?"

Rose cuts in quickly, grabbing my arm.

"Look, you can forget all that stuff, all right? This place just happened to be in my family before… It doesn't belong to anyone now. It's just a place that was available, that's all. That Lady of the Manor thing has gone, dead. Hitler saw to that."

"She's right. She has no title to it, my friend. Do you know what? Just keep your English nose out of our business, okay? Now get out, the pair of you, before I really lose my temper."

I stiffen, but sense I am fighting a losing battle. In the end I give Max a long stare, as if to tell him not to mess with me. He treats that with the contempt it deserves, jamming his pipe back in his mouth. Before I can think what piece of empty bravado to produce next, Rose has hauled me out of the room and the freezing night.

§

In spite of everything, Rose is in high spirits. Her moods change like a feather in the wind.

"I'd be free!" she cries. "Just think – the only lover I'd ever going to have again is you! Isn't that wonderful?"

We stop long enough for me to kiss her a long passionate kiss, as the occasion clearly merits. She is slim and warm and utterly lovely, and it is a long time before we break apart and move on down the street. Her enthusiasm is infectious, and we are grinning at each other like naughty children escaping from school. She puts her head on my shoulder as we walk along. Then reality seems to dawn on her.

"What are we going to do, though, Adam?" she whispers anxiously. "He's serious, you know. I'm finished there really."

"I know, darling," I say soothingly. "Let's find this restaurant and we'll talk about it there. If we cut across the canal… mind this building…"

We swerve to avoid a tall teetering structure which looks ready to collapse at any moment, and take a circuitous route round an enormous crater. Half a street has disappeared into its depths, and it is now surrounded by barbed fences and admonitory notices.

### *'KEEP AWAY! DANGER! NO ENTRY!'*

Below them is an old British Army of Occupation notice, torn and faded.

> *'Don't make friends! Be suspicious!*
> *Every German girl is a funeral march!'*

Rose points it out to me and we giggle again. Suddenly nothing seems to matter any more.

We walk for fifteen or twenty minutes as briskly, Herr Klumpf grumbling, but our mood lightening at every step. The exercise has revived our spirits. I say something innocently about my leg getting stiffer, and the beautiful girl on my arm laughs into my face and says something rude and I hold her more tightly as we walk along together. Our breath freezes together into a single cloud in the frosty air. I am suddenly seized with joy.

The few people we meet mostly keep their heads down, though one woman with a baby smiles at us and offers us a cheerful greeting. I realise we must present a picture of hope, the tall young man and his merry girlfriend defying the devastation all around us. A grey haired man looks at us with something keener than mere envy, and hurries on.

We have come to the remains of a cobbled street at the back of the Cathedral, where the remaining cottages still bear signs of having formed part of the church community. The ancient bulk of the thousand year old building looms high above us, and although two walls are missing and the roof has collapsed, much of it has miraculously escaped the worst of the bombing. A gargoyle's head stares balefully down on us among the exquisite tracery of the medieval stonemason's craft, and the flying buttresses soar up to heaven, gladdening the heart.

We find the house I have been advised to look for. It has a portico with a carved stone arch over it and a hollowed worn doorstep. I push the ancient brass bell and it rings reassuringly within the house. After a moment the door is opened by a plump dark girl.

*"M'sieu 'dame?"*

"I was told to ask for Jean- Pierre, and to enquire if by any chance you have a table for tonight?"

*"Mais bien sur! Entrez, s'il vous plait."*

We are politely shown through into a small dining room, furnished with dark red embroidered drapes and heavy antique tables and chairs. A Mozart serenade is playing from a hidden apparatus. A delicious smell of cooking heavily flavoured with garlic comes from the kitchen.

A dozen or so other diners fill the room with merry chatter, the clatter of cutlery, and the heady aroma of Gauloises cigarettes. A small bald youngish man in a blue apron is busy serving a party of four with plates of casserole and side dishes piled high with green vegetables and roast potatoes. A flask of wine stands on their table and one of the diners is pouring it out.

The girl shows us to a small table in the corner lit by an oil lamp, and politely takes our coats. The room is comfortably heated, in contrast to the bitter chill of the evening, and we luxuriate in the warmth. She disappears into the kitchen and we settle back in our chairs, again smiling at each other conspiratorially.

"This is the life," I say, rubbing my hands together and looking round at the scene. "Civilisation again at last. Oh boy."

Rose doesn't answer for a moment, and when I look at her I see tears in her eyes.

"What's the matter?" I say anxiously. "Don't you like it?"

"You've no idea," she whispers. "Oh, yes, I like it."

She takes my hand and squeezes it.

"Adam? Promise me something?"

"Of course."

"We'll stick together? I'm never having to go back to that – that nightmare life?"

I look at her for a long moment. She is perfectly beautiful, a picture of youth and loveliness in her long dress. The oil light catches the deep tones of the silk as in a Rembrandt painting, matching the blue of her eyes. But there is a sweetness in her which goes beyond mere physical looks. She has an integrity, a courage, a merriment which survives the devastating tragedy of losing her family, and the dreadful things she has experienced.

I stare for a moment or two at a small painting on the wall behind Rose – a Paris street in the rain, Utrillo at his not very convincing best – and then at Rose, stroking her hand.

"It's not going to be easy, darling. I've got no magic wand. But the war's over, and you and I are free to try to make a life together. God knows it's not going to be a piece of cake, but by Jingo, we're going to give it our best shot."

She frowns slightly, and then I realise that I've lapsed into English again. I don't know how much Rose understands – we almost always speak in German together. I begin rehearsing in my mind how to translate what I've just said. But I have obviously been looking so serious that she starts to giggle.

"All I understood there was 'a piece of cake'," she says. "*Ein Kuchenstück, nicht wahr?* Are you talking about food? Perhaps the English are always thinking about their stomachs?"

"Well, I am at the moment, I must admit," I say, giving up my attempt at an heroic speech and changing the subject with some relief. "I could eat a horse!"

"Well, you're in the right place, I think? A French restaurant?"

She shrieks with laughter, and some of the other diners look round at her. We dissolve into giggles again just as the proprietor comes up to the table.

"*Bonsoir et bienvenus chez Cecile, m'sieu 'dame,*" he says. "*Je m'appelle Jean Pierre. Ah, pardon – vous parlez francais, m'sieu?*"

I hesitate, preparing to embark on choppy waters. My French is like that of Chaucer's Prioress, '*after the school of Stratford-atte-Bowe, for French of Parys was to her unknowe.*'

But happily Rose takes command, speaking rapid French like a Parisienne, charming the little man and making him laugh. He spreads his hands and appears to be apologising for the limitations of his cuisine.

She turns to me, seeing me baffled.

"He says there's not much choice, obviously. We have to take what he's got. But there's vegetable soup to start with, then rabbit casserole and potatoes, or he could do some fish – and whatever wine we want as long as it's red! Ooh, and he's got gateau for dessert, and ice cream, and real coffee, and some Napoleon brandy too, but don't say it too loud, because…" I cut her short and smile at the man.

"*S'il vous plait, m'sieu,*" I say, doing my impression of a Gallic shrug. "We are only too grateful…"

He inclines his head courteously and backs away from us, towards the kitchen, seemingly unwilling to take his eyes off Rose as she smiles her thanks. I kick her under the table.

"Put that poor little man down!" I hiss. "You've

got him in a such a state he'll be ruining the food!"

"He'd better not," she says. "Because I need plenty of nourishment to give me the energy for what you and I going to do after dinner..."

"Hey, hang on!" I protest, though my legs have turned to jelly. "Listen – I don't even know where we're going to sleep tonight, let alone anything else. We can't go back to your place together, and I can't turn up at Frau Teck's with you in tow and explain to her that I found you lying in the gutter."

She smacks my hand with a large white rolled table napkin.

"I was not lying in the gutter!" she says. "I was sitting having a quiet cigarette in the fresh air, minding my own business, when this Englishman came along and dragged me against my will into this – this den of depravity!"

I throw my hands up in mock remorse.

"I can only apologise," I say. "We will of course cancel the meal, leave at once, and I'll take you back to where I found you."

Before she can reply, Cecile appears bearing a painted wooden tray which holds a steaming marmite of soup, a warm crusty baguette, a plate of olives, and two glasses of dry white wine as an aperitif. I realise suddenly how hungry I am, and not just for food.

For the next ten minutes we say not another word of any consequence to each other, but just occasionally smile across the table in perfect contentment as we eat. For this brief instant of time nothing seems to matter, and the world is once again a beautiful place.

Then I have to ruin it.

"I want you to know a little about what I do at the

office," I begin carefully, as we push our plates away and wait for the next course. "I want to clear up a misunderstanding that everybody seems to have about what my job is."

She leans forward, fluttering her eyelids roguishly.

"I'm all ears," she says. "I just hope it's very shocking indeed."

My eyes are cast down at the table. "It is shocking, because I am living a lie," I say quietly.

She stares at me. Apart from my work colleagues, I tell her, everybody who knows me automatically assumes that my task is the prosecution of the countless numbers of sadistic citizens who have taken part in the unspeakably brutal Nazi elimination machine.

The truth is different. I am one of the few military lawyers whose job is to defend, not prosecute, these dislikeable people. This has to be done in order to uphold the impartiality of the law, but until now it is a function allotted to one or two junior lawyers like myself, with the unspoken understanding that we are to go through the motions but not get in the way of the real business of detection and punishment.

So I spend my days listening to the shrill self-righteous testimony of people who for the most part have thought nothing of bullying, torturing, and generally ill-treating the wretched victims of Nazi persecution. "Those were my orders – what could I do but obey them?" is what I hear day in and day out from the NCOs, foremen, factory managers, drivers and policemen. They are ordinary people who came to terms with, but often took a surprisingly sadistic delight in the hideous daily duties they were obliged or chose to perform.

"So you see," I conclude, grateful for the wine which Cecile has unobtrusively brought and poured out for us, "I get paid for doing something I dislike, finding excuses for the inexcusable and standing in the way of these low life scum getting the punishment they deserve. It's despicable."

Rose is listening intently, lightly gripping the stem of her wine glass in her lovely long fingers. She has exquisite manners, as befits someone of her aristocratic lineage. For a moment I think I've gone too far. Then she leans towards me, making a dismissive flicking gesture with her fingers. Her hand catches her glass of wine, which rocks dangerously for a moment but recovers its balance.

"Did you expect me to be shocked? Me, of all people?" she says passionately. "That you do a job for money serving people you detest? Darling, what the hell do I think I do, if not that?"

Her low infectious giggle breaks the tension between us.

"You're just another whore like me, don't you see? Only you've got a fancy legal title and you get to keep your underpants on while you're working! Otherwise we're two of a kind. Oh, Adam, you don't know how good that makes me feel!"

Her reaction is completely unexpected. The similarity between our occupations hasn't even occurred to me until that moment, and at first my mind rejects it. Then I suddenly see the truth of it, and start to laugh as well.

"We're just a couple of old slappers, you and I!" she shrieks, bare shoulders shaking with laughter. People at other tables turn to stare at us, then quickly look away. She raises her glass to me. "Two whores together!"

I swallow hard. "Here's to the oldest profession in the world," I say, raising my glass towards hers without touching, in the German tradition of a toast, and holding her eyes.

"Yes, the legal profession," she murmurs. "Between the two of us, we've got it made."

"Well, I didn't actually mean…" I begin.

Then we look up, abruptly aware that Jean Pierre is standing smiling by the table with two *assiettes* of rabbit casserole. Behind him is Cecile with the vegetables. There is a rapid exchange of French. He says something to Rose and she translates for me.

"He says, he hopes we are still hungry?"

"I hope you said yes."

"Yes, but I told him you would really prefer horsemeat."

"Oh, you did, did you? What did he say?"

"He took me very seriously and said he would make sure to save you some for next time."

I open my mouth to speak, then notice they are both smiling.

Then she says something else to him, and he nods.

"*Avec plaisir. Bon appetit, m'sieu 'dame,*" he says, and leaves us.

Someone has turned up the wireless. Edith Piaf is singing *La Vie en Rose,* her smoky voice the very essence of a smoky Parisian style bistro. The music blends into our brains as intoxicatingly as the finest Bordeaux.

"This is your song! How do they know your name?" I whisper, but Rose has closed her eyes and is swaying her head in time with the music.

The Little Sparrow sings huskily of eyes that kiss

hers, a laugh lost in her throat. The room is swimming.

"Do you think they will let us dance a little afterwards?" Rose says dreamily, her thigh pressed against mine under the table. My leg begins to throb, but for once not with pain. In fact it isn't hurting at all.

"Yes, *cherie*. I'm sure they will. But the *casserole de lapin* is truly delicious. You haven't even tried it yet."

"Adam?"

"Yes?"

"I hope you don't mind, but I asked him something else too."

I add some more vegetables to our plates, and pour out more wine.

"You did? What?"

"I asked him if they have a room to let for the night," she whispers.

"What?"

"And he said yes, but he was desolated – we would have to share a bed. And I said that if I asked you nicely you very probably wouldn't mind too much."

"Do you know what," I say, pushing my casserole aside and putting my glass down carefully to give her a kiss. "I think – I think – you're very probably right."

# 13

*Hamburg, 1947*

Outside the office window I can hear the sounds of a work party clearing the piles of bricks from the remains of a large building. The labourers are mostly *Trümmerfrauen,* the women workers. They form long lines, passing the bricks from hand to hand and piling them neatly up, ants patiently rebuilding an overturned nest. The task is daunting, but it offers a glimmer of hope in a desolate landscape, hope that one day a new city will rise phoenix- like from the ashes.

A woman's voice calls out a shrill order, and the sound of the work ceases. No doubt they have come across something useful - furniture, some valuables. Or perhaps they are warned by the smell that they've come upon something worse.

Then the work is resumed. A false alarm.

It's been another long exhausting interview with van Reen. I just wish he didn't remind me so much of Professor Jellicoe. I keep half expecting him to get up and pour me out a glass of sherry, and put a fatherly hand on my shoulder.

"Going back to the murder of the Greek islanders…"

"Excuse me."

He winces. For a minute I think he's going to protest mildly at my lack of good taste in introducing such an unseemly topic into our pleasant conversation.

"I'm sorry, sir, but my damned prostate again…?"

This time I have made sure Bletcher has left me the key to the handcuffs. I get up and release van Reen from his seat, clicking one of the cuffs onto my own wrist as I do so.

He senses my embarrassment and smiles kindly at me. Against all my better instincts, I find it hard not to respect his air of dignity, his erudition, his undoubted charm. It is impossible to imagine me handcuffing Professor Jellicoe and leading him to a lavatory.

I just manage to stop myself apologising. Van Reen waves his free hand as if to say, it's nothing, we cannot help these silly little rules.

I slip the key into my trouser pocket, and we walk out together through Helga's office in our little convoy. She studiously ignores us and taps harder than ever on her typewriter keyboard. I have the strong impression that her private life is not going well and her temper, never sweet at the best of times, is shorter than ever.

The little cloakroom down the corridor is shabby, and its smell a sharp reminder of its function. A roll of shiny Izal toilet paper, standard Army issue, hangs from a nail on the wall and a tap drips slowly into a dirty hand basin. The lavatory has no seat, something we have all complained about. A dirty khaki overall hangs on the back of the door.

I unlock my own cuff and start to fasten van Reen clumsily to the down pipe leading from the cistern. I am finding this acutely embarrassing.

"I'm going to have to stay with you…" I start to say.

Then to my utter astonishment I feel a steely hand gripping the back of my neck. My head is thrust forward, banging my forehead with extreme force against the wall above the toilet. SMACK! Sparks are flying in front of my eyes. I literally see stars.

I cry out, partly with the pain, but also with surprise and shock. For an insane second I think it is an accident, and that van Reen has somehow slipped on the dirty floor. But then the action is repeated with even more force, and this time my nose is squashed against the wall. Blood spurts out immediately and gushes down the rough plasterwork. The pain is intense now, both in my head, which I can feel swelling up, and in my broken nose. This is horror.

Instinctively I kick back as hard as I can, and have the satisfaction of feeling the heel of my stout army issue footwear hit van Reen on the shin. He gives an 'oof' of pain. But now my left arm is being twisted behind my back and given a vicious extra wrench that almost dislocates my shoulder. I try to scream, but my head is being forced down, down, down into the toilet pan. Filthy brown water comes up my nose. Van Reen holds me down in this position with my head half underwater. I am unable to breathe. I feel myself beginning to black out. There is a drumming in my ears like thunder.

*Thomas, you bastard. Why are you and the other boys*

*laughing while I'm dying? I'll give you my sweet ration. Just stop it, stop it… I can't breathe! Please, Thomas!*

AAAH!! Another twist. Now my arm is breaking, and I'm drowning. So this is what it's like to die, like poor Clarence in his butt of Malmsey. *O Lord! Methought what pain it was to drown!*

Can't breathe, can't breathe…

My lungs hurt. Consciousness is mercifully drifting away – the pain and the roaring noise in my head will stop now. Will stop… will stop…

Suddenly my head is yanked roughly back by the hair. More pain. But now the room judders back into focus, slowly at first and then in a rush, as I gasp and gasp again for air. It's a miracle. I can breathe again.

It is not death. I see van Reen's face very close to mine. The gentle scholar has been replaced by someone almost unrecognisable. The eyes are staring and the mouth is twisted into a grin. This is the face of a vicious killer, enjoying the agony of another human being. How could I have been so stupid about him?

"One peep out of you and you'll go under again. And this time you'll stay there," he hisses. His knee is in the small of my back and I am pushed against the chipped china pedestal, half sprawling on the floor. Van Reen has the key in his hand and is fumbling with his handcuff. The other is still on my own wrist, on my good arm.

Now our roles are reversed. It is I who am being shackled by both wrists to the down pipe, a helpless prisoner, blood pouring from my nose, an agonising pain in my shoulder. Van Reen has picked up a filthy damp rag from the metal bucket in the corner of the room and is binding my mouth tightly with it. It stinks of urine, and the smell alone nearly chokes me again.

His hands are going through my uniform pockets, and he pulls out my battered leather wallet. I remember suddenly that there is quite a lot of money in there, along with my identity papers. I try and speak, but only a mumble comes out. Out of the corner of my eye I can see him pulling the overall off its hook. It will conveniently serve to cover his prison clothing. I hear the door shut quietly, and then there is silence. He has gone, stealthy as a cat.

Slowly and with a great effort I take stock of my situation. It is grim in every way. My head is hurting like hell where my forehead hit the wall, and I wonder if the skull is cracked. Blood is still pumping from my nose, and my arm feels as if it's been wrenched out of its socket. The filthy gag in my mouth is threatening to make me retch, in which case I will choke to death on my own vomit, and unwilling to be left out of this catalogue, the old wound in my knee is reasserting its right to be felt.

Clearly I must raise the alarm as soon as possible and alert the authorities that a dangerous escaped prisoner is on the loose. But even more urgent is the need is to get the gag out of my mouth before I choke to death. I look around. Then I see a tap sticking out below the cistern. I rub my mouth against it, trying to hook the cloth round it, and after a few moments I am able to ease the gag down from my mouth to my throat. That is a blessed relief. I spew the filthy contents of my mouth out into the toilet pan, and gulp in the stale air of the cloakroom as if it is the purest Alpine ozone.

Gradually my lungs stop thumping and I start to breathe almost normally again. I can even imagine that my skull is not fractured.

I manage to twist myself round so that I am sitting sideways on the lavatory, and bring my handcuffed wrists round in front of me round the downpipe. I try to staunch the flow of blood from my nose with the toilet paper, but the wretched shiny stuff is non-absorbent and just as useless for this task as for the purpose for which it has been so inappropriately designed.

But I find I can bend my torso over towards the washbasin, and with my arms at full stretch painfully turn the tap on. I stretch my face under the flow of water. The blissfully cold stream washes away most of the blood from my nose and revives me.

It also soaks the horrid gag round my neck in clean water and renders it less obnoxious. I sit back breathing raspily, weak with my efforts.

It is beginning to dawn on me that, in addition to all my physical woes, I have lost a prisoner. This is a court martial offence that could well see me in a military prison. At the very least I shall be lucky to keep my job. On top of that is the knowledge that, having completely misjudged van Reen's character and veracity, I probably don't deserve to be in my job anyway.

But there is no time to consider this any further. My obvious immediate course of action is cry out for help to Helga down the corridor. Absurdly, my habitual English reticence makes me hesitate. The embarrassment of having Helga find me in this state, shackled to the toilet covered in blood, my prisoner fled, is almost more awful to contemplate than the alternative. But of course there's nothing else for it, and I take a deep breath and start shouting, "Help!

*Hilfe! Hilf mir!'* and variations on the same theme. My head thumps with pain as I shout.

There is no response, and after a few minutes I stop. It is clear that Helga cannot hear me from behind the closed door of her office, and very few other people in this part of the building use this cloakroom. But Helga must surely soon wonder why van Reen and I are taking so long. Perhaps she is waiting, out of timidity or mere indifference, for Bletcher to return. He is due back soon. Meanwhile of course van Reen will be long gone.

I begin to shout again, but it useless. I sit back again, and find my eyes are closing. Blood is still trickling down my head and I am dimly aware that I am beginning to lose consciousness. Then I hear footsteps coming down the corridor. The door opens and in comes a stooped bespectacled figure, a file tucked untidily under his arm. It is Pinkerton, God bless him. Never have I been so pleased to see the old chump.

"Pinkie!" I try to cry, but it comes out as a strangled squawk.

His mouth literally drops open, and he stops dead. He peers at me myopically as if he can't believe his eyes.

"Good gracious me!" he says. "Is that you, Adam, old chap? Whatever have you been up to?"

At last he moves forward as if to inspect me more closely. He perches his bulging file precariously on the wash basin, from where it immediately slides off and spills its contents all over the floor. He ignores it. He has noticed the handcuffs for the first time, and fiddles with them, trying unsuccessfully to detach them from the downpipe.

"Good Lord, you are in a state. Let's try and clean you up a bit, then we'll have to get these things off."

He wets a clean handkerchief from his pocket, and dabs ineffectively at the wound in my skull. I wince, and he desists.

"Look, I'm going to get some help," he says, straightening up. "You need a doctor. Won't be a moment. Let's see now – your office is down that way, isn't it? There'll be someone there."

At the door he turns and looks at me again, then shakes his head as if in despair at the sort of scrapes young people get into these days.

"Now – stay there and don't move. I'll be back in a jiffy."

"I couldn't move if I wanted to…" I start to try to say, but the door has slammed. I feel nausea rising in my craw, and new waves of blackness coming over me. There is a banging in my head, and noises in my ears. I lose track of my surroundings, and am floating, floating away…

Now a rasping noise near my head is getting louder and louder, going through my skull. A rough voice is saying, "It's all right, sir. We'll soon 'ave you free. Just try an 'old still."

Bletcher is standing beside me sawing steadily at the chain of the handcuffs, while somewhere in the background a woman is sobbing hysterically.

I half open my eyes to the unlikely sight of Helga clasped in the arms of Pinkerton. She is clinging to him so tightly that he can't move, and he is saying, "Now, *Fraülein*, now *Fraülein*…"

"Will he be all right?" she is screaming. "Is he dying? Is he dead?"

Bletcher steps back with the severed handcuffs in

one hand, the hacksaw in the other.

"No, 'e's not dead," he says. "An' I don't think he's dying, neither. But we'd better get him to 'ospital quick."

He turns to Pinkerton.

"Sir? Will you notify the colonel right away? Prisoner's gone missing, and 'e'll need to put out a search party, sharpish."

By this time Pinkie has managed to detach himself from Helga's embraces, and straightens his spectacles nervously on his nose, smoothing his thin hair down with his other hand.

"Right you are, sergeant," he says. "But let's get the captain somewhere more comfortable first."

He comes over to me where I am being helped to my feet by Bletcher.

"No, sir! Leave 'im to us," says Bletcher sharply. He puts his arm around me to support me, and signals to Helga to assist him. I gasp with the pain.

"Tell the colonel – now!" he barks at Pinkerton, adding "… sir!" a little too late. Pinkie jumps nervously. He opens and closes his mouth, then turns to obey.

"There'll be all 'ell let loose if we don't catch 'im quick, I can tell you that for nothin'," says Bletcher, steering me through the door with Helga, still sniffling, gripping my other arm. "I never did trust that bugger van Reen. An' I said so, straight I did. Come along, sir. Easy does it."

He's right enough about van Reen. But his voice seems to be coming from a distance, and it's very difficult to think straight with this thumping in my head and everything going round. Very difficult…

§

Although it is daylight I am still in bed in my own room.. The colonel hadn't been any too gentle with me and was much more concerned with organising a search party for van Reen than in my cuts and bruises. It was left to Helga and Pinkie to do their best in that department.

"Patch him up and get him home," Foxy had ordered curtly, glaring at me. "I'll see you when you've recovered enough to come back to work. I'm warnin' you now, Adam. Losin' a prisoner is a dismissible offence. We're still under military law in this office. You might be subject to court martial."

"Sir!" Pinkie had said in an anguished tone. "You can't be serious!"

"I'm damned serious. Now get him out of my sight."

And so we had stumbled through the streets to my warm bed.

There is a knock at the bedroom door. It is Ernst, standing crookedly in the doorway and peering in at me.

"My friend! I have only just been told! Whatever has happened to you?'

I try to sit up.

"No! Lie back. I am a doctor, you know - had you forgotten? Just keep still while I go up and get my things. I think I know where I …."

He had hurried off upstairs with something more of a spring in his step now that he had a medical mission, and returned with an ancient cracked leather briefcase.

"Now, let's have a look at this nose. Oh dear me,

yes…. But I am much more concerned about your head wound. Now, just a little pinprick….It will take some time to take effect."

Frau Teck must have lit the fire in my bedroom, a hitherto unknown event, and it is glowing quietly and comfortingly. Evening has descended, and the windows are dark with rain. Ernst is sitting by my bed, quietly reading. When he sees that I am awake he puts the book down and leans forward eagerly.

"How are you feeling now, my boy?"

"Much better, thank you, doctor," I say drowsily. "You have not lost your touch."

He grins almost boyishly. He looks so much younger when he is not brooding over the past.

"But you have had a very bad bang to the head. There may be internal bleeding. And your arm is badly wrenched. I am ordering you to stay in bed until you are fully recovered."

I am too exhausted to argue. And not too keen to rush back to the office either, if the truth be told. Minutes pass before I open my eyes again.

"What are you reading?" I ask curiously, after a period of companionable silence. "It looks well thumbed."

He glances down at his lap.

"It is one of my old diaries, from the war days," he says quietly. "I had forgotten it was in my briefcase. I have several of them. I do look at them from time to time. This one is indeed battered, isn't it? Blood stained too. Or shall we pretend they are just coffee stains? But still legible after, what – nearly thirty years."

"Ah, the other war," I say, understanding now.

He smiles thinly.

"Yes, the Great War. The war to end all wars, they called it. As it should have been, if it hadn't been for…"

"Your little friend Adolph?"

"Yes. One man, one evil man. I fear I have always been in the shadow of Hitler. It is a destiny I can never escape. I have just been reminding myself…"

I fervently hope he is not about to set off on his familiar theme, his delusion that he could have saved the world from the destruction of another world war if only he had acted to eliminate Hitler. I am powerless to escape, trapped in my bed.

"…of how you met him?" I ask bravely, prepared for a long conversation. At least I can close my eyes without seeming rude. The fire in my bedroom is dying down now.

"Oh yes indeed," says Ernst, putting the diary down again.

"I met him several times of course. The last was on the Somme in 1918, in the final month of the war as it turned out, though we thought it would go on forever. I was working in a large field hospital we had set up in a ruined farmhouse, behind a little town called Pasewalke. I well remember…"

Hard as I try, my eyes are closing. Ernst notices and closes the book.

"But you are tired. What am I thinking of? What you need is rest."

"Ernst?"

"Yes, my friend?"

"Do you think you could read them to me? I know they're private but…it looks as if I'm going to be here in bed for a few days, doesn't it? I should be most interested."

He hesitates, then nods reluctantly.

"Well, they are private, of course. But that isn't going to concern me for very much longer. And they may distract you a little, that's true. There are several of them, and I don't expect you would want to wade through them yourself."

He leaves the room again and comes back with a cardboard box containing notebooks of various kinds. I reach down and look at one of them while he puts more fuel on the fire. He is clearly settling in for a long night.

The diary is written in crabbed, faded handwriting, but is legible enough. The date on it is July 1903.

"Shall I sit here and re-read them while you rest? Perhaps they will help me to tell you something of my life. An old man likes to look back…"

My head has started throbbing again. Whatever drug Ernst has given me is making me feel very strange. The diary drops from my hand, and I sink back onto the pillow. His voice is hypnotic.

"I shall start at the beginning. I had not long been qualified as a doctor when…"

I am transported into a town in Austria over half a century ago, to an era that after the first world war would be gone forever.

# 14

*Leonding, Austria, July 1903*

Flies buzzed against the window panes and skinny babies wouldn't stop crying. When one stopped, it seemed another would begin. They were punctuated by the groans and cries of other patients, of whom the town seemed to have an endless supply.

It was a lovely summer's day outside the surgery window, with the sun catching the tips of the Alps on the horizon. But Dr Ernst Mann was in no mood to appreciate it. It is not enjoyable for a young man to be stuck indoors in a surgery full of sick people, and with not enough medicines to go round.

It was a busy time for Ernst. Recent heavy rain was constantly seeping into the mine workings at the big coal pit at

Bressingheim, testing its rudimentary safety precautions to the maximum and failing miserably. Every day brought its quota of accidents, many minor, but some hideous. Dr Bloch and Ernst were kept fully engaged dealing as best they could with mangled arms, legs, and fingers, in addition to the usual day to day quota of dust- choked lungs. The lack of proper medical supplies added to the problem. It was exhausting work and Ernst found it emotionally and physically draining.

The long day wore on. The crowd in the waiting room in the surgery had finally thinned out when it was the turn of a latecomer, a skinny boy of about fifteen. He wore a grubby shirt and the usual Lederhosen shorts. He bowed politely, as was the custom.

"Yes?" said Ernst, stretching stiffly in his chair and beginning to dream of a long, cold lager. "What can I do for you?"

"It's my Vati," said the boy, pulling a bit of paper from his pocket. "He's coughing a lot again – can't sleep at night, he says. He is cough, cough, cough. And he has a pain in his lungs, he says. He's sent you this note, Herr Doktor."

Ernst glanced at the scrawled letter and knew from the signature who the father was: Alois Heidler, the senior customs officer in the town, a notorious puffed up bully of a man. He was a heavy drinker, rumoured to have a nasty temper. Ernst had seen him once or twice in the local Gasthaus, and avoided him.

He read the scrawled demands on the note, sighed and opened the doors of the big cupboard on the wall.

"Here you are," he said to the boy. "Take a bottle of that brown stuff. That should soften the cough a bit. And tell your father from me that if he doesn't cut down on that pipe, it'll finish him off. That'll be five pfennigs."

As the youth stretched up a bony arm to take the bottle, something caught Ernst's eye. He frowned.

"What are those scars on your arm?" he demanded.

"Nothing!" said the boy, reddening slightly and turning to leave. Ernst caught his sleeve.

"Hang on. Let's have a look at you, then. Take your shirt off for me. What's your name?"

"Adolph," was the mumbled response. "But it's nothing really."

As the shabby blue shirt was reluctantly pulled off, Ernst caught his breath. The boy's upper back and arms were covered in vicious welts, some of them crusted with scars and others still a livid red.

"My God! Who did this to you?"

There was no reply. The doctor took

some cream from the cupboard and started to rub it over the injured back. Adolph winced. "This'll sting a bit, but it'll help you heal. These wounds aren't funny. This is your father's idea of discipline, I take it?"

Adolph made no reply, pulling his shirt back on and placing some coins on the desk. Ernst thought for a moment. This sort of thing was very tricky, and it was all too easy for a well-meaning outsider to make matters worse. But these marks indicated more than an everyday minor domestic matter. "You live in that little yellow house on the way up out of town, don't you? I pass it every day."

Adolph nodded again. Ernst thought a moment.

"I'd like to call in on you in a couple of days. I'll drop another bottle of linctus off for your father."

He saw a look of alarm in the boy' eyes. "It's all right – I'll be discreet. Just say hello," he smiled. "I think I've seen your sister? She's very pretty, isn't she? Perhaps she'd welcome a caller sometimes."

*"You stay away from her!"*

Adolph had stiffened, and advanced on the doctor, his eyes wild.

"She's... she doesn't always know what she's doing. You leave her alone!"

The doctor stepped back instinctively. The young man's reaction frightened him, and he raised his hands in a calming gesture.

"All right! I'm only joking! No need to get so worked up."

The boy gave him a final glare and was gone. The door slammed and the doctor slowly let out a breath. For some reason he'd gone quite cold, and his hands felt clammy. Then he told himself crossly to pull himself together, and called in the next patient.

The young doctor was oddly disturbed by the incident. He couldn't get the white, angry face out of his mind. Later that day he decided to have a word with Dr Bloch. He tapped on his office door when the last patient had gone, and they spoke as usual for a little about some of the day's cases.

"There's another thing, sir..."

Dr Bloch was rinsing his hands in a chipped stoneware basin. He looked tired, and his broad face was crinkled like an old map under the neat grey beard.

"What's the problem, Mann?" he asked, peering at his young assistant over his wire-framed spectacles. He wiped a hand over his forehead. "It's hot, isn't it? Sheesh."

"Oh, it's just a patient I had today, sir. Well, he wasn't strictly the patient..."

The older man listened closely to the story and sighed. "Heidler. Yes, I know the family," he said. "My advice is to steer well clear. Heidler is quite an important man in this town, and not someone you'd want to cross swords with."

"Do you know them well, sir?" asked Ernst diffidently. He felt a strange curiosity about them, but wasn't sure why. Perhaps because he had more than a few unpalatable memories of his own father's strict parenting procedures.

"A little. His wife Clara is a nice little thing, very much under Heidler's thumb," said Bloch, carefully drying his hands. "I've had to see her several times over the years. They lost more than one baby to diphtheria. And another one to measles, if I remember rightly."

He shook his head.

"Very unhappy family, one way or another. There's a daughter too – Paula? Something like that. And there was an older brother who has disappeared abroad somewhere."

He wiped his forehead with a damp handkerchief. "In fact I delivered Paula, now I come to think of it. Very difficult birth. Yes, a tricky one"

"She's damaged?"

"A little slow, shall we say?" he said, spreading his hands out. "Pity. A lovely looking girl."

"I think I've seen her. But the boy?"

"Bit of a bad lot, I believe. Always in trouble at school. Won't fit in. You know the sort of thing." He looked at the young man and put his hand on his shoulder for a moment.

"He'll survive, you know, Mann," he said kindly. He turned to a pile of paperwork on his desk. "They always do. He'll be as tall as his father before long, and that'll probably make that schmuck Heidler think twice about taking a stick to him. Anyway, he'll be leaving school soon, I should have thought. Maybe move away altogether, like his brother did."

He picked up his pen and some paper from his desk.

"I don't know, sir...."

"Leave it, Mann. There are a lot of things going on in this town we're better keeping out of. Let us concentrate on treating their medical problems. The good Lord knows we've enough on our plate without our turning childminder as well." He smiled kindly. "But now you're here, Mann, I could really do with your help with these requisition orders for the new vaccines? It's bit complicated."

"Of course."

"This is the one we really need, but..."

Ernst reluctantly took the other chair. The lager would have to wait a while, it seemed. Ice cold, in a long glass...

§

A week later Ernst was walking slowly up the long hill above the town, basking in the pleasure of having got another long day's work behind him. Several people greeted him respectfully as he passed them. He was becoming known in the town now, and he imagined them whispering to each other, "That's the new doctor at Dr. Bloch's." It was a good feeling.

It was another lovely evening in that warm summer, but with a hint in the air now of autumn days to come. He noticed that the swallows were already clustering in the treetops, noisily planning their long migration back to Africa. Squirrels were playing in the trees, romping from branch to branch.

He decided to call in at the Gasthaus Wiesinger before going home. It was too tempting to pass the door. You were always guaranteed a good welcome from big Karl and the plump barmaid with the wide smile, and the beer was the best in town. He enjoyed coming here sometimes when he'd been paid his weekly wages.

Tonight was quiet in the tavern, and apart from a couple of nodding acquaintances, Ernst found no-one to chat with. After a couple of steins of lager, he left and took the road up the hill. It was beginning to get dark now. The first stars were just detectable against the dark blue sky, and the air was crisp and clean. He was passing the little yellow house where the Heidler family lived, which was normally quiet.

He remembered the visit to his surgery, and the weals across the boy's back. Tonight he thought he could hear raised voices, and slowed his pace a little. Then suddenly there came a sharp cry.

Ernst still hesitated, Dr Bloch's warning ringing in his ears. It really was none of his business. He turned away and continued to walk up the hill, putting the problem behind him, until a sudden piercing scream, almost a shriek, split the air.

That was a girl's voice, he was sure of that, and there was a note of desperation in it. It was impossible to ignore. Caution thrown aside, he went back nearer the house. He instinctively drew into the shrubbery to avoid being seen in the gathering gloom. The curtains on the window to the living room were barely closed, and he could see through a crack to the scene inside.

What he saw rooted him to the spot.

In the middle of the room stood a big, moustachioed man in a dark blue uniform. His face was red and he was shouting at the top of his voice, swinging his arm up and down against a form bent over a sofa. In his hand was a baton, a part of his equipment as a Customs Officer. Ernst had seen such an object before. It was made from polished black malacca, with an ornamental silver handle, part of the official regalia designed to impress rather than to be used. But used it was certainly being now, and to brutal effect.

From the ceiling hung an oil lamp on a chain, which was swinging slowly to and fro in the darkening room. It cast long shadows as it swung, lending the scene an added touch of horror which it scarcely needed. A broken wine flask lay on the floor, the glass shattered and a dark red stain oozing from it.

As Ernst's eyes took in the details, he saw two women clinging to one another by the kitchen door. He recognised the daughter, Paula, who was holding her hand across a welt on her bare arm, tears streaming down her face, while her mother clasped her protectively. At their side a little black and white sheepdog was yapping furiously, crouched down and glaring at the master of the house.

Ernst knew that the recumbent form taking the blows belonged to young Adolph. As he watched, unable to make his limbs work,, he saw Adolph struggling to his feet, twisting his body towards his tormentor.

"Stop it!" he shrieked. "No more! Stop now, Father, d'you hear!"

It was an unequal confrontation however, as the older man wielding the weapon was twice the boy's size.

"I'll stop when I please!" Heidler shouted at the top of his voice, raising his baton again. "And you call me Sir! Have you no respect for my office?"

"You tore up my paintings!" sobbed Adolph. "How could you?"

"Paintings? Is that what you call that worthless trash? Get down. Take that!"

*Whack!* went the cane. The girl moaned quietly, rocking her head up and down. "Please, papa! Leave him alone now!"

Her father ignored her. "Get your head back down!" he bellowed, seizing Adolph by the scruff of the neck and forcing him back over the sofa. "I haven't finished with you yet!"

*Whack!*

At that the dog broke free from Paula's restraining hand and threw himself at Heidler, barking like a mad thing. Heidler swung his stick across the dog's back with his full force, and knocked it halfway across the room. Paula screamed and gathered her pet into her arms, blubbering with grief.

Heidler ignored her. Swinging his arm with his full force yet again, he spat out, "Artist! Art! What! You dare bring that up again! Going to Vienna and loafing around with a bunch of long-haired pansies masquerading as painters! After all I've done for you? Art? Over my dead body, you useless little piece of *Scheisse!*"

*Whack!* The tirade was punctuated with blow after blow of the pitiless stick, and Adolph's choking cries rose in pitch.

*Whack! Whack!*

"And don't you go blabbing to that Jew doctor again either! That assistant of his has been asking questions about me in the Wiesinger. Unless you want another hiding tomorrow?"

Mann's fingernails were digging deep into his palms as he watched. Assistant? That's me, he thought.

He was not by nature a pugnacious man and was disposed to avoid confrontation wherever possible. He knew in his heart that trouble could result if he interfered in a family matter, but he could not bear this scene for much longer. The boy could be seriously injured at any moment, and the punishment was too horrible to witness.

On an impulse he put his hand on the doorknob, and at that moment he saw Clara rush forward and interpose herself between her husband and her son.

"Alois!" she screamed. "That's enough! All the time the same thing! He can't take any more. And neither can I!"

She looked terrified, but she gripped the baton with her hands and stared into Heidler's mottled face.

"In the name of the good Lord above, stop it – now!"

Heidler wrested the stick back from her, but hesitated, and for a moment Ernst thought he was going to beat her too. Then he turned away with an expression of disgust.

But she wasn't done yet. Now it was her turn to berate him. She crouched in front of the big man like a wiry little tigress prepared to leap on her assailant to protect her offspring.

"Call yourself a father?" she shrieked. "You're nothing but a drunken bully! You've driven his poor brother away, with your drunken violence and cruelty, and soon you'll drive Adolph away too. And now you've started hitting your sweet daughter too, who can't defend herself! And even Peppi!"

The dog was licking its side in the corner, and whined at the sound of its name. Clara went back across the room to put her arms round Paula again, tears now streaming down both their faces.

"And then you'll have no-one left to take your temper out on except her! And me, of course, as usual! You're a monster, that's what you are."

She shook her head, clenching her teeth

like a terrier holding a rat.

"And monsters breed monsters too. You'll be sorry for that one day, you mark my words. God is not mocked."

She gestured as she spoke to the large crucifix hanging on the wall.

Heidler was shaking his head like a baited bear. He started to say something, then thought better of it. Then with a muttered curse he threw the baton to the floor, grabbed his coat from a hook on the wall, and made for the front door.

But in his rage he accidentally stepped on the stick. It rolled away under his foot, taking his full weight with it. He staggered for a moment, arms flailing in a desperate attempt to regain his balance, then went down onto his back like a felled ox with all the wind knocked out of his body.

For a few seconds there was silence. Clara took an automatic step towards him, perhaps to help him up, and then stopped herself. The three spectators in the room stared at the huge recumbent figure on, struck dumb by the scene.

Then the silence was broken by an odd sound. It was a mixture between sobbing and laughing, and it came from Adolph. Unable to speak for the gales of hysterical laughter which were sweeping him, and half sobbing with pain, he could only point mutely at the sight of his father, who still seemed unable to rise.

It seemed that no-one else in the room could share his mirth however, and gradually his laughter subsided. Slowly Heidler pulled himself up into a sitting position, and began groaning, rubbing his back. He stretched out his other hand and looked around at his family, mutely pleading to be helped up to his feet. No-one moved. Finally with a huge effort, he pushed himself erect with the aid of his treacherous baton, and tottered to his feet, one hand holding his injured back.

He looked at the faces of his family one by one. Still nobody moved. Then he turned again towards the door. He gave one glance at them, but getting no response, he stumbled out, snarling a curse.

Ernst was just quick enough to pull back into the bushes without being detected. He waited with his heart beating so hard he thought it would burst. Once the man had staggered out of sight, no doubt heading down the hill to the tavern, Ernst took a deep breath, knocked briefly, and went into the house.

The people in the room stared in amazement at the slight figure of the young doctor standing awkwardly in the doorway The lamp had stopped moving now, and quiet was gradually returning after the violence.

Paula gave a little gasp and turned her

face away, nursing her injured dog in her arms. She was slim, with long brown hair in ringlets, and a dignity of bearing even in her present distress. But her eyes had a permanent air of bafflement, as if the whole world was beyond her power to understand. She presented a tragic figure, like some image from a Renaissance painting, and the young doctor felt unbearably sorry for her. Then Clara stepped forward, her face a picture of mortification.

"Who... who are you, sir?" she asked. "And what are you doing in my house? With all this..." She looked round her in a dazed fashion as she spoke, as if awakening out of a nightmare which hadn't yet ended. She rushed to pick up the broken wine flask and straighten the worn carpet as she did so, ashamed that a stranger, whoever he might be, should see her home in this state.

Ernst swallowed and was about to reply when his eyes were drawn towards Adolph. The young man was half leaning against the shabby sofa, pushing his shirt back into his shorts, and trying to stand upright. His hysterical laughter had ceased, and his breath was coming hard. He winced as he spoke.

"It's all right, mama," he said, the words coming in gasps. "It's Doktor Mann from the surgery. Please, Herr Doktor. Leave us.

Everything is – in order."

The doctor saw that the young man's arms, and his legs too, were covered in bloody weals. "Adolph," he said, moving forward. "Let me have a look at you. You need attention."

The expression in the staring eyes in the white face took him aback however, and he stopped in his tracks.

"Please, Adolph."

"Mind your own damn business!" screamed the boy. "I'll deal with this my own way. This a family matter."

"But I..."

"Get out! Now!" shouted Adolph, making towards Mann with his arm raised. "And don't come back! I shall deal with it." A twist to his bony face and the set of his jaw convinced the doctor that he meant what he said. It suddenly came to him in that moment that this was no mere frightened boy. It was someone to be mightily reckoned with, who meant what he said and whom nothing and no-one would deter.

"Very well," he said quietly. "I shall take my leave."

He bowed to Clara, and to Paula, who stood mutely in the corner of the room with her shawl to her face, her big eyes with the long lashes still wet with tears.

"Please accept my apologies for intruding, *meine Damen.* I bid you good night."

And with that he left. It was quite dark outside now, and a chill had set in. But he breathed in the air in gulps, like a man just saved from drowning.

# 15

A month or so had passed since the incident in the Heidler household, and summer had slipped into autumn as imperceptibly as an apple ripens on a tree. The lovely woods up in Märchenholz were ablaze in shades of flame, scarlet, amber and gold, and in the far distance the summits of the Alps were lightly dusted with white, gleaming in the brittle sunlight.

As a relief to the pressure he was under at work, Ernst was enjoying the occasional company of a local girl called Ilse. She was a merry blonde he had met at the baker's shop where she had just found a job, soon after leaving school. It may not entirely have been Ilse's intellectual properties which had attracted him, sensible and uncomplicated girl though she was. Her long plaited fair hair, blue eyes, and suntanned limbs may have had something to do with it too. And she had a sweet smile.

She had a knack of teasing him while still being able to listen to him talk about the day's challenges, and she would laugh at his feeble jokes. She made him remember he was young, on days when he felt very old.

Ernst was examining a young miner with a nasty gash to his eye and a broken finger, and thinking of Ilse as he worked. The man was stoical and spoke little. Ernst was trying to make him say a few words in an attempts to relax him, when Dr Bloch put his head into the room. He was wearing his distinctive wide brimmed hat, which made him a recognisable figure in town.

"I'm just going up to the Gasthaus Wiesinger, Ernst," he said. "Apparently your friend Heidler has had a stroke there after enjoying his usual morning tipple. Sounds as if it may be fatal. I'll be back as soon as I can – I've got a room full of patients."

Ernst was taken aback. So Heidler might be dead, or dying. What effect would his death have on the little family? Surely it would bring nothing but relief, though what the financial implications of the loss of the main breadwinner might be, he could not guess. But otherwise he could hardly imagine that Heidler would be much mourned.

He tied a bandage round his patient's head, trying not to hurt him.

"Off you go now, Schultz. And no going back down the mine till that eye's healed, d'you hear?"

The man looked at him a moment, smiled slightly, bowed, and left. No work meant no pay. No pay meant no food. And he had a wife and three months old baby to feed. Today and tomorrow and every day, bad eye or no bad eye.

That evening Ernst and Bloch exchanged notes as they usually did as they were closing the surgery. Bloch sat wearily back at his desk. The room stank of chlorine and vomit and blood.

"Heidler? A pleural haemorrhage," said Bloch. "I've been expecting it. Little wonder, given the quantities of food, alcohol and tobacco the man apparently consumed." He shrugged. "I doubt if the family will be sorry to see the back of him. He was... a pig."

There was no more insulting epithet he could have used. He reached for a file from the pile on his desk.

"You pass their house, don't you, Mann? Would you mind dropping the death certificate in for them on your way home? They'll need it for the coroner."

"Of course, Herr Doktor."

Ernst took the document.

"Good night, Mann."

"Good night, sir."

He'd drop in at the Wiessi for a beer first, he thought. He'd been keeping away from the tavern recently, not keen on the possibility of bumping into Heidler after what he had witnessed. But there was no risk of that now. Well, that was something to celebrate.

The tavern was buzzing with the impact of Heidler's death. Ernst bought himself a stein, lit his pipe, and found himself a stool at the end of the bar. He sipped his cold beer and listened idly to the conversation.

"Sick everywhere, he was," Karl, the landlord, was telling an attentive group of regulars. "Sick as a cat. It was 'orrible. He bought his glass of Burgundy and took it over to 'is table.."

He shook his head thoughtfully. "Didn't look quite as full of 'imself as usual, I 'ave to say. Most days he'd be in 'ere shouting and laying the law down, wouldn't he? Arrogant bastard... God rest 'is immortal soul. But, no, 'e wasn't 'imself at all. Polished off 'is wine all right, though!"

He wiped along the bar with a damp cloth, and served another customer. The air was thick with pipe smoke, and the barmaid was bustling in and out of the kitchen with plates of Bratwurst and Sauerkraut, all piping hot. She had to run the gauntlet of the men's ribald comments, and hoots of laughter rang out as she deftly dodged stray hands.

Karl was intent on his story. The smell of the food made Ernst feel agreeably hungry.

"Then suddenly 'e gets up and rushes out to the back room. 'e'd gone as white as a sheet. When he didn't come back for a while, I puts my head in to see to see if 'e 's all right."

"Yucking it all up, was he?" cackled a greybeard. "All last night's beer? Heh, heh, heh! Bet he stank even worse than usual, and that's saying something!"

The other men laughed. There was little love lost for Herr *Zollmeister* Heidler in the tavern, it seemed.

"Ja, he stank something awful," agreed the landlord. " 'e was lyin' on that leather sofa, groaning and clutching that big fat belly of his, hollering out like 'e was dying." He paused in pulling a pump. "Which 'e was, of course, now I come to think of it."

Another roar of laughter rocked the bar.

" 'e was a good spender, though, I'll say that for 'im. I'll miss 'is cash, that's for sure! But that's about all, if I'm honest."

He wandered down the bar towards Ernst.

"All right, *Herr Doktor*?" he said. "Ready for another?"

"No, I'm good," said Ernst, draining his stein and preparing to leave. He knocked his pipe out in the communal ashtray. A thought struck him.

"Tell me something, Karl? There must have been a lot of blood in the vomit? Blood everywhere, I suppose. Hell of a mess."

The landlord laughed. "No, nothing like that. Just 'is breakfast, I reckon. There was enough of that to be going on with."

"You're quite sure?"

"I should be! It was me that 'ad to clear it up afterwards!"

"And did he die straight away?"

"God, no. 'e was a long time groaning and retching. 'e was in a lot of pain. I sent Betti down to your place to fetch Doktor Bloch pretty sharp. We did what we could for 'im, like. Givin' 'im water to drink and tryin' to calm 'im down." He took Ernst's empty glass. "But by the time the Doktor got 'ere, 'e'd gone quiet." He shook his head. " 'e was dead then, I reckon."

"Right," said Ernst. "Thanks. A nasty shock for everyone. Well, I've got to be off. I'm calling at the house with the death certificate."

"They'll be in a right state, I expect," said Karl. "Mind you, that lad's a cool enough character. Shouldn't think 'e'll be sorry to see the back of 'is father. 'e'll go off to Art College now, I shouldn't wonder."

As Ernst left the landlord called after him.

"Give my best to Frau Heidler for me, will you? And that poor daughter. They deserved better than 'im, I reckon."

Ernst was inclined to agree.

§

Ernst's welcome at the Heidler household could not have been in greater contrast to his previous visit. When he knocked at the door it was opened by Frau Heidler, who greeted him warmly.

"Herr Doktor! Come in, come in. Adolph, Paula, see who's called to see us! It's Doktor..."

"Mann," he said, ducking his head politely. "Ernst Mann."

He stepped into the little room and smiled back at the two ladies. Adolph was sitting on a low chair in the corner, and looked up irritably from a book he was engrossed in. He half rose reluctantly to his feet. They nodded at each other.

"You'll have to excuse the mess!" said Frau Heidler, straightening cushions, clucking around like a mother hen surprised in her chicken run. "It's been quite a day, what with ..."

"Yes," Ernst said. "May I offer you my deepest commiserations for your sad bereavement. It must have come as a great shock."

"Ah well, yes indeed," she said, and made a brave attempt to adopt a sad expression. "A great shock indeed."

But the smile broke through again, matched by her daughter's. It was as if the sun had come out unexpectedly after a long period of filthy weather. Even the barely furnished room looked somehow brighter and more appealing.

"Can I offer you some refreshment, *Herr Doktor*? Some cordial perhaps? I'm afraid we do not drink alcohol."

She reached for a large stoneware jug on the table.

He thought it polite to accept. As he sat down, he reached into his coat pocket. "I have the death certificate here from Doktor Bloch," he said, feeling a little awkward. "You will no doubt be needing it."

Frau Heidler reached out for the document rather dubiously. But Adolph was there first.

*"Let me see that!"*

He peered at the form, with its scrawled particulars, read it carefully, then handed it to his mother.

"You will see that the cause of death is stated to be pulmonary haemorrhage," said Ernst. "That means... "

"I know what it means," Adolph snapped. "It hardly matters, does it? My father was a man of many excesses. It was clear to everybody that he was killing himself with his greed. The medical definition of his death is neither here nor there."

He went back to his chair, picked up the book he was studying, and made to go upstairs. He stood still a moment in thought. Some of the tension seemed to go out of him. Then he said, "If you'll excuse me, Herr Doktor, I have some studying to do. I find my bedroom much the quietest place in this household."

He turned to his mother. "I'll have my meal at eight o'clock, if you please."

She looked startled.

"But Adi, you know we always eat at seven! Your father... "

"Eight o'clock."

There was silence in the room. Then Frau Heidler nodded, a little smile on her lips.

"Very well, Adi. Eight o'clock it is. You are the master now."

Adolph looked round a moment, bowed stiffly to Ernst, and was gone.

His mother said quickly, "Don't mind him, Dr Mann. He's a strange boy. Always has his head buried in some book or other. History, politics - it's not right for a boy of his age! I tell him, he should be out in the fresh air getting some exercise."

His sister looked up. She seemed

anxious to contribute to the conversation, but there was a dullness behind her eyes, and a hesitation in her speech, as if she expected all the time to be rebuked.

"He does go out, mama," she said timidly. "You shouldn't keep nagging him. He went walking in the woods only yesterday, didn't he? Brought back those wonderful mushrooms we had for breakfast."

His mother brightened. "Yes, that was kind. Alois was very pleased, I think, though he doesn't – didn't -- show it easily. You know, I had hoped those two might gradually stop quarrelling..."

She broke off, near to tears.

Ernst stood up hastily. It was time to leave. But the beers and lemonade had had their effect. "Before I go, I wonder if I might use... ?" He gestured towards the outside yard.

"Of course, *Herr Doktor*. But please be careful – it is getting dark."

Once outside, he looked around in the gathering gloom. A silent beehive stood in one corner. Near the small shed that he guessed contained a bucket to serve as a toilet, lay a large sack into which the household waste was tipped. A black cat was scavenging near it. It snarled at him and darted away over the fence, startling him.

He noticed idly that among the kitchen

scraps were the remains of some large mushrooms. They were now blackened, though with a greenish hue, and had rusty stained stems. The family's breakfast, no doubt. He glanced involuntarily up at the upstairs window. A dim light glowed where Adolph would be poring over his books, he thought.

As he glanced up, he caught a glimpse of a white face with staring eyes. He jumped involuntarily, and moved to an area of rough grass by the fence. The face had disappeared. Ernst delicately preferred not to investigate the shed, but stared up at the sky as he relieved himself. There was something nagging at the back of his mind, but he couldn't identify it.

Overhead the bright unwinking stare of Venus made her look close enough to touch, and beyond her, a million million more pinpoints of light filled the clear sky. It was very still. The personal affairs of one tiny speck of dust on one minor planet in an insignificant galaxy should have seemed very trivial. But that was not how it felt to Ernst as he gazed up into the night sky.

§

As Ernst walked to work the next morning, many unbidden questions were forming in his brain, perhaps the products of his subconscious mind during sleep. They were to do with Heidler's death.

Why, his suspicious mind demanded, had young Adolph seemed oddly relieved by the wording on the death certificate? Wasn't that wording itself in fact disquieting? Dr Bloch had certified the cause of Heidler's death as pleural haemorrhage, the logical result of the tobacco fuelled chronic lung disease for which he had long been treated. By its very name this implied massive bleeding as the wretched lungs finally gave way and choked the patient to death.

And yet Karl, the landlord, had said definitely that there was no blood in the dying man's vomit. He had apparently died in great pain from stomach contortions, presumably caused by something he had eaten.

Those mushrooms... it always came back to them. Mann slashed irritably at the nettles by the side of the road as he walked from the outskirts into town. Hadn't their remains looked rather odd in the starlight? Was there a connection? And why had an excellent doctor like Bloch certified a completely false cause of death? It didn't make sense. Another thing - if Heidler's breakfast had in fact brought about his demise, how was it that the rest of the family was unscathed by consuming the same meal?

One thing was not in doubt, the fact that Adolph had everything to gain from his father's death. Release from the fear of constant terrible beatings, a new freedom to choose his own career path, an end to the misery of his mother's married life, the unaccustomed light in his sister's eyes – these would be reward indeed.

It was not difficult for Mann to picture a desperate, driven schoolboy planning and executing a solution to all his problems at one bold stroke. Even on a brief acquaintance, he did not doubt Adolph's capability for such ruthless action.

His mind kept returning to the mushrooms. Every countryman knew that fungi can be poisonous. Mann himself had treated many cases of painful stomach cramp incurred by a careless forager. A few – by no means all – of the fungi that grew wild and abundantly in the damp Austrian forests could actually kill, often in contrast to their agreeable taste and innocent appearance. Very often they were deceptively similar to their harmless cousins, but were all too easily gathered by any walker in the woods.

And yet Clara had clearly implied that the whole family had eaten the mushrooms Adolph had gathered for their breakfast yesterday, surprising them by his thoughtfulness. But how could Adolph have contrived that they poisoned only his father and not his mother and sister as well?

Ernst grimaced to himself as he walked. There had to be a logical explanation. It was just a matter of finding it. There was a volume on fungi among the surgery's collection of reference books. He'd often browsed in it, being fascinated by the subject at one time. It would be worth consulting it. He had a clear recollection of the shape and colouring of the scraps in the Heidlers' yard. A shaggy inkcap perhaps, he thought, but unusually large. He could not be certain. He'd have to look it up.

The surgery was as busy as usual, but much later in the morning there was finally a lull in the flow of sick citizens, Ernst slipped into the little storeroom by the waiting room where the medical reference books sat neatly arranged on shelves.

But there was an empty space where the fungi book belonged. Someone must have borrowed it. Damn, he thought. No! There it was, thick and dog-eared in its cracked leather binding, but on quite the wrong shelf, in among the textbooks on tropical diseases. He picked it up but had no time to consult it.

His attention was immediately distracted. There was a stir in the waiting room. Two miners came in carrying a figure on a makeshift stretcher. It was a boy of no more than twelve, his face black with coal dust but daubed like a clown's with bright scarlet streaks. He was unconscious and breathing hoarsely, moaning in delirium. His clothes seemed to have been torn off him, leaving only rags.

"Firedamp. Blew him down the shaft," said one of the men briefly. "Can we leave him with you, Herr Doktor?"

Firedamp was what they called the explosion that occurred when methane gas, which might have been lurking for countless years in a cavity below the earth, was suddenly exposed to air. It was what all miners dreaded, the more terrifying for its unpredictability. The men left abruptly after a few mumbled words of farewell and a glance at the boy. Their time was money, and money meant survival.

Ernst called for hot water and cloths, and told his very competent nurse to wash the coal dust off the boy and deal as best she could with his injuries with unctions and bandages – he would look at him later. He passed his hand gently over the young forehead, sighed, and went back into his office, the leather tome under his arm. He wondered absently who had been looking at the book. But of course any member of the nursing staff, or even a patient from the waiting room, could have consulted it. It meant nothing in any case, he told himself. Pure coincidence.

"Next, please!"

But all afternoon his mind raced as he doled out medicines, bound wounds, tapped chests, and looked down infected throats. The injured boy, the most dramatic patient of the day, had been taken home by his tearful mother.

Once the last patient had left and the surgery door had been locked, Ernst lit his pipe and started looking through the book. It had some very accurate drawings of various fungi, and descriptions of their appearances and characteristics. He had a good recollection of the remains of the Heidler family breakfast that he had seen in the yard, and searched by shape, colour and appearance through the pages.

Ah! There it was. The shaggy deathcap, *involita pudens…*

*"Good to eat, but deadly poisonous if taken along with alcohol. Even if the alcohol has been consumed in the previous twelve hours, the effect is speedy and violent. Further intake of alcohol even several hours after the mushroom has been eaten will cause…"*

Ernst banged the table with his fist.

That was it! It was clear in his mind now. Adolph would know that his father had had his habitual heavy intake of wine and beer that evening. Even if his mother or sister by any chance tasted the mushrooms when Adolph had brought them from the woods, they would have been quite safe, as the strongest thing either of them ever touched was their homemade blackcurrant cordial.

Adolph would have been equally sure that his father would take himself off to the Wiessi immediately after breakfast on his way to the Customs office, as that was his invariable practice. The effect of the alcohol already in his stomach from the previous night, added to just one glass of wine in the morning, would then inflict violent, almost certainly deadly, food poisoning.

Even if Dr Bloch had correctly diagnosed the cause of death, the fact that the rest of the family had eaten the same breakfast would have ruled out the mushrooms as the cause and drawn away any suspicion of foul play. But as it happened, Heidler's medical history made a sudden stroke at some point almost inevitable, and Dr Bloch had clearly leapt to that assumption. Adolph was in the clear. It was a bold plan, resourcefully plotted and executed. The more he thought about it, the surer he was that he had found the truth.

The boy had murdered his father. But

what in the world was he, Ernst, going to do about it?

Finally Ernst let himself out of the surgery and set off walking. It crossed his mind to call at Ilse's house and see if she was free for the evening, as he did sometimes, but he dismissed the idea. He needed to think, not to be distracted by soft lips or blue eyes. In any case they had a date to go to the tavern the following night for a special musical evening.

§

The woods in Märchenholz were cool and welcoming after the day's muggy heat, and Ernst picked his way carefully down a leaf-strewn path to the little stream that meandered through the valley. To his left were the caves that the children called the fairy grottoes, scene of a hundred tales of magic. His arrival startled a young deer that was lapping at the water. It raised its head and stared at him a moment, and then with a defiant twitch of its white tail it was gone, disappearing into the greenwoods. All around him were celandine and woodruff, and the strong smell of wild garlic filled his head.

He stepped on the rough wooden bridge and stared down at the water as it burbled along. A thrush was singing its sweet piping song somewhere high above him, and the first fat wood pigeon of the evening fluttered in to settle in the trees where it would spend the night. It ruffled its feathers noisily and made itself comfortable.

Mann drew on his pipe, leaving a cloud of aromatic smoke to embellish the softly scented air. His correct course of action was clear. He should inform Dr Bloch of his suspicions, which would then be reported to the local police force. They would undoubtedly pay attention to such a report by a local doctor, and would embark on some form of investigation.

Clara and Paula would be submitted to a deeply unpleasant experience, at the very time when they would be trying to adapt to their new circumstances and recover from the shock of Heidler's death.

That was distasteful enough. But what the civil police would inflict on young Adolph in an interrogation cell did not bear thinking about. The grey, forbidding Police Headquarters on the corner of Lindenstrasse was a place that the average innocent citizen of Linz walked past as quickly as possible with averted eyes. The sounds issuing from it were harder to avoid. Ernst shuddered.

*"Ach, nein!"*

He spat into the stream, shaking his head, his knuckles white from gripping the thorny branch that formed the rail of the bridge. His pipe had gone sour in his mouth, and he impatiently knocked the tobacco out into the running water. He stuffed it into his pocket with the bowl still warm against his trouser leg, and turned back up the path.

There was another matter to be considered too. His own employer, the infinitely kind and dedicated Dr Bloch, would have to admit to a serious blunder in assessing the cause of death. It would be a matter of major embarrassment for him, and apart from other considerations, seemed unlikely to enhance Ernst's own career prospects. So what should he do? The question wouldn't stop hammering against the inside of his skull.

Say nothing, then? Why not? Heidler's body would be buried next week, and with it any remaining trace of Adolph's misdeed. The family would learn to smile again, Adolph would choose his own career path, and the world would have been freed of an unpleasant excrescence on its face.

And yet... Ernst quickened his step now, as darkness drew in and the first low hoot of an owl came mysteriously from somewhere within the wood - what would the effect be on the boy himself? At – what? fifteen? – he would have learnt that he could, literally, get away with murder. What would that knowledge do to a young mind already tormented by the cruelties of an unhappy childhood, steeped in the study of politics and history, with its messages of social injustice and violent remedies? Could a lack of action on Ernst's part allow the nurture of a monster? Wasn't that the word the boy's own mother had used of him? A young person of strong character imbued with such a strong sense of injustice that he might dedicate himself to trying to change society, and ruthless enough to carry out such changes feeling invulnerable to opposition, might be formed. The characteristically adolescent certainty of knowing himself to be right but always misunderstood, would now be reinforced by the knowledge that he could remove obstacles by violence and never have to pay the penalty for it. Who knew what that might lead to?

It was almost completely dark now. Ernst quickened his step, conscious now that he was hungry. His landlady was a good cook, and tonight being Friday, there would probably be a fish stew waiting for him. With a young man's healthy appetite, he felt noticeably more cheerful at the prospect. What he needed was a hearty meal and a good night's sleep. Time enough in the morning to think things out again.

# 16

The noise level was so high that Ernst and Ilse could hardly hear themselves speak above the accordion music, the spontaneous singing, and the shouts of the customers, some of them already dancing. The Gasthaus Wiesinger was in a mood to suit their own, it seemed. The seductive aroma of roast pork, cabbage and potatoes was in the air, and the waiters were busier than ever.

Ilse caught sight of a young couple in the corner of the bar, and she dragged Ernst towards them, clutching him by the sleeve.

"Do you know each other?" she cried. "Ernst, this is my former teacher, Herr Professor Schliemann. May I present Doktor Mann, sir?"

A burly, bearded young man, hardly older than Ernst, rose grinning to his feet. He leant forward to give Ilse a very hearty embrace and a wet kiss. "No Professor tonight!" he boomed. "You have left school now, Ilse! Call me Fritzi. Everybody does. Either that, or Hey, you!"

He shook Ernst's hand firmly. "How do you do, *Herr Doktor*? And this is my poor wife, Magda!"

His wife was plump, bespectacled, and smiling. It seemed she was well accustomed to her husband's bonhomie and took no offence from his embrace of Ilse.

"Please – won't you join us?" she asked, motioning to the two empty chairs. "Fritzi – where are your manners? Give our new friends some wine."

Fritzi poured out the sweet rough red wine of the region from a large jug into their half-empty glasses, spilling a little, and speaking above the music to make himself heard.

"No, really – " protested Ernst, but it was hopeless, and soon they were all laughing, joking, and playing the fool together as the crowd grew denser and the tobacco smoke became so thick that they could hardly pick out each other's faces in the lamplight.

"Shall we eat?" cried Fritzi. "I am absolutely starving. Magda never gives me a thing to eat at home."

He ducked a blow from his wife and waved at the pretty waitress, who was too harassed to do more than nod briefly.

"Pork for four! And plenty of crackling, d'you hear?" he shouted. "You have four starving people here. And this man is a doctor! Who will deliver your babies if you let him die of hunger?"

The waitress stuck her tongue out at him as she passed with two mountainous plates of steaming food held high for another table, and they all laughed. It was going to be a good evening.

Ilse was in particularly high spirits, and kept holding Ernst by the arm and smiling at him. She seemed to find his lightest remark funny, and for once in his life he felt quite a wit. With some more red wine and a good meal inside him, he was even able to keep up with Fritzi's ever wilder banter.

The women meanwhile, though pretending to be shocked at some of the badinage and fluttering their eyes in horror, had no shortage of things to talk about between themselves. They discovered that, despite a small age difference between them, they had many friends in common in the neighbourhood.

It was much later that the music finally stopped. The dance floor had emptied and the customers began to leave. The ladies retreated together to the rear room for mysterious feminine reasons, putting their heads together as soon as they left the bar, while the two young men slowly drained their glasses and knocked out their pipes.

Now that the evening's entertainment was over, Ernst's dilemma had come back to haunt him, like a migraine that wouldn't quite go away. He pursued a thought that had crossed his mind earlier.

"Tell me, Fritzi," he said. "Have you a young student called Heidler in your class by any chance? Adolph Heidler?"

For some reason he felt he knew the answer.

"I have indeed," Fritz said. "Hasn't his father just died?"

"Yes, here in this very place."

They talked a little about the event.

"Tell me, Ernst – why did you ask about the son?"

Ernst hesitated. Should he confide in his new friend? He would certainly welcome someone to talk things over with, and somehow he trusted the schoolteacher's judgment beneath the cheery outgoing exterior.

"Oh, it's just that I've come across him recently. He intrigues me, that's all. How would you weigh him up, would you say? Troubled? Difficult?"

Fritzi screwed up his eyes. "Difficult? More like different, I should say, I think."

He stared unseeingly across the room, which was emptying rapidly. "You know,

Ernst, I've been teaching for over ten years now, and I've met some hard cases. Kids from bad backgrounds, naughty boys, spiteful girls... but I've never come across anyone quite like your 'troubled' friend, Adolph."

"In what way different?"

"There's something about that boy that actually frightens me. Yes, me, his teacher. I can't bear him looking at me with those staring eyes."

"Is he badly behaved?"

Fritzi looked down at his empty glass.

"No, not at all. There are many worse. It's just that he's deep. Not quite with us."

"Problems at home?" asked Ernst, knowing the answer.

"Well, yes. His father is, was, not a man one would warm to, shall we say. But, no, there's something else. Adolph has a way of dismissing anything that he considers trivial, as if school is just a process to endure before he can go on to something a lot more meaningful. Things like homework, or school rules. I've had to beat him a couple of times. Irritating little bugger."

He tapped his glass. "Fancy a refill before the girls get back?"

Ernst raised a hand, and the girl came straight over from the bar to collect their glasses and replace them with full ones. She smiled at the two young men, leaning over the table just a fraction longer than seemed necessary. As she no doubt intended, the eyes of both men for a moment went to her low-cut blouse. Fritz grinned at her and took a long pull of his beer, wiping the foam from his lips with a sweep of his large hand.

"Oddly enough I've got another boy like that in the same class. The two of them are really very similar. Not that that they get on with each other. Ach, Gott, no!"

"Who's that then?"

"Oh, a boy named Ludwig. Heir to the Wittgenstein millions. And don't we know it."

Ernst was interested.

"Aren't they the richest family in Austria?"

"I believe the Rothschilds have that distinction. But, yes, pretty close, by all accounts. Young Ludo is driven to school every morning by a chauffeur in a Mercedes Benz motor car. Can you imagine? Fabulous beast. I'm still hoping for a ride in it. Not that the boy seems to appreciate it, though. To be fair, I think he'd rather walk to school barefoot."

"He's not a show off? Some of these Jewish kids can...? "

"*Mein Gott*, no. He's rather shy. Got a bit of a stammer, though he talks very precisely. The other kids mock his upper-class accent. He's a fierce little intellectual, really."

"Clever boy, eh?"

"Cleverest boy I've ever taught. But he's another one who can't stand his father, it seems. The old man's a bastard. Very strict. A real tyrant. Won't let his other sons go to school at all, I've heard. Has them privately tutored at home to become captains of industry like him."

"So Ludo and Adolph…"

"Oh, they've got a lot in common, all right. But it doesn't make them friends. I get the feeling Adolph's jealous of Ludo, a bit in awe of his brain power perhaps. No, they don't get on at all. In fact Adolph seems to actively dislike him, calls him names. Maybe it's the Jewish thing he doesn't like. I wouldn't know."

Their tankards were already half empty again. Ernst thought quickly. The girls would be back in a moment.

"Could we perhaps meet tomorrow?" he asked. "There is a matter on which I would welcome your advice."

Fritzi paused a moment, then the grin returned.

"Certainly, my friend!" he said. "I think a drunken reprobate like you could do with a little religious instruction. Do you know the Theresienkirche? Magda and I are worshippers at that august institution. I hold a modest position there, in a minor capacity. Shall I expect to see you there at

Evensong tomorrow?"

Ernst had intended to spend the evening quietly, avoiding any religious celebration. And that particular church was known to be very High and the sermons accordingly long, not a palatable thought for a young Freethinker like Ernst. But still...

"And afterwards we could invite you to our humble home for something to eat, if that suits your Honour's inclination?"

There was nothing for it but to concur. Ernst smiled in his turn.

"I shall be delighted to accept your kind invitation, gracious sir," he said, bowing deeply. And at that moment Ilse and Magda returned, shrugging into their coats while still chattering away to each other.

"Come on, Ernst! Escort me home before my father comes looking for me," cried Ilse, taking Ernst's arm.

"Why, will he bring his shotgun?" Fritz asked innocently, earning a kick on the shin from his wife. The four young people went out arm in arm together into the late summer evening. They were basking in that glow of contentment that good company, alcohol, and the precious, fleeting gift of just being young can sometimes achieve. The world and all that was in it lay before them, brimming with promise.

§

*"Dominus nostrum, pater noster, nunc dimittis......"*

The plaintive wailing went on and on, seemingly unto Eternity. Ernst sat through the hour and a half long service in a sort of stupor. He decided the words and the rituals actually meant nothing, to him or anyone else. They were simply a form of soporific. Indeed they seemed to go on into eternity, itself in fact a recurring theme, and no wonder.

His eyes kept returning to the sight of a solemn faced Fritz in a richly embroidered alb. Apparently he was a lay official, whose clerical duties seemed mostly to consist of carrying a large censer very slowly up towards the altar, waving it about so that the air was filled with the sickly cloying smell of incense, which made Ernst's stomach heave, and then just at the same tedious pace bringing it back again.

To Ernst he just looked stupid. The whole thing had about as much to do with the mystery and magic of life and the Creation as a child's marionette show, as far as he was concerned, though that was an opinion he kept to himself.

He shifted again in his seat. Truth to tell, Ernst was in a bad mood, which was not helped by a nauseous stomach and a strange sensation of everything happening at one remove. He had consumed a great deal more beer last night than he was used to. Even the singing by the small choir failed to move him, surprisingly good though it was. The glorious Toccata and Fugue in G minor by his beloved Bach. It was energetically played on the organ by a small man with a mop of unkempt white hair that bobbed up and down as he struck the keyboard. The music served only to add to the pain of Ernst's throbbing head and the churning of his guts.

He was torn by conflicting emotions. From time to time during the long service his mind went back to Ilse, and the recollection of their previous afternoon between her sheets. Images of her body close to his ran repeatedly through his brain. He was no longer a virgin, an amazing thought. Far from being satiated, he was now in the mood for more of the same, and the thought made him twist restlessly in his hard pew, stifling a groan. A sharp-faced woman in a black bonnet next to him glared at him, pursing her mouth into a moue of distaste.

At that moment he became aware of a slight but perceptible shift in attitude of the congregation, a kind of collective catching of the breath. It was as if an icy draught had cut across the room on this otherwise sunny day. A thin figure in a black suit was at the pulpit and had started reading one of the lessons. His high, reedy voice had an unpleasant edge to it that grated on the ear. The wintry sun reflected on rimless glasses above a thin, lipless mouth.

"An eye for an eye, a tooth for a tooth..." he intoned with some relish.

A heavyset older man in a nearby pew dropped his hymnbook with a clatter. Nobody moved. The cold glare of the lector switched to him for a long moment. The old man hurriedly bent to pluck his hymnal up. His face had gone white, and he looked as if he were about to faint.

At that moment Ernst realised that he knew who the reader was. This must be Goetz, the police chief, a man who could only be described as infamous. His name alone was enough to inspire terror in the hardest criminal. He was known as a man whom pity could not touch.

There was a long pause before the reading was finally concluded. Goetz closed the large bound copy of the Bible and walked with almost feline deliberation through the silent congregation back to his seat. At last the rituals seemed to be signalling a close, and finally after another agonisingly long delay Ernst was able to join the line of worshippers leaving the church.

They filed past the clerics, with their solemn, self- satisfied faces and shook their hands respectfully. One of them was Fritz. Their eyes carefully did not meet, but Ernst was gratified to see that his friend's face was showing at close quarters a certain waxy pallor not unlike his own, suggesting that he too was regretting the last stein or two.

After the service Ernst waited outside the church in the chilly sunshine, and was in time to see Goetz being ushered by two acolytes into a small black carriage with two horses, which trotted smartly away once he was inside. Somehow the air felt fresher after he had gone. He was the man, he reflected, to whose tender mercies Ernst would have consigned Adolph if he had reported his suspicions to the police.

Ten minutes later Fritz emerged from the building, dressed now in more conventional clothes, and accompanied by Magda with her usual cheerful expression on her face, smiling and chirping merrily away.

Fritz took Ernst's arm and whispered, "Come on... let's get home quickly. I have an urgent need for a lavatory."

"I too," said Ernst sincerely, and the three set off to walk at a brisk pace round the corner. Of the three conflicting sensations in his head, his loins, and his bowels, the latter had now assumed supremacy. Oh God, how far away was this house?

It was with difficulty that he maintained a polite conversation with Magda about the quality of the sermon and the beauty of the singing of the choir. At last they reached a pleasant little cottage, one of a row of three. A mongrel with a worried face and a furiously wagging tail barked over the garden wall at them, frantic with relief at their return. Smoke came from the chimney.

"Down, Struwwel! Behave! This is a friend," said Fritz, fondling his long ears as they opened the front door. "Come in, Ernst! *Willkommen!*"

It was welcome indeed.

Some time later, the two men were sitting in the small, tidy sitting room, gratefully enjoying cups of hot strong coffee. Ernst stretched luxuriously back in his chair. Magda had shut the door firmly behind them, no doubt detecting that they would prefer to be alone. Ernst noticed skis propped up in a corner of the room, and a row of cups on the mantelpiece.

'Right, Ernst," said Fritz, leaning back to match the attitude of his guest with a loud sigh of appreciation for the coffee. "Time to tell your Onkel Fritzi just what is on your mind. Sit down, Struwwel. Be quiet!"

The dog looked at his master reproachfully, then lay down slowly and curled up in front of the fire.

Ernst was silent. What he had to say might have very serious consequences, and Fritz was after all a professor at the academy and an official of the local church. But somehow Ernst trusted him. And he badly needed to get advice from somebody, and could think of no-one else to turn to.

"It's about young Heidler, isn't it?" prompted Fritz.

Ernst swallowed, pulling at his earlobe.

"Yes, it is. But if I tell you my worries, Fritzi – do I have your word the matter is in complete confidence? You are not obliged to report what I tell you to your Headmaster, for example? Or to the Bishop?"

Fritz laughed. "My goodness, it is serious, isn't it? No, my friend, I have no such obligations. Whatever you tell me will be strictly between the two of us, I promise."

He produced a pipe from his pocket, and offered the pack of tobacco that accompanied it. Ernst accepted gratefully and filled his own pipe, tamping the tobacco firmly down with his fingers. Once it was burning well, he leant forward. He felt he could be content with Fritz's assurance.

"It's about Adolph's father's death, you see," Ernst began. "It's only my theory, mind..."

Gradually, sometimes correcting himself, he told the whole story. The boy's wounds he had seen in the surgery, Adolph's chilling demeanour, the cruel chastisement Ernst had witnessed, the tale of the mushrooms, the misplaced book, Dr Bloch's misdiagnosis. He omitted nothing

"So you think the boy planned the whole thing? Researched it in a book, went out into the woods, found a mysterious fungus that only poisons you if you've drunk alcohol?" said Fritz, screwing up his face. "Then served it up to the whole family the next morning, and calmly went off to school, hoping that it would kill his father? And in a particularly painful way?"

Ernst nodded carefully. His head was still throbbing a little. Rooks cawed raucously in the treetops beyond the garden, and Struwwel snored softly by the fire.

"Yes. I do. He knew that if his mother or sister ate the mushrooms too, which they probably did, they wouldn't be affected. But his suffering and that of the whole family would be ended, and the brute would be dead."

"And that's what you think really happened? My God! Is the boy a monster in the making?"

Ernst puffed on his pipe, but without enjoyment. He put it down.

"To be honest, I just don't know. Is he capable of murder? Going just on my impression of him, yes, I think it's possible." He sipped his coffee. "That's all I'm saying really. It's possible. But that's all. And in any case there's nothing I can do."

Both men were silent. Ernst stared out of the window, squinting behind his glasses. The sky was still blue, and he watched the rooks quarrelling and shrieking at each other, wheeling and clamouring round the top of a clump of tall trees which were dotted with their untidy black nests. What was it that made them so permanently angry with each other? It was a mystery, something to be investigated at another time. Jealousy, territorialism, sexual rivalry, hunger? Who could say. But they made a hell of a racket, that was for sure.

*"That little shit!"*

Struwwel looked up startled, cocking his head, as Fritz suddenly burst out.

"Yes, you're right, you know, Ernst. I think you've got it. It's completely plausible. The little bastard is certainly capable of anything. Murder wouldn't bother him, don't you worry. Not even of his own father. And you know something... " Fritz clenched his fists. "...if you and I don't stop him now... oh, God knows where..." He breathed out heavily. Ernst was beginning to regret having spoken.

"Look, all I'm saying..." he began.

"No!" cried the teacher. "What you are saying is that you think this boy is a murderer! But you hardly know him, and what I'm saying is that I do know him, and what's more, I'm damned sure you are right!"

"How can you be so sure?"

"It's his whole manner. It's as if he's on a mission to change the world. And if anybody crosses him – and that includes teachers – you can look out. He'll let nothing and nobody stand in his way, of that I am certain."

He blew his cheeks out angrily.

"The other kids don't say much about him. But you can see the way they avoid his eye. He's... just different, somehow, as I said. It's hard to explain. There are tales about his poor brother Theo, and why he left home so suddenly. They say the father had given him a bad time, too. I don't know what happened exactly, but he's gone. Like the others."

"What others? Dr Bloch said something about it."

Fritz shrugged.

"All Heidler's kids, apparently. My aunty

used to know the family a bit. Heidler was known to be very handy with his fists when he was drunk. One baby after another reached no more than two years old, and then took sick of something, and died. One of them – Edmund I think – made it to six. Then he went too. Measles, that one, they said."

Ernst jumped to his feet.

"For God's sake, Fritzi!" he cried. "This is absurd. I'm beginning to wish I'd kept my mouth shut. This is all just hearsay. Babies die all the time. I should know. There's hardly a family in the town that hasn't lost a child in infancy. Did they blame the father for all them? What's the man supposed to have done?"

Fritz poured out some more coffee.

"Do you want some brandy with this? I think we've got some somewhere. Just sit down."

Ernst shook his head, but resumed his chair, a scowl on his face.

"All I know is, the father was a real brute," continued Fritz. "A – what's the new word? – psychopath? He's drunk, baby's crying, he loses control, swings it round, belts it to stop it crying... who knows. There's a lot of diphtheria around, so what's one more dead infant in the town?"

"So Adolph grows up in that household, sees violence as the answer to every problem, and when the time comes..."

"Old Heidler gets what's coming to him."

Both men are silent for a while. Then Ernst burst out.

"Oh, this is ridiculous. The boy's a thinker, a loner! Just because he's different from the others, he gets blamed for every damn thing that happens!"

Fritz softened his tone a little.

"Look, all I'm saying is that he's the kind of person who attracts such stories about himself. But in itself, doesn't that tell you something? That you are right about what happened to his father?" He leant forward, banging his hand into his fist.

"I tell you, Ernst – that boy is either going to end up ruling the world, or swinging from the gallows."

"Hmm."

"Ernst - it's obvious. It's your duty to inform the authorities, and get the old man's body dug up. He'll hardly be cold in the ground if they get a move on. If they do an autopsy on him, they can tell exactly how he died. Then dear shy little Adolph will get what he deserves."

"And what's that exactly? The garrotte? The noose?" asked Ernst.

He looked Fritz straight in the eye and held his gaze. Ernst picked up his coffee, but it had gone cold.

"Because that's what we're talking

about, isn't it? Do you and I want to have that on our conscience for the rest of our lives? To condemn a child to lengthy police interrogation, imprisonment, and then no doubt to the gallows? Jesus!"

Fritz held his gaze for a moment, then looked down. He seemed to hesitate.

"The police. Yes, I must admit that would not be pleasant. No, not pleasant at all. I suppose you saw Goetz in church today?"

"Reading the second lesson?" said Ernst. "Yes, I wondered if it was him. I've heard of him, of course, but never seen him before. I thought he looked a nasty piece of work. The way he glared at that old fellow who dropped his hymnbook."

"That was Willi, the postman. His son was arrested by Goetz last year over some trivial accusation, something about some confidential mail that went missing. It was found later, gone to the wrong address. But the son's in a wheelchair now – they say he'll never walk again."

He shuddered.

"Yes, God knows what *Polizeibeamte* Goetz would do to a suspected teenage murderer like Adolph. He'd enjoy questioning a young boy like him, that's for sure. Take his time over it too."

Ernst sucked at his pipe, but it had long gone out. He tapped it on the fireplace, watching the grey dottle fall into the grate. The quietly burning wood was mixed with coal, which gave off a yellow gas flame with a little popping noise. It was at odds with the comforting dull red glow of the oak logs. He looked up.

"Exactly. You see, Fritzi, we can't be absolutely certain Adolph murdered his father, can we? It's just my suspicion. If I breathe a word of this to the authorities – or you do, for that matter! – it would set off a chain of events that I or anybody else would be powerless to stop. And I couldn't live with that."

"Well, if you're sure..." began Fritz. They looked at each other.

"Quite sure," said Ernst firmly. "The matter is closed. Thank you for your advice. It has helped me make up my own mind."

"It's up to you, but..."

Fritz shook his head in despair, and opened his mouth as if to argue further. But then came a cheerful call from the kitchen.

"Fritzi! Ernst! The meal is ready. Stop gossiping. Don't let the food go cold!"

Ernst stood up and clapped his friend on the back as they left the room together. "Thank you, my friend. I feel a hell of a lot better now I've told someone about it. Now let's forget the whole thing and enjoy this meal – I'm starving."

"And I've got a flask of red wine that'll

go down with it very nicely too!" said Fritz happily, his spirits reviving. The two young men, who earlier that day might easily have been persuaded to sign the Pledge, went into the room where Magda, red-faced with her efforts, was laying the table. All thoughts of Adolph and his possible destiny could not survive the wonderful odours arising from the roast lamb and potatoes and the steaming Sauerkraut.

§

"Right – let's change the subject," said Fritz, after they had taken their seats round the heavy beech table and said Grace. "Are we going to teach those damned Serbs a lesson? We need to show them who's boss."

"Dangerous, though," said Ernst, politely helping his hostess to wine and pouring some for himself and Fritz. "The Serbs are just looking for trouble. And they're desperate for land access to the sea."

"Well, Germany's backing us to the hilt," said Fritz, who was engaged in carving the lamb with a surgeon's skill.

"Of course they are!" said Ernst. "Nothing our German friends like better than a fight! Their army's growing bigger every day. They say they've got Russia in their sights after Serbia. And that goes for

England too, don't forget. They'll ally with Russia soon."

"Ach! England would never fight Germany!" cried Fritzi, tucking his napkin into his shirt front. "They're cousins! The English royal family speak German to each other! They'll stay out of the whole thing, you mark my words. All they care about is their precious British Empire. That keeps them busy. And very prosperous too."

"Although..." began Ernst, but Magda interrupted, banging on the table with her knife handle.

"Right, you boys, that's enough! I've had enough politics!"

They fell silent, abashed.

"We'll speak of something more pleasant, if you don't mind! Now, Ernst, I want to know a bit more about you and Ilse. What a lovely girl."

She heaped their plates high with cabbage and potatoes and hot steaming gravy. "How did you two meet? You must tell us the whole story. You know she is too good for you, Ernst!"

Struwwel lay flat on the floor by their table, front paws stretched out in front of him in a pose that said, as clearly as if he could speak, *"You know I'm too well bred to beg, of course, but if by any remote chance the odd scrap should just happen to drop my way ..."*

They ate and talked and waved their hands around, sometimes serious, sometimes yelping with laughter, as their glasses emptied and their plates refilled.

"Fritz! If you're already having second helpings, at least offer them to our guest as well. My God, I've married a greedy swine. You're getting fat, do you know that? As fat as a farrow in a farmer's field!"

"You can talk!" he replied. "You're as plump as a pie in Pieters' patisserie!"

"So maybe it's time we had some little piglets?"

It was a long time before Fritz pushed aside his empty pudding plate and got up.

"This has been the best Sunday ever!" said Ernst.

"We should do this more often! Just the three of us. What do you say?"

"Let's see what Magda thinks. She's done all the hard work," said Ernst, ever the diplomat. "But I'll drink to that!"

Magda had already piled the dishes up on the table by the sink, while Fritz filled the old iron kettle to put on the dying embers of the fire to heat up some water. He smacked Magda's bottom as he returned.

"Is it a deal?"

"On one condition," she said firmly, removing his hand from where it had crept round her tummy, and reaching for her glass. "That this time next year we don't wake the babies up with our noise."

Fritz looked irritated for a moment, then caught Ernst's eye. Ernst smiled and shrugged his shoulders, and they all laughed together. The grandfather clock in the hall startled them with its deep solemn tones. They clinked their glasses, looking into each other's eyes.

They stood with their glasses raised.

"Here's to us! To peace and prosperity!"

It is fortunate that mankind does not have the gift of looking into the future. For had they but known it, within a decade they would be part of the biggest conflict the world had ever known.

And the boy they had discussed would start a chain of events that would bring about over one hundred million deaths little more than forty years later.

"Ernst! What's the matter? Someone walked over your grave? Drink up! Get your accordion, Fritz. It's time for a dance!"

Struwwel jumped to his feet, woofing madly and eager to join in this sudden new excitement.

"Music! Music!"

"Any more wine?" cried Fritz. "Anyone for any more? Forget the washing up!"

And with laughter and hope the young people danced the evening away, to the music of Strauss and the barking of a scruffy dog.

# 17

*Pasewalk, the Somme, June 1918*

Ernst was so tired he could hardly stand. He looked with longing at a bed which had just been vacated, bloodstained though it was. How wonderful it would be to lie down there and close his eyes. Never to have to cut, poke, slice, stitch or bind another broken body...

Two men had died on the makeshift operating tables in the last ten minutes, one silently slipping away almost apologetically. The other had been choking on gas and clawing the air in his efforts to breathe before a final louder rattle had signalled his death.

Ernst shook himself and looked around wearily for the next stretcher. But as sometimes happened, there was a sudden unaccountable lull in casualty admissions. The thunder of shellfire in the distance too had temporarily unabated.

He seized the opportunity go out into the field among the tents and shelters, fumbling in the pocket of his gown for a cigarette. He leant wearily against a damaged stone wall. His hand trembled violently as he struck a match, not a good symptom in a field surgeon. Somehow it stayed steady for hours as he worked, but now it was twitching like a thing with a life of its own. He watched its movements absently in the intermittent flashes of light from the shell bursts a mile or so away, thinking of nothing else at all except his need for sleep.

For a blissful few minutes nobody called for his attention. Then a badly battered mud-soaked army vehicle roared up out of the darkness and slewed to a halt. The passenger door opened, and a figure was roughly helped out, to stumble for a few paces before collapsing. The vehicle turned and roared off back in the direction from which it had come.

§

Ernst watched as the young man slowly pulled himself to his feet. His eyes were roughly bandaged with a dirty piece of cloth, which he was pressing hard against his face. Ernst didn't move to help him. He was too exhausted, and this was only one of dozens of patients needing him.

The new arrival called out gruffly, "Can anyone help me? I can't see. Anyone?"

There was no-one else nearby, and after a moment Ernst reluctantly threw his cigarette away, watching it as it arced through the black night in a feeble parody of the spectacular light show on the skyline a mile away.

"All right," Ernst said, going over to the man and taking his arm. "I'm a doctor. Come this way."

The wounded man didn't speak, but came with him into the operating room, his hand still pressed against the bandage. He was lurching at an angle in the way that men do when they come out of the trenches after a long spell. Standing upright without needing to keep your head below the parapet was a skill that needed to be relearned.

It seemed to Ernst then that he knew him from somewhere, but the thought hardly had time to form. He led him to a gore soaked canvas chair, and went to fetch a bowl of water and a relatively clean piece of cloth from a side room.

"Right. Let's take a look at your eyes," he said, untying the clumsy knot. As Ernst wiped away the mud and blood and suppurating yellow mess as gently as he could, he recognised him. He was several years older than when Ernst had seen him last, and he had grown the conventional handlebar moustache. But the white face was the face of the boy who had murdered his own father.

Ernst stopped his work for a moment, drew a breath, then resumed his ministrations.

"It's Heidler, isn't it? Adolph Heidler? I am Doktor Mann from Linz."

Dark sightless eyes turned towards the doctor.

"Hitler now," he said. "Adolf Hitler."

In the distance the bombardment had begun again, more menacingly than ever.

§

There was a sudden hubbub at one end of the makeshift building, as another party of stretcher bearers came wearily in with their dreadful burdens. It was difficult to think straight.

"So it's Adolf Hitler now, eh?" Ernst said. "Well, Adolf. Let's see what we can do about this," he said. "I don't think the damage is permanent. Temporary loss of sight is a frequent symptom of battle fatigue. What section of the trenches were you in?"

Adolf shrugged.

"All over. Runner," he answered succinctly. "Anywhere they – *ach*! That hurts!"

259

"I'll put a fresh dressing on, and then give you something to make you sleep. Have you any other wounds?"

The patient shook his head silently. Ernst picked up the syringe that lay on the table beside him. It held a drug which used in a small dose would act as a mild painkiller. But with an extra push of the thumb, it would become a potent poison to put dying patients out of their misery. It caused a massive heart attack in seconds. It gave the doctors the power of life or death, and in peacetime would have only been used after lengthy consultation with senior doctors. But here it was employed it every day with hardly a second thought.

Ernst performed a brief injection with the adeptness of long practice. He beckoned an orderly, who led Adolf away to the big room with its long line of recumbent men, some shrieking and writhing, most lying on the floor, whether with their eyes stuck together, their bodies covered in yellow festering blisters, or their lungs choking with gas. It was a scene from the seventh circle of Hell.

Ernst worked the rest of the night with only occasional periods of relief until the morning – a total of fourteen men treated, six dead. One was still dying noisily, screaming, gagging.

For some reason, during the long night, Adolf Hitler's face kept coming back to him. Later the next day, when he reported back for duty after a few hours' sleep, he enquired about Hitler in the long room. A young doctor named Matthias checked the ward lists and told him he had discharged himself, though still blind.

"Did you know he had the Iron Cross?" asked the doctor, fair hair matted with blood where he had absently brushed his hand across his forehead, his bloodshot eyes shining with admiration. Ernst said he didn't.

"Well, in fact, he had two. Can you believe it? He didn't tell me. They were in his pocket. He was a real hero, a runner – worst job of the lot, they say."

Matthias rubbed a hand over his chin. He badly needed a shave.

"Funny type though. Seemed furious that we might be surrendering. No manners either. I told him his blindness was temporary, shellshock and nothing physical. Never thanked me. He just turned on his heel and went, I don't know where. *All right, all right! I'm coming!*"

The doctor turned back into the ward into which he was being urgently summoned. "Could you help me over here, sir? This one's lost both arms, and I don't like the look of his leg."

Ernst was already kneeling by the stretcher. The two men worked together in silence for a while, the patient gasping and choking.

"*Scheisse.* It's no good, it'll have to come off."

Matthias moved away to fetch a blood-soaked saw from the pile of instruments on a nearby table, exchanging a few words with another medic and even laughing. When he returned, Ernst was straightening up.

"No need now," he said briefly. "He's gone."

Matthias made a wry face. They tidied up briefly in silence, and the younger doctor beckoned an orderly to remove the body.

"Time for a smoke?" he asked Ernst.

The two doctors stood outside the long building together, both numb with fatigue and almost oblivious to the sound of the constant bombardment in the distance. It was an endless drumbeat, going on day and night, which in the end the brain ceased to register. But not far away, men were cowering in their trenches as a hundred shells a minute fell along the frontline, in the greatest orgy of destruction ever known to mankind.

Matthias drew deep on his cigarette. He was so pale that his red rimmed eyes looked like clumsily applied clowns' makeup.

"Have you heard? They say it's only a matter of time before we surrender. The navy's on strike. The Kaiser's fled the country. And since the Americans came into the war..."

Ernst could only shake his head. All that horror. All the deaths. All the wounded. All that long misery ending at last. It was too much to take in.

"Come on," he said, grinding his cigarette butt under his boot. "Back to work we go. Our war's not over yet, not by a long way."

The screaming bedlam of the emergency wards had not slackened either. Ernst plunged back into his nightmare work. There was little opportunity then or later to allow his mind to dwell on his encounter with the young man from his home town.

He could not have known it, but the next time he was to see him, Adolf Hitler would be addressing a crowd of ten thousand people in the *Sportpalast* in Berlin, as Chancellor of Germany.

# 18

*Hamburg, 1947*

"No!" says Rose sharply. "That's enough. Don't be greedy. You're obviously not up to it. Just lie there quietly and stop being a fool. You should be in hospital."

"But Ernst said I needed to spend plenty of time in bed!" I protest, running my hand gently down her bare arm. "I'm only obeying doctor's orders."

"Yes, but I don't think he meant me to be in bed with you too, darling." Rose pretends to press her finger onto my nose and push me down into the bed. "He meant you to rest, as you very well know. You shouldn't really have come here. That head wound is still looking nasty. And this nose…"

"Ow! My nose! Don't do that!"

"And you know I've got to go out in a minute. Max will be up here shouting at me when he gets back."

My nose isn't broken, it seems, but it's still very tender and has a plaster strapped across it. Nor does my skull appear to be fractured. I sink back onto the pillows all the same, but secretly I have to admit I'm still pretty queasy. There's a permanent dull ache in my bandaged head, and my right arm is strapped up in plaster of Paris.

Rose is nuzzling my neck. Changeable as ever, she now seems reconciled to being part of the Lion House again.

"Sorry, sorry, sorry. But I still think you could have got a message to me somehow, *Liebchen*," she says in a silly little baby voice, playfully pinching my arm. "Your little Rose was nearly out of her mind with worry, wondering where you'd got to - you know that? I missed you. We all did."

"How was I going to do that?" I ask crossly. "I could hardly send Pinkie into the Lion's den here, could I? He'd have had a fit. Half-naked women lying around all over the place, and people planning violent insurrection in the kitchen."

"I haven't even met Pinkie yet. You keep promising to introduce me."

"He's not your type," I say. "But if it wasn't for him, I'd probably have been handcuffed to that toilet until I bled to death."

"You were never bleeding to death, from what you've told me. Just shocked after what that awful man did to you." She wrinkles her nose prettily. "By the way, Max should be back soon. You said you wanted to talk to him. What's all that about, anyway?"

I hesitate, then decide there's no harm in telling her. There aren't many secrets in this house.

"I'm just wondering if he can help me, that's all. See if he's heard anything about van Reen. Our lot haven't a clue where he is, but he'll have gone to ground somewhere. I just want to see if Max has got any ideas." I reach for my cigarettes. "I'm in very bad books at the office, I can tell you."

And I give her my Foxy impersonation, which always makes her laugh. *"Damn bad show, what? Got a good mind to take a horsewhip to you."*

"I don't believe he's really like that!" she giggles. "You're always exaggerating!"

She jumps abruptly out of bed and walks over to the wardrobe, hunting through the rail. I just lie and watch her.

She is as beautiful from behind as she is from the front, with her perfectly modulated back, slim waist, and long legs. There is a little bump where her blouse has ridden up above the place where the bottom of her spine reaches her buttocks. I suddenly feel an urgent need to kiss it, but I have enough sense to sink back onto the bed and do nothing. She pulls out a brightly flowered blue, scarlet and yellow dress in a crisp cotton fabric. She stops in front of the long mirror and holds the dress up against her body, her head on one side as she contemplates her image. It is a long moment.

I turn my head away. The sight of her getting dressed up to entertain some other man is too much to bear. "Who is it tonight?" I growl.

"Oh, just dinner with some old guy," she says, lipstick in hand, peering intently at her face in the mirror. "Do you think I should pluck my eyebrows? The other girls do."

This is too much for me. This business has got to stop. No, don't say it, I tell myself. Don't start a row now. Whatever you do, don't say it. Don't say, this has got to stop.

*"This has got to stop!"* I hear a voice saying. Oh, marvellous. It's my voice. I blunder on. "For Christ's sake! We can't go on like this. Well, I can't, even if you can. It's torture for me."

"Well, it's not very nice for me either, darling!" she says, staring at her reflection as she pulls her dress on, and adjusting the shoulder straps. "Do you think I like making love to strangers?"

"No, of course not."

"So what do you suggest I do?"

I'm sitting up again now.

"Look, darling, in bed I've had time to think. Listen. We can't live together, I know that. It's against army regulations. My future's already hanging by a thread as it is. But we'll find a room for you somewhere – I'll pay the rent – and then you can get a job. A proper job."

"Like, what, exactly?"

"Well, I don't know. Working in a shop or a café or something. Anything's got to be better than…than selling your body."

"There are no fucking shops or cafes! The city's been bombed flat, remember? There's no city left to get a job in!"

"Yes, there is," I say. "It's getting better all the time, you know it is. There are new places opening up again every day. There's that new artists' cafe opened just this week, for one, round the corner from the office in Flindersstrasse. They say it's pretty good."

She is still for a moment.

"I don't know. I'll think about it. God knows, I can't be a – a whore for the rest of my life. But – I know it's silly, Adam – but these people are my friends. I can't just abandon them. And this is still my house, you know."

Downstairs we hear the front door bang. Max is talking to someone in the kitchen.

"Get up and have your chat with Max," she says. "I've got to go. I'm late."

She is fully dressed now. She puts her fur coat on and comes over to the bed to kiss me goodbye, the very image of a professional woman going out on a business appointment while her lazy husband is still lying in bed. Sometimes I wonder if she actually enjoys her job. No, that's a monstrous thought. She peers out of the window.

"God, it's still freezing. Will this winter never end? Right – I'm off. See you tomorrow, all right? Now you look after yourself, *Liebchen*!"

She blows me a kiss from the doorway, and is gone into the icy night.

Max is sitting in the kitchen hunched over the table, warming his hands on a chipped mug of thin vegetable soup. Kaspar is standing by the stove stirring something in a large saucepan. I say good evening to him, but as usual he ignores me.

"Ah, the gallant wounded hero. My God, you look a mess!" says Max, cheering up visibly. "I hear you fell down the toilet! What happened, did you pull the chain too hard?"

He laughs uproariously, and even Kaspar does a half-grin. He even offers me a mug of soup, and I take it gratefully from his skinny hand.

"Yes, very funny," I say, and pull up a chair. "Serves me right for dropping my guard. The guy had me properly fooled."

"What happened?" enquires Max with genuine interest.

"Oh, I was handcuffing a prisoner – a client, if you like – to a toilet when he wanted a slash. We'd been having a good chat all afternoon, nothing too confrontational. Then – bang – !"

I tell the story briefly. Both men listen intently, not smiling now.

"So where is he now, do you know?"

"No, I don't know, and frankly Max, I could do with your help. I'm in a hell of a lot of trouble at the office over this. Our lot have no clue where he might have gone. And if he's not caught, we…let's say it's not good for my career."

Colonel Fox-Martin had been very agitated indeed. He couldn't have been more upset if he'd taken a hedge badly and had to have his favourite hunter put down. His face had gone bright pink and his ginger moustache positively bristled as if it had a life of its own. He had summoned me for a second interview, and walked up and down his office, banging his fist on his desk from time to time.

*'Losin' a prisoner! Losin' a prisoner is unheard of, no, never heard of such a thing in all my long career, utter carelessness, whatever could you have been thinking of, do you realise you are still a serving Army officer and could be court martialled, what?*

*'Thought you had more bloody sense, how wrong can you be about somebody, met your father once, damn good chap, great loss etc., God knows what he'd have thought of you, had you shot I should think. And if it wasn't that you cut such a pathetic figure in your bandages I'd have fired you on the spot and as it is, I'm minded to take my riding crop to any part of your miserable anatomy that is still visible under your bandages. Have you any idea how I am going to report this to London, Christ knows they're on my back enough already…"*

I was to stay out of his bloody sight and hope to God that the British military police had located van Reen and hauled him back into jail before my leave was over and in the meantime he was docking my pay.

I'd had one big problem with all this. I agreed with every word the colonel said. So did Max, clearly.

"Are you surprised? Who was this man?" he grunts.

I hesitate. Oh well, in for a pfennig…

"Fellow named van Reen. At least that's the name we knew him under. He was out in Russia for a while."

"Van Reen? You had van Reen – and you let him go?"

I've never seen Max so angry. Is there anyone I'm not infuriating these days?

"You know of him?"

"*Ja, natürlich.* He's one of the bad guys on the top of our list. We'd like to find him, for sure."

I stare at the floor. "Truth is, we've no idea where he might be. None at all."

"Has he any money? Any contacts that you know of?" demands Max.

"Some money, yes. Bastard stole my wallet," I say ruefully. "I don't know about contacts. All his old mates in the regiment and the SS, I suppose."

Max thinks for a minute, drumming his fingers on the table.

"I know where he'll go. The Dead City. That's where all the scum hang out. It's out of police and army jurisdiction. But there's quite a gang of them in there, hiding from the law and planning their escape routes out of the city. There's a network organised for ex-Nazis. He'll be hiding out, waiting for the wheels to turn. Like a trapped rat."

He gets up abruptly.

"We've got fingers in a few pies in there. I'll put out some enquiries. It may take a few days, but if he's in there, we'll go and find him."

"What about the army?" I say nervously. "We're looking for him. My colonel..."

Max laughs shortly. "Your colonel won't touch the place, I can tell you. Your lot wouldn't survive ten minutes in there. No, this is a job for us. Now clear out and leave me to it."

I am only too glad to obey. My head is hurting like hell, and I'm off to crawl home to bed.

# 19

*The Dead City, 1947*

The path we are taking might once have been a prosperous main street lined with stores and grand houses, or just a sordid backstreet alleyway. It is impossible to tell now. We are shivering as the snow falls faster from the night sky, and I am moving as quickly as I can, which is not saying much. The moon casts long shadows, the stark chiaroscuro of a demented celestial set designer. Everywhere there are tiny rustlings as we pass.

Max is impatient and snarls "Keep up, damn you!" over his shoulder. Rose sticks her tongue out at him from the safety of the darkness, and I stifle a giggle. It has only taken Max a couple of days to get word of where van Reen has been sighted in the Dead City. He didn't want me to come with him and his gang of thugs, let alone bring Rose along, but she has insisted, and so have I.

We have broken through the perimeter into the Dead City through a disguised entry point, under Max's impatient orders to keep an eye open for police patrols. The area was still forbidden territory, plastered with stern notices reading *Restricted Zone*. Now we follow him, stumbling through the broken landscape charged with its hideous ghosts. I am quite lost, but Rose keeps looking round her alertly. Then she puts her hand to her mouth.

"Oh God. I know this place, Adam," she whispers. "*Tante Gretl* – my nanny – her little house was here, down a little cobbled lane, a tiny, medieval place, like a witch's cottage. And she had a cat! But she wasn't a witch, she was a dear, kind person."

We swerve to avoid a burnt out vehicle and I try to prevent Rose seeing the petrified corpses still inside it.

"She retired here when she was too old and frail to carry on living with us in the farm. She must have burned to death that night, Adam. She was all alone. Except for her black and white cat, of course."

She smiled tightly.

"I used to call him Adolf, because I said he looked like Hitler. She used to tell me off. Walls have ears, she'd say. And she was right."

The smile threatens to turn into a sob as tears fill her eyes. She stops and holds me. I gently squeeze her shoulder.

"Come on, darling. Tell me later. We've got to keep moving. Come on."

After a moment she swallows, and takes my arm. Now we are half running over the humps and dips in the darkness, huge empty eyeless buildings looming up unexpectedly and disappearing again into the gloom. A surprising number of chimneys have survived, their long sad twisted fingers reaching out in sad entreaty. If you only knew the sights we have seen, they seem to say.

*"Shit!"*

I have tripped over an object sticking out the ground and fall full length, hitting my good knee on something sharp, and in trying to save myself drop the handgun I was clutching. Rose reaches out a hand to help me to my feet. I look back curiously to see what the obstacle might be. It is some buried metallic structure, perhaps one of the hundreds of household relics in this landscape of fire blackened bricks and masonry. It is all mostly overgrown by weeds, and tonight covered by a dusting of snow.

Perhaps, I say to Rose in a low voice, it could be part of a crashed Allied aeroplane? There are said to be several in the Dead City. Some poor sod of an English – or American – pilot may lie buried beneath it, among the many thousands of other unidentified corpses. Perhaps an eager boy on his first mission, or a hardened veteran half dead with exhaustion. Good, Rose would say, and I understand why all too well. She shushes me, anxious too for us not to be delayed.

"Wait. Where's the damned gun?" I hiss.

To my dismay we cannot find it, even with the torch. It is an impossible task in the darkness amid the chaos. After wasting a couple of precious minutes we give up the search. I am more concerned about losing contact with our colleagues than finding this unfamiliar handgun, which was an encumbrance to my progress anyway rather than an asset. In any case Max and his men are well armed. But there is no sign of them, and the road in front of us is deserted. They must have pressed on without us.

Rose pulls me close, laughing.

"Look!" She points to her coat pocket. "It's all right! I've got a knife! I grabbed the biggest one I could find in the kitchen as we were leaving. That'll do!"

It's all a fairy tale adventure to her, I realise. She is still partly a child. I start to say something, then she freezes, and points silently ahead. Ah! There is a figure in the pale moonlight, a swift slight wraith. I quicken my step in relief, until I realise it is not one of our party. Is it – by God, is it... ?

Yes, it's van Reen, slipping into a side turning. The others must have missed him. He is wearing an overall, and has some sort of cap jammed onto his head, but his jaunty angular silhouette is unmistakable. We've found him when the others have failed. Thank God for that. What an amazing piece of luck. Perhaps I have a career ahead of me after all.

I stiffen, heart beating fast, then seize Rose's arm and turn a corner. We are just in time to see van Reen pushing himself awkwardly into a space behind a broken wall and then immediately vanishing. We approach the spot as quietly as we can, every nerve alert. Where has he gone?

Ah, there's a narrow gap between some structures which I would otherwise have missed, and behind it the remains of a large doorway, entrance perhaps to some public building. Dare we go in after him? It is strictly against both common sense and Max's instructions. We both stand indecisively, my hand against the wall.

I peer closely and see part of a metal sign sagging by an ornate pillar. The moon has disappeared again now, but I point the torch at the object, careful not to betray our presence. It is blackened by smoke like everything in the Dead City, but I can just make out an elaborate typeface in pale red and blue colours, and trace out the letters "…RBAHN".

I snap the torch off. My God, that's it. The city had a small but highly efficient underground train service before the war, the *Unterbahn*, destroyed in the bombing as far as I knew. This must be the entrance to one of the stations. I whisper this in Rose's ear, and she nods.

I make my mind up suddenly. There is no sign of the others, and we may never be reunited with them now. There are very few recognisable landmarks left in the Dead City, and I have no idea in which direction Max was going. He has told us nothing, but just abruptly instructed us to accompany him and his three men. But our mission is to catch van Reen, and this is our chance, with or without Max.

I don't feel in the least heroic, but I look at Rose and her mouth tightens. She is as scared as I am, but neither of us is going to admit it. I take a deep breath, and then we squeeze one after the other through a narrow gap into the uninviting black cavity behind.

*Lasciate ogni speranza, voi ch'entrate.*

Dante's dreadful warning to Virgil comes unbidden into my head, but I push the thought away. We may indeed be entering Hell, but I am not ready to abandon all hope just yet. We feel our way cautiously down the concrete steps which betray themselves to our probing feet as we descend. Now we have reached level ground, and walk for perhaps a hundred yards along a dark corridor. Finally we come to an area that is slightly better lit, where a long line of greater darkness stretches endlessly out.

We are on the platform of the deserted station, standing among great puddles of oily water and fallen brickwork. To our side and below us we can see in the dim light the glistening line of the railway track. On the walls we can just make out large elaborately tiled Art Deco murals, depicting scenes from a distant pre-war era. The place has an eerie beauty, which in different circumstances we might have had time to gaze at. But the unique smell of corruption, which still lingers over the whole of the Dead City, is even stronger down here.

But now I see with a shudder that the numerous humped shapes which litter the platform, covered in dust and grime and distorted into weird angles, are dead bodies. They are decayed and skeletal, though in places grotesquely fat maggots are crawling over them. They must be feeding on other bodies buried deeper, more remains of people who came down here to escape the raids. A faint stink of death still pervades the air.

Where have I seen such a thing before, I wonder numbly. Of course! The mummified corpses in ancient Pompeii, frozen in their death agonies, victims of a similar phenomenon two thousand years earlier, though theirs was a natural catastrophe.

There is no time to pursue this thought. Something brushes past my foot and makes me jump, and Rose gasps and clutches my arm. As we turn a bend we sees rats as big as cats scampering along the platform and down the tracks, their eyes glinting red in the dim light.

We stumble on grimly, until the sound of the scraping of some object against a wall brings us to a halt. We listen, senses almost as acute as those of the hundreds of bats wheeling on their urgent missions far above our heads. To our left the passageway branches off, perhaps to another platform, and that is where the noise has come from. Van Reen may well have created some kind of refuge down here, to which we have found him retreating. Down here in these echoing caverns would be an ideal place to hide while he awaited instructions.

Treading as delicately as possible, we turn the corner. Then I blink. Moonlight is streaming down onto a huge pile of rubble. Broken benches, seats, planks, wheels protrude from it at crazy angles. A jagged section of the roof above it is missing, to admit a glimpse of the night sky, now dancing with snowflakes. I peer hard around me, Rose's hand clasped firmly in mine, both clammy with fear. There is no sign of our quarry.

Now yet another passageway branches off to our left, back into the sticky black darkness.

Uninviting as it is, a sudden instinct tells me to search it, and I look at Rose, eyebrows raised. After a second she nods. We grope our way down it. The walls are slimy, and our path is treacherous. Herr Klumpf is complaining loudly now, but I tell him sharply under my breath to shut up. I grip my heavy torch for some sort of comfort with one hand, and Rose with the other, and we stumble on.

As it comes to my dull brain that without her courage to inspire me I would halfway back to my bed by now, I come to an abrupt stop, my face within a whisker of a hard surface.

"What is it?" gasps Rose.

We have struck a wall and can go no further. We stop and take in the situation. The passage is a cul-de-sac, with what looks like a storage area off it, perhaps an abandoned offshoot that the underground railway authorities turned into storage and office space. We can just make out shelves, tables, and bulky heaps of equipment, all charred by the firestorm and covered in black dust. I swear through clenched teeth, and turn to take us some way back to the lighted area by the collapsed roof. Then I freeze, my heart thumping in my chest as if it is trying to burst out.

Twenty yards ahead of us, the light behind him, is the silhouette of a man. He is crouching on the pile of rubble and blocking our exit. The moonlight is behind him and I can see only a dark shape, but I know it is van Reen. He is holding a pistol. And it is pointing straight at us.

It is a heart stopping moment.

"Halt, *Herr Kapitän!*" calls out the well-remembered voice, harsh and startling in the gloomy silence. "Don't move a muscle!"

His voice echoes in the confined space. We both duck instinctively behind a neatly stacked pile of sleepers, a legacy of pre-war station administrative tidiness. I open my mouth to shout, "Give yourself up, you fool! You'll never survive down here!" or some such nonsense, like the hero of the propaganda war films they're making in Hollywood, but no sound emerges from my dry throat.

*Ah, perhaps the whole thing is a film and I've dropped off to sleep in a cinema somewhere. We can't really be crouching here in a deserted tunnel with a mad Nazi trying to kill us, can we? Please, God, tell me it's all a nightmare and I'm about to wake up any moment!*

Then van Reen fires, and the shock of the loud bang brings me back to reality. The rattle of small stones falling onto our heads from the domed ceiling above stings my forehead. The noise of the shot is exaggeratedly loud in the confined space. I look at

Rose, who is brushing dirt back out of her long hair, but she seems unharmed, and even manages a half smile.

I hear van Reen laugh.

"Brought your little tart with you, have you? That's very brave of you, *Herr Kapitän!* Needed someone to hold your hand, did you?"

He is merry now, intoxicated by the prospect of the kill perhaps, and well in command of the situation. Has he always been insane, I wonder? Probably. And there was me making excuses for him. The old bastard always managed to fool me.

"This is the end, *Kapitän!*" he cries. He points his gun towards us in a steady sweeping movement. It looks to me like an old Wehrmacht issue P-08 Luger. I push the thought away. I can see him quite clearly now, clambering down. We are some way away, probably out of accurate pistol range. That thought does little to console me as he comes steadily nearer.

The moon chooses this moment to re-emerge from behind the dark snow laden clouds directly above the hole in the roof, highlighting the silvery surface of the revolver as van Reen nears the bottom of the big heap of plaster and broken bricks.

Dear God, let us live. But the gun, now pointed steadily at our hiding place, goes off again without warning. A chunk of stonework explodes into fragments by our heads and I am blinded for few moments by brick dust. We cower back as far as we can behind a section of wall that offers a certain amount of protection, but I know the next shot could be fatal. I'm going to die now. That's it. This tale told by an idiot is over before it's scarcely begun.

Rose is beside me, screaming into my face.

*"Do something, for God's sake! What's the matter with you, Adam! Are you just going to let him kill us?"*

But my limbs have turned to water and I am quite unable to move, though at this second I'm more worried about Rose, crouching white-faced beside me, than I am about myself. What a sickening waste of a beautiful person. She is so much braver than me.

But she is no longer beside me now and I realise she has moved further down the primitive tunnel. In this nightmare chaos it is hard to tell shadows from reality. Something is flashing in her hand. It must be the kitchen knife, and she is brandishing it like a pirate boarding a ship. I am frightened to act, but she is Lady Macbeth. *Infirm of purpose, give me the daggers!*

She is now quite close to van Reen. At first he doesn't seem to have seen her in the darkness and confusion, but then I see him turn his head and turn the gun towards her, peering through the gloom. The moon in the sky far above has lost interest in our silly antics and moved on, leaving us in semi darkness. My paralysis is broken at last. I shake my head, half blinded by sweat and dust and trembling with emotion, and move forward to Rose's side, screwing up my eyes to prepare for death as I do so. At least we can die together.

I can dimly make out van Reen, his gun raised for the *coup de grace* as he manoeuvres for a better position. Time seems to have been suspended. Images are flickering across my sight like a black and white newsreel running uncontrolled. Rose is nearer to him now, knife in hand. This is madness. Then I see that he is about to place his foot onto something metallic protruding from the rubble. Idiotically I cry out "No!" as if to warn him, knowing in a telepathic moment what is about to happen.

I leap towards Rose. I drag her down with me, hugging my arms round her and rolling our bodies into a ball. Now I am covering my ears with my hands and holding my breath. This is the end of the world. I hear Van Reen shout something, perhaps another cry of triumph.

But instead of the expected gunshot there is a tremendous explosion in a *WHOOMPH* of displaced air. Van Reen disappears in a bloody dusty mass under a storm of falling masonry. The whole structure of the tunnel judders behind us. Rose and I are both hurled backwards against a hard surface, stuck together like a pair of discarded rag dolls as the air is sucked out of our lungs. The last thing I am aware of is a steady roar as brickwork collapses around us, and breathing becomes impossible. The darkness is now total.

# 20

*The Dead City, 1947*

"Adam! Adam! Oh, tell me you can hear me!"

I am shivering with cold and lying on my side. It is pitch black. I try to sit up, but every movement hurts. Unseen hands pull my coat gently round me and a voice begs me again to speak, but it seems easier to allow myself to drift away. I have a feeling this has happened several times already.

Now I become aware that pale daylight is suffusing the cave. My head is thumping. I put my hand up to feel a sticky patch on my temple. Rose sits up beside me in a flash.

"Adam! Oh, Adam! Are you all right?"

I manage to speak. "I think so. God, it's cold. Oh, Christ, my head…" It registers on my brain that my feet are bare. My boots must have been blown off in the bomb blast. We are both still in our coats, which are covered in bloodstains, and we are lying propped up against a broken wall.

"Where else does it hurt?"

"My shoulder… Never mind me. What about you?

Are you injured? What happened?"

She shushes me. "I'm fine, darling. You were hurled backward, but you must have protected me from the full force of the blast. I didn't even lose consciousness. Got a few cuts and bruises…" She glances down at her legs and shrugs. "But you've been out for hours. I've been so worried. *Ach mein Gott…*"

I squeeze her hand feebly. The dim daylight is enough now to allow me to inspect myself. I am bruised and battered, and my shoulder has been hurt when I was thrown against the wall by the blast. Now that I'm fully conscious, my body begins to call attention to its several injuries. My bad knee is swollen and even more painful than usual, and my arms and face are scratched and bloody.

Thankfully the headache is easing as my brain comes to life. I can move my limbs relatively freely, though I groan like a sea lion when I experiment with my back.

I look slowly around, trying to take in what has happened. It is obvious that van Reen stepped on a wartime bomb, presumably an anti-personnel device rather than one designed to blow up buildings, or else the devastation would have been much greater and we would not have survived. I start to tell Rose this, but she brushes the information away.

"For God's sake, Adam, what does it matter what sort of bomb it was? It damn nearly killed us, that's all I know!"

Behind her, part of the rubble is stained dark red. It shows where van Reen was standing. Mercifully most of the evidence has been buried. There can't be much of the bastard left. He's gone.

*Ashes to ashes, dust to dust, van Reen. Perhaps there will be someone to mourn you, a distant wife or child perhaps, something I was once going to find out. But the families of the villagers you murdered won't be included in their number, and neither shall I.*

Rose has done what she can for my wounds, which is little enough, and straightens up stiffly. Her legs are covered with bloody grazes, and she pats at them ineffectively with the cloth  she has soaked in snow.

"Adam, you know something?  We're completely trapped down her. I'm so scared."

She reached a hand down to me, and I seize it mutely. Her calm is deserting her, and she is starting to break down. Now panic wells up in both of us at the enormity of our hopeless situation. We are seized with despair and sit hopelessly trying to take in our situation. We must lie here like this for hours, unable or unwilling to stir.

Without warning Rose starts to sob, sinking down beside me again, crying in great choking gasps. I smooth her long hair with my free hand, trying to find some words of comfort.

"You were so brave, darling. I was a useless coward."

She does not contradict me, but just shakes her head through her tears. I am frozen with misery and self-contempt, and can find no words to comfort her. Finally she stops crying, and sleeps, huddled in my arms. But I am wide awake.

This is stark reality, not a nightmare I shall soon wake up from. We are trapped in a kind of cavern formed by the collapsed building of the underground station. All around us is debris and bomb rubble. A little daylight has begun to reach us from the opening thirty feet or so over our heads, allowing in freezing cold air above the huge pile of stones and bricks. At least we won't suffocate. But at the moment that seems scant consolation.

We are both injured, I don't know yet how badly. We have no apparent means of escape, no food or drink except snow water, and face the prospect of a slow death from starvation and exposure. And this is the stark truth, which I can only acknowledge and then try to put aside. All in all, this is not one of the best moments of my life.

§

"You know," says Rose dreamily, "there's something wonderful about this. Our situation, I mean. *If* we do get out alive…"

Her mood of despair has miraculously vanished. She is gazing at a weed in her hand that she has plucked from a crop growing on a corner of the masonry, its tiny scarlet flower no bigger than a drop of blood.

I am still lying propped up against the damp wall. It feels to be much later in the day. I am still in a soporific state. The loss of blood from the wound in my arm, which Rose has wrapped in a makeshift bandage torn from her blouse, must be making me weak. It is agony to move my shoulder, and my knee is hurting. I stir uneasily and start to say something. Rose looks as if she has been up and active for some time. The sleep has restored her spirits. She bends and puts her finger to my lips.

"*Ja*, that is a big 'if', I know! But if we do survive,

we shall never forget this time as long as we live. And, do you know what – when we are old and fat and rich and have loads of possessions, we shall remember this day. Us in our cave, wounded, with nothing, only hope."

She laughs suddenly. "It's like one of those fairy stories that my nanny used to tell me! The two little orphans in the wood!"

She cocks her head and looks at me, her long fingers trailing gently down my face. I can't help smiling up at her. We can expect only to die slowly of starvation. Yet her optimism is infectious.

"Look at this straggly green stem, and this tiny flower," she says, gazing as intently at the poor thing as if it were a precious jewel, turning it round in her hand and half closing her eyes to inspect it more closely.

"Yes, it is a weed. A nothing, you might say. Something we wouldn't even notice normally. And yet, a miracle."

She pauses.

"Just imagine. A seed blew here through that hole in the roof, among all this hideous destruction. It landed in this mess. A little nourishment fed it, some snowflake perhaps, and it slowly began to take root and grow. And look at it. Look at its long elegant stem, with its little prickles that allow it to defend itself. It is perfectly formed, and totally beautiful. I think it's the most beautiful thing I have ever seen."

"It's just a rotten little weed," I groan. "You're delirious. Your mind is wandering."

*'Nein!'* she says. "I am not. Don't you see? It is part of a creative force at work, something far beyond any possibility of our comprehension. This tiny little

thing is part of the life force! It has demanded to be born, but had to wait, maybe for decades, until the firestorm. And here it is, for us to wonder at. It is our own little bomb weed."

Our cave is silent, though never completely. Slow dripping noises come from somewhere some way away, and occasional weird creaks startle us. It is as if the whole edifice is groaning with pain, like an old wooden ship battered by storms, about to sink at any minute.

Sometimes we hear small birds twittering, but we've never seen them. We have seen no rats in here yet, thank God. I am trying not to think about drinking a long, clear glass of water. Melting snow is dripping down in places, but we have no means of catching the water.

"It is part of the divine plan, just as we are. Don't you see? It is a miracle."

"I didn't realise you were religious," I say, moving my back stiffly against the wall to try to relieve the pain between my shoulder blades. "Ah, this damn shoulder. It's agony."

"*Ach*, I'm not religious. You know that. Can't stand all that stuff. Doesn't mean I don't know there's something going on that I don't understand, though. The bloody Catholic church doesn't understand it either, that's for sure."

She gets up suddenly to her feet, bored with trying to make me understand. Sometimes I'm not sure if she even likes me very much, it comes to me suddenly, an ugly thought that I push away.

"You know what we're going to do?" she asks excitedly. "I've suddenly thought. You know all these railway timetables in that little office place down the

288

other passageway? Why don't we take them up to the top of the heap and light a bonfire? The smoke will show where we are. Max is sure to be looking for us – well, this is how he'll find us!"

I think about this. She is right. It's worth a try and I try to struggle upright, looking down the corridor where she is pointing. But then I shake my head. "Just look at it. It's blocked by the explosion. There are piles of bricks in the way."

But Rose is already there, pulling out blackened bricks and throwing them behind her.

"I can see through here. There's some light going onto that area. We can clear a way through and get to the books. And I might find something to catch the drips in."

She is scrabbling furiously now, and I wince at the noise.

"For God's sake be careful, Rose! The whole bloody lot can come down on top of you. At least let me help."

But it's no good. I can't even get to my feet, and fall back defeated.

"I can't do it," I say. "I'm too feeble. I just can't move. I'm sorry."

I feel pathetic, but it is true. There is no strength left in my battered body. Secretly I'm worried that my shoulder may be broken, but I don't tell Rose.

"Just stay there, darling! I can do this. Just get better *am schnellsten.*"

I'm not at all sure if she's being sarcastic. She hurls another couple of bricks onto the growing heap behind her.

"All right," I groan. "But for God's sake slow down. You'll burn yourself out. Take it nice and steady and you'll get a lot more done."

Rose starts to argue, then thinks better of it. I watch her for another hour, trying not to cry out with pain as I shift on my hard makeshift bed. Finally she wipes an arm across her brow and comes to sit down beside me, panting with her efforts.

"Look!" She points. "Another hour or two and I can crawl through that doorway. Then I can reach the timetables and chuck them through the gap. But that'll have to be tomorrow, I'm afraid. I'm absolutely whacked." She uses the English word with a pout, mocking me.

"*Vacked*, are you?" I say. "Yes, and then tomorrow someone's got to climb up this other mountain of rubble and light a bonfire on top. And I'm afraid that'll mean you too, sweetheart."

"You may be better by then, you never know!"

She puts her arm round me, and I wince.

"Ow. Jesus!"

"Oh, I'm sorry, darling." She plants a moist kiss on my forehead.

"Are you very hungry?"

"No, I'm fine," I lie. "But you must be starving."

"I could eat a horse. Or a rat if we could catch one. No, on second thoughts, forget that. It's going to be dark soon. I'll get some more snow in a minute. At least we can drink some more of that in the morning when it's melted."

We sip the icy mush out of the rusty can she has found, and pretend it is the finest champagne. I raise my can in a toast, and try to smile at her. My job is to offer encouragement.

"Bottoms up!"

She giggles.

"Bottoms up?"

"Just another quaint old English expression. Look, I'm beginning to think you might just be right. If we can get all that paper out in the morning and we can light a bonfire, there must be enough books there to keep a fire going for a couple of days. There'll be plenty there – you know how you Germans love your paperwork. Max will see the smoke for sure."

It is a long shot, and I know it. Max may well have written us off for dead and be reluctant to waste any more effort and manpower on a hopeless search. We are not exactly indispensable to his ambitions.

"How will he know where to look, though?" she says doubtfully.

"They'll have heard the bomb go off and know roughly where it happened. There'll be recent disturbance at street level. He'll guess we had something to do with the explosion – we weren't far from the place where we all lost contact."

Rose bites her lip.

"He'll think we were killed in the blast."

"But when he sees the smoke, he'll know we're alive!"

We smile at each other in the gathering darkness. It seems we have not yet abandoned all hope. Stick that in your pipe and smoke it, *Maestro* Dante.

§

*"My God!"*

Rose's voice is shrill with excitement. We have both passed a terrible night. Frozen, sore, stiff, hungry, and able to sleep only in brief snatches. But since first light she has been working away at gaining access to whatever lies behind the chaotic mess left by the bomb. I want to help but am genuinely unable to do much. Now we can see daylight pouring quite strongly through the gap she has made.

"Oh my God, Adam. You won't believe it."

"What is it?" I croak, trying unsuccessfully to get to my feet. "What have you found?"

"Oh, Adam. It's not just piles of books and paperwork. It looks like the railway workers used this place to sleep in. There are blankets, a sort of bed, shelves, buckets. I'm just going to…"

Her voice breaks off.

"Be careful, darling! Watch out for metalwork. There might be another bomb there."

"What in heaven's name do you think I've been doing, you fool? Poking at unidentified metal objects to see if they go off? Listen – you won't believe this. There's a tin of cocoa here, a kettle, cooking things – ach, more tins! Food!"

"God. What's in them?"

My stomach gurgles at the thought of food. It's been two days since either of us have eaten or drunk anything except snow water, and there's not much of that left that's accessible to us now. It appears to have stopped snowing in the outside world, in that Promised Land beyond our reach.

"Ham! Beans! Four, no five, tins. And ach, guess what – a pocket sized bottle of schnapps, half full! There is a God!"

"Hey, that's terrific! I'm glad you didn't say half empty. We need all the optimism we can get."

Suddenly my spirits have lifted.

"Anything else?"

"No, not really. Yes! Some cigarettes. Some

mouldy bread. That's all. Oh, *Scheisse…*"

I can hear her scrabbling around for a while.

"What have you found now?"

No answer.

"Rose?"

"Bodies," she says indistinctly.

"What? I can't hear you…"

"Bodies, for God's sake! Two of them. They're in railway uniform…These men must have been down here in their office when the firestorm came. They thought they were safe, poor bastards. They tried to crawl into a corner… Oh, it's too horrible…"

She breaks off. A minute later her head appears in the gap, and she is crawling through, arms full of tins, and the little bottle of schnapps. With a superhuman effort I heave myself to my feet and stagger over to her, every bone in my body screaming for mercy.

"Here, pass those to me. It's all right, I've got them."

"I'm going back for more papers. Can't get the bed through obviously, but I'll fetch the blankets."

She disappears again. After a dozen trips she stops, exhausted, and we assess our spoils.

"The label's come off this can, but for God's sake open it up before I faint with hunger."

She isn't entirely joking, and neither am I as an awful thought strikes me.

"Yes," I say. "I suppose you've brought your handy portable tin opener with you?"

She tilts her head on one side, and points a delicately raised finger. I see to my joy that the tins are the kind that have a little metal key on the top to open them. Rose watches me starting to fiddle with the thing, her hand to her mouth.

"Oh my God! Be careful! If you break it off, we'll never…"

There is a moment of supreme tension. These little gadgets are very flimsy. If it breaks off we are sunk. But in the end the little key pulls back quite smoothly, revealing the precious contents. We can breathe again, and smile into each other's face.

Rose has also produced two spoons, which she wipes in the snow.

"Dig in. It's corned beef."

"Ugh. Can't stand corned beef," I say, making a face and pretending to push the can away. "I used to hate it at school."

"Adam!"

"Oh, all right then – in this case, and not to hurt your feelings, I'm going to make an exception and try it."

"Very good of you, I'm sure. A little schnapps with your breakfast, sir?"

"I hope you realise I'm breaking the habit of a lifetime here?"

We tip the colourless liquid into two battered enamelled cups embossed with the brand name of the underground railway company. We raise them in salute to each other. The drink tastes like ambrosia, and I gasp with pleasure. With the addition of some hardtack biscuits, it is the finest breakfast I have ever eaten.

For five minutes, we say nothing at all, savouring every mouthful. The only sound is of dripping water. It is much milder today, thank God, and the snow on top of our prison is beginning to melt.

When our tin is empty, we sit back and look at each other.

"We're going to get through this, Adam. If we're careful, there's enough food here to keep us alive."

"Yes, for four or five days perhaps, at starvation level. A week maybe, with the snow water. Then what?"

"Then what? We'll have a fire going on top of the big pile all that time. The smoke will tell someone where we are. We'll be saved!"

Her enthusiasm is infectious, and I haven't the heart to squash it. But there are a lot of ifs. If the fire will burn properly, if Max bothers to carry on searching, if the weather doesn't turn worse again bringing more heavy snow, if we don't go stark raving mad cooped up down here waiting for rescue...

I take her hand. "You're right, *Liebchen*. Someone up there is looking after us. We're going to be all right." It is amazing what a difference a little food and drink can make to a starving couple.

# 21

*The Dead City, 1947*

It is the third day of our captivity. We have strategically placed empty tins to catch dripping snow in, which slakes our thirst. We have assembled a reasonably sized stack of old timetables, letters, and magazines onto a little platform we have made as near the top of the big heap of rubble as possible. Rose has done most of the hard work, but I am now more mobile and able to crawl slowly up and down a rough track we have formed on our route skywards.

I bring my tin matchbox out of my torn trouser pocket to light our signal fire. I have six matches left, and a few cigarettes. But neither of us have dared smoke much since we conceived this plan, for fear of using up our precious means of ignition. And I am desperate for a cigarette. I take a deep breath. "Right," I say. "Here goes."

I cup my hands to shield the flame of the first match, but it still splutters and goes out. I try one more, but the same thing happens. This is agony. This is desperation. This is the end of the world. This is everything. How ridiculous – everything depending on a little flame.

And for some idiotic reason, I feel not despair, but an almost trancelike elation, like the effect of an ice cold bath. I am not here, but looking down on the scene, hovering above it. It's electric blue, it's creepy, it's life-or-death – and it's real.

"It's so damp up here, with all this snow lying around," says Rose, squeezing her eyes shut in anguish. "Adam, if we can't get this fire lit, we'll never be found. We're going to die, here, you know that?"

Her optimism has vanished.

"Shush!"

I'm still somewhere else. Certainly not in this hell pit. I feel cool, detached. Very, very detached. I turn my body round and back myself into a more sheltered spot. Even the pain is at one remove. I note that certain parts of my body are complaining, excruciatingly, but it's happening somewhere else, to someone else, poor sod. But it's not me. I'm very calm.

"Do you know what? I think this is the moment I'm going to have that cigarette. Pass me a very dry piece of paper, will you?" I say. "And have another two or three ready."

She nods. My third match is struck, fizzles, fizzles again in my cupped hand – and is going out. Out, out, out.

Aeons pass. And then suddenly – oh, please God yes – the cigarette catches the flame. The uncertainty is all over in a millisecond, and it is lit. I draw the smoke into my lungs deeply, luxuriously. Now I can use it to light the paper, which starts to burn fiercely. I can feel the heat on my hand. I pass it up clumsily towards Rose, too tense even to smile, and she adds the next piece of paper to it. Now they are both ablaze, and with a little squeal  she plunges them into the little pile of stationery we have formed.

There is another moment of suspense. No, the game is not over yet. Again the world waits. But then a bright flame appears, spreading swiftly, and before we know it, the bonfire is aflame.

Now the fire is going so well we have to draw away from the heat and clamber down. The warmth is so welcome, so strong, so unexpected, as we crawl back astonished, and start grinning. But more importantly, a column of black smoke is beginning to rise vertically from the fire and escape through the gap above into the cold blue daylight. It rises in a thin pencil line against the bright sky. We sit back on our floor, mesmerised by the sight. Everything is still. All motion has ceased.

Our breathing has slowed down to normal. All I can perceive is the warmth of Rose's leg against mine, and somehow as part of the same feeling, the beauty of the black line soaring into the sky. A tiny money spider skitters through my hair, and I brush it impatiently away.

It is ages before either of us speaks as the fire crackles. I take another drag at the cigarette and pass it to her. She draws on it, and blows an elegant smoke ring. Then she turns to me, and now I am drowning in the deep green depths of her eyes.

"Are we safe now, Adam?" she says softly. "Will we live?"

For a long moment I just look at her. I love this girl, I think stupidly. I really love her. We should spend our lives together. Her life is my life. God, that's a good feeling.

I grip her hand tightly and move my face nearer hers, so near that our mouths are touching.

"Ya betta fuckin' believe it, baby," I say in my best American accent, and then our mouths fuse together and electric shocks run down my spine. Herr Klumpf gets jealous and starts to screech oh God not again, please.... But I ignore him. He is just being grumpy, I know.

We kiss and kiss and kiss, and somehow the pains in my body have gone away. Now we are lying down on the hard cold floor, hugging each other as though we never want to be parted again.

"You have the most wonderful neck. It is made for kissing," I say indistinctly into her neck, nuzzling into it. "Do you know what we're going to do when we get out of here?"

"I think I can guess," she murmurs, running her hand down my body. "My trained senses are picking up certain indications..."

"No!" I say urgently, clasping her roaming hand tightly. "We are going to get married! And have lots of babies. And live in the country. And live happily ever afterwards."

"What? But what about our beautiful home here?" she gasps, looking about her. "You can't mean to take me away from all this, just as I'm growing to love it? Why, with a bit of wallpaper, and some new furniture..."

I put a finger to her laughing mouth.

"Look, I'm serious. When we get out of here I'm going straight to Foxy to tell him we're going to get married, and if he doesn't like it he can lump it."

She pulls away.

"Let's concentrate on getting out of here first, shall we?"

She has risen to her feet, and seems suddenly angry. I shall never understand women.

"And then maybe we can get out of this city and get married and have children and become *Herr und Frau Normal?*"

"Yes, if I can wangle my way out of the army and find another job, and…"

"You know something? We can have a baby anyway without doing all that boring stuff!" There is a wicked look in her eyes. She giggles, her hand probing inside my torn and dirty shirt.

"Look," I protest feebly. "I can hardly stand, let alone… Come on! Be sensible!" Her hand is moving down my stomach. I groan, but this time not with pain.

"Ooh look! I think there's still a bit of you that isn't injured! Ah yes, definitely. Now isn't that a miracle?"

She starts undoing my trousers.

"It is a bloody miracle," I say. "But honestly…"

"Think of our new baby," she coos, slipping off her dress, so filthy that the original pattern is unrecognisable. The nipples stand dark and erect on her finely rounded breasts.

"Mind my shoulder…!" I start to yelp, but she covers my mouth with hers. It can't be broken after all, because suddenly it doesn't hurt any more. She pulls herself up.

"What are you doing?"

"Let's just make sure this fire doesn't go out, shall we? I'm going put some fuel on. Or neither of us is going to marry anybody. Be back in a moment – don't go away."

She is right, of course. And the thin, wavering, black pencil line of smoke snakes its way up through the sky, the signal that we are alive, the plea for someone to rescue us.

§

All the rest of that day we take it in turns to keep the fire going. We crawl into the office area from time to time for more paper, files, folders, and pieces of wood. By night time we are exhausted, but we take shifts, staying awake beside our beacon, our only hope of survival.

Our surroundings never sleep, but quiver slightly like some dreaming wounded prehistoric monster. During the night there are little unidentifiable sounds, tiny scurryings, mysterious muffled squeaks. The walls and piles of masonry issue occasional creaks, as if still settling themselves into unfamiliar locations, and once a sudden crash as a broken piece of wall gives way and we grab each other in terror like frightened children. The grey dawn offers some relief, though my empty stomach twists with dread at the thought of what may transpire in the coming day.

But our optimism is failing as yet another night and day pass, with little  food and few comforts left. Our supply of combustible material is virtually exhausted. Most of the time my mind is blank. Neither of us speaks much, lost in our own forebodings. Sometimes we touch accidentally, and then stare at each other. Then we bend to pick up another burden or heave some more stones aside, too weary to talk. My body hurts continually, but gives some indications of recovering slowly.

Then, when my mind had almost stopped working for fear of thinking the unthinkable, there is a moment of something different, a new sound. Something is happening in the world above our heads.

There are indistinct noises, then the crash of stones being moved, and finally indistinguishable voices. We look at each in anguish, not knowing if these are friends or foe. We seize each other's hands, like skeletons, undisturbed for centuries, stirring in a grave. We scarcely dare to breathe.

I have just decided that we must take the risk and answer anyway, when a muffled shout is directed straight down the opening in the roof towards us.

*"Adam! Rose! Can you hear me? Are you down there? Hello? Adam? Anybody?"*

My God. The voice calling our names is angry and raucous. But no angel from a celestial choir could have sounded more melodious. After a second we both start yelling together.

"Hello! Max? Hello!"

"We're down here! Hello! Hello?"

"Rose? Adam? Is that you? You both there? Are you all right?"

The voice is coming from far away, but it is recognisably Max's. He doesn't sound sympathetic, but we don't care.

"Yes! We're all right!"

There is a long silence, during which we can hear sounds of activity high above our heads. We hardly dare to breathe. Then Max's voice comes again, harsher than ever.

"We're going to have to get some tackle and some

other things. We'll be back as soon as we can. But it is dangerous. There are a lot of men living here, *Kriminale,* all around."

"Understood!"

"We'll be back as soon as possible. Do you need water? Food?"

"Yes!" we shout. "Water! Food!"

"And cigarettes!" I yell as an afterthought.

"Hang on. I'm throwing down what we've got. Then just wait. And put that bloody fire out before someone else sees it."

Another long pause, punctuated by bangs and scrapes. We gaze at each other mutely. My heart is thumping, and Rose is gripping my hand.

"Food," she whispers. "Ham. Cake. Bread."

Then there is a yell.

"Coming down! Stand by!"

Something is crashing down the pile of stones and bouncing off projections before it lands. Eagerly we rush to it. It is an old haversack, stained with what looks like rust. Rose grabs it and pulls out the contents.

"Thank you!" I shout weakly, remembering my manners, but there is no acknowledgement. I open a flask half full of a liquid, as visions of whisky swim before my eyes. Rose watches me anxiously.

"Well?"

I wrinkle my nose. "Water."

"Thank God."

I hand it to her, and she drinks greedily, then passes it to me. She is opening the other packages.

"Stale bread," she says. "Some old sausages. What's this — meat, I guess. Some Sauerkraut. Oo, some black chocolate. Two squares. And, yes, a packet of cigarettes. Matches. And… that's it."

We stare at each other, then begin to laugh.

"Manna from heaven," I say, and we giggle again.

"Shall we tuck in to the lot now, or spin it out? Come on, let's eat it. They won't be long now."

But they are long, and the thin daylight has started to filter through the opening in our roof before we hear any sounds again. We are both fast asleep when a stone rattles down, bouncing off the pile and ending up a couple of yards from my head.

"Shit!" I cry, pulled violently out of a nightmare about being back on the beaches of Normandy, shells hurtling round our heads. "What the hell was that?"

Rose is instantly on her feet, staring upwards. At the top of the shaft we can see dim lights, and some movement. Then Max's voice.

"Hallo? Can you hear me?"

"Yes!" we both shout.

"Thought that would wake you up. I'm coming down on a rope. We've rigged up a block and tackle here which will lower me down. Then you can come up, one at a time. Are you injured?"

"Yes! Adam is. Quite badly."

*"Scheisse.* Can he stand?"

"Just about."

"So. Get yourselves ready. I'm coming now."

For twenty minutes for the sound of falling stones and loud obscenities precede the dust-caked figure of Max. He curses again as he comes close to the ashes of our beacon, which we have extinguished but which is still hot enough to burn.

Finally he stands before us, peering furiously at us in the gloom.

"How fucking stupid can you get, coming down

here alone, anyway? Why didn't you wait until we could back you up?"

"We found van Reen."

"Yes? YES? And?"

"He's dead. He…."

He cuts off my feeble attempt at an explanation with a wave of his arm.

"He's dead. Good. God knows why I'm bothering to rescue you two though. You're nothing but a bloody liability, both of you."

He examines my physical condition cursorily, and merely grunts.

"Right, let's get you into this thing. You first."

It is agonisingly painful being crammed into the rudimentary harness, but I am determined not to show it. Finally Max is satisfied, and calls instructions up the shaft to his unseen helpers.

It is not the most comfortable ride I've ever taken, and more than once I think I'm hopelessly trapped, but eventually, battered, bloody, almost fainting with the effort, I emerge onto the surface. I take great gulps of the fresh night air as rough hands grab me and dump me without ceremony onto the ground. Dawn is breaking over the grim, ruined landscape, but whatever horrors it undoubtedly conceals, it looks good to me.

The rope and harness have descended again immediately, and after what seems an eternity, Rose's head appears above ground, and she is dragged to safety. She looks so ridiculous caked in dirt and scratches that I start laughing, but I cut my hysteria short when I see her exhaustion. She comes over to where I am lying, one of the men watching her anxiously, and immediately checks my wounds. Her shoulders rise and fall as she gets her breath back after her ordeal.

"Fine pair we make," I whisper. "What wouldn't I give for a hot bath and bed."

She says nothing, but continues tying a dampened bandage round my arm, which has started bleeding again. The men have sent the rope down for Max, and seem to be taking an inordinately long time dragging him up.

Rose finishes her work and plants a kiss on my forehead.

"There you are, my wounded hero," she starts to say. "At least now you..."

A loud crash from inside the shaft interrupts her. There is a babble of chatter among the men, one of whom, Kurt, a thickset powerful looking fellow, is peering down the void and calling Max's name. After another brief discussion, another rope is produced, which he wraps rounds his shoulders and waist before he disappears from our sight down the gap, a torch on his belt strapped against his leg.

We all wait tensely. It is much lighter now, and I recognise one of the helpers, a surly young man with badly scarred arms. He comes near us, pulling a cigarette out of his pocket and lighting it with some difficulty.

"What's going on?"

He shrugs. "I think Max must have got stuck. We can't pull him any further, and he's not responding. Maybe a rock fall. Kurt has gone down to look. We must wait."

We wait endlessly, cold and aching and hungry. Once Rose helps me up, and we go to join the men round the winch. Two more have gone down to join

Kurt, and we can hear muffled orders and curses. Kurt emerges eventually, and angrily gestures us to get out of the way.

"But what is happening?" says Rose, her face tight with worry.

'Max is stuck," says one shortly. "There has been a rockfall, and we cannot shift him. He is not speaking." He turns to fetch another tool. "Please keep out of our way."

It must be the best part of an hour before there is a shout from the void. They all start pulling on the rope until finally Kurt emerges. He has a nasty gash on his forehead, and is shaking his head. The men mutter together, then Kurt starts untying the rope from round his body. When he is clear of it, he speaks to the others, and then comes over to us. I catch the younger man saying something about "the Englander and his whore," but I'm getting used to that.

"Bad news," Kurt says shortly. "Max is dead."

We stare at him.

"Dead? Dead?" says Rose, her hand to her mouth.

"He must have dislodged some rubble. Quite big stones. He got trapped in the shaft underneath them. They bounced down and hit him on the head. We've only just reached him."

"You're quite sure he's dead?" I say, struggling uselessly to my feet.

"Of course I'm sure," Kurt grunts, wiping a filthy forearm across his sweating forehead. "Horrible mess. Nothing we could do for him. Right, on your feet, you two."

He turns to shout instructions to the others, and they start dismantling the block apparatus, still muttering among themselves.

"Sooner we get out of here, the better. Bad place to be found in daylight, I can tell you. They don't call this the Dead City for nothing."

We are a silent party as we make our difficult way back to our entry point. We are both limping and supporting each other, and my progress in particular is agonisingly slow. None of the men seem willing to help us, or to talk to Rose or me, and it is not difficult to understand why.

We see a few shadowy figures, and more than once Kurt tells us to halt and maintain strict silence, until he beckons us on. Finally we reach our entry point. But there is no sign of the civilian police who regularly patrol the perimeter, and are liable to shoot trespassers on sight. We painfully manoeuvre ourselves out through the barrier, and back to the place we call civilization, and to blessed sleep.

# 22

*Hamburg, 1947.*

The doctor is now sicker than the patient, I reflect sadly, seeing Ernst half shut his eyes and wince as he changes my bandages. It's been two weeks since our ordeal in the Dead City, and the trees in the street outside my bedroom window are putting out bright green leaves in the annual miracle of spring.

"*Ach!*"

"Are you in pain, Ernst? Leave it. I'm all right now."

"I'm good. Now keep still."

But his face is white and when he has expertly finished his task, he lowers himself slowly onto the chair by my bed. I sit up on my pillows to try to help him, but he waves me down impatiently and closes his eyes again.

After a while he says, "You're doing very well, Adam. The shoulder and your head are healing nicely. You are almost ready to go back to work. You just need rest, good food and drink, and the care of a good woman."

He opens his old bright blue eyes now and looks at me. I think he is trying to smile. Rose has been to the house once or twice in the last few days, bringing me some snacks, though she has not dared to stay long in the face of Frau Teck's withering disapproval of her.

*"Pah! That girl is no good. Selling her body! Whatever would her parents have thought? I remember when she was a schoolgirl, always so cheeky. And stuck up too. Lady Muck! You can do better for yourself than that, Herr Kapitän."*

And so on. But I have introduced her to the doctor as well. She made a very different impression on him, being sweet with him, teasing him about his rumpled clothes and telling him he needed a haircut.

"That is a nice girl you have found," says the doctor. "I think you are important to each other, *nicht wahr?*"

"Yes, I think we are. But of course there are difficulties, you know…"

"Of course. I think you are very serious about each other though, and hurdles are there to be overcome. What will you do? Marry her and take her back to England with you? Ach…"

He shifts in his seat and grimaces with pain.

I pretend not to notice.

"Steady on, Ernst. Let's not rush our fences, hurdling or not. I don't think my employers will allow that, for a start. And anyway it would be very difficult for Rose in England now. It's going to be a long time before people there will accept a German girl. You know that."

"Yes. Oh, my God, yes. We Germans will all be evil monsters forever now. And by God, some of us were." He shakes his head sadly. "You will know that about us better than most, Adam."

I shrug.

"We humans are all frail."

There is a long embarrassed silence. There is not a lot more I can say to any of this, quite apart from the fact that I have become none too confident recently that Rose wants to marry me anyway. It is time to change the subject.

"Ernst?"

"Yes?"

"May I ask you something?"

"Of course, my friend."

"How ill are you? Really?"

He laughs.

"How ill? Ach, yes, I'm ill enough."

He blows a stream of air out of his mouth with a *pffff* sound.

"Very ill, my friend. The dying kind of ill. It is cancer, you see. I've seen enough cases in my time to know that. My lungs. Kidneys too. And maybe more. The lymph glands, I suspect."

"Jesus. Have you seen a doctor? Can I get one to come to the house?"

"Doctor? I'm a doctor. What will another doctor tell me? What I've just told you and then prescribe some magic cure? There are very few medicines to be had, Adam, and even if there were, there is nothing that can help me now, except painkillers. And there are none of those around either."

"Let me try our British doctors. We have our own medical supplies."

His voice is sharp. "No! Forget that! I am not begging favours from the English. With due respect, my friend."

Something suddenly strikes me. "I'm going to ask Rose. She is an expert on herbs and medicinal weeds. Cannabis is one – it is growing wild now in the ruins. It's a wonderful painkiller, and pleasant to smoke as well. It's so agreeable, it's a wonder they haven't banned it. It can only be a matter of time. Will you let me get some from her?"

His face is creased, and he closes his eyes. When he can speak again, he nods and whispers, "That is kind, Adam. A good idea. I can smoke it in my pipe. It may help me now in my last few days."

"My God! Is it that advanced?"

"Oh, yes. My whole body is riddled with the cancer now. My vital functions are beginning to shut down."

He winces. "I make you a proposition. You can bring me the cannabis tomorrow. I shall be grateful. And I must tell you something you do not know. And will not like."

"It's a deal. I'm getting up now anyway. I'm not lying here a minute longer. Just look at the lovely day outside the window."

I hobble out of bed and go to my wardrobe. Ernst raises a hand as if in protest, then shrugs and lets it drop again. I start to pull my clothes on.

I don't know what to say. What words does one use to an old man who has just told you he is about to die?

"I'm so sorry, Ernst."

"*Ach*, I am ready, Adam. My time has come. My wife, my friends – they are all gone. There is only me left. My good friend Fritz has gone of course, some years ago."

"He died?"

"Oh yes. Of pneumonia, not so long ago. He commanded a brigade at Verdun you know, but he lost both legs there. He was never the same man after that. Hardly surprising that he hated war with a passion after that. And he had loved skiing so much."

"Poor old Fritz. He was the man who told you that nonsense about Hitler's love child being alive in my village?"

"Yes."

I laugh. "How can that possibly be true?"

"Nonsense, perhaps. But stranger things have happened. Now – I am going to lie down. Enjoy the day. And do not do too much – you are still convalescent. It is hard to escape the shadow of Hitler, you must understand. Even for you. Remember that, Adam."

His eyes are staring at something I cannot see.

§

*Hamburg 1947*

It is spring, and we are alive. Rose and I are strolling along the waterfront, hand in hand as all young lovers should at this time of the year. She has not returned to the Lion House, which appears unlikely to continue to function after Max's death. She has found rooms nearby, but I have not been invited to visit her there. Something has changed in our relationship, and I don't know why. But today it seems we are friends again.

I am wearing a bandage round my head under a knitted cap, and an old sweater. Since my release from the Military Tribunal Service, my uniform can stay in a cupboard, at least for the time being. We present a curious picture, both of us clearly recovering from injuries and wearing odd clothes, but in fact quite unremarkable among so many others in a similar condition.

Even Rose's long-legged stride is reduced to a hobble, but we laugh at each other, and gaiety is in the air. Herr Klumpf is drawing less attention to himself these days, perhaps from having to take his turn now among a long list of other bodily ailments vying for supremacy.

It is a noisy scene. Around us hardly a building in the old port has escaped damage or destruction, and sunken shipping still fills the bay. But miraculously, cranes have appeared recently – the mechanical variety rather than the avian – and there is a bustle of activity. There must be over a hundred men working on the harbour side. Everywhere rebuilding work is taking place at a feverish pace, set against the incongruously melancholy backdrop.

"It's like looking at an ants' nest that someone's kicked over," says Rose. "Have you ever seen one? The ants scurry around, all with different jobs - supervisors, workers, soldiers, scouts, lines of porters carrying crumbs or eggs ceaselessly, all day long, rebuilding, rebuilding…"

She gestures at the scene. "Are we so different? We're ants too, Adam. We think we're more intelligent, but we're not. Just different, that's all. We couldn't do the things they do, and they can't do what we can."

She breaks off.

"*Ach*, see, is that a little workmen's cafe over

there? I'm starving. Shall we go and get something to eat?"

"What do ants eat?"

I tease her. "It's probably just grass or worms or something. Don't think I fancy that very much!"

In reply she yanks me by the arm into the doorway of the little cafe.

I stifle a yelp of pain, and with some difficulty we find ourselves a table. All the other customers are men, and Rose attracts a barrage of admiring glances. She ignores them and smiles sweetly at the old waiter, who comes over to us immediately. She always looks so haughty and aristocratic when she is pretending not to notice the effect she has on men, I think. And when the waiter has gone with our order I lean forward to whisper in her ear and tell her so, brushing her cheek with my lips.

"I'm so glad you've got rid of that awful straggly beard," is all she says. "Are we going to have something to drink? I've had enough of dying of thirst recently, thank you."

"They'll only have beer," I say, glancing round. "And of course sausages and potatoes!"

"Beer will do very nicely, thank you."

As she speaks and exactly on cue, two large steins of lager are being borne towards us on a tray by the waiter. I look at him in surprise.

"Wonderful, but…?"

"With the compliments of those men."

He sets them down on our table, jerking a gnarled thumb backwards at two men sitting at the bar. They laugh and bow to us, and say something in a foreign language.

"Russian prisoners, I'll bet," says Rose, raising her

glass to them and smiling prettily. "Celebrating their freedom. *Nostrovia!*"

"*Nostrovia!*" they call, bursting into laughter, and turn away from us back to the bar.

"Poor bastards," says Rose quietly, pulling the beer towards her. "They put Russians like them into a camp not from our farm. Hundreds of them. They starved to death there that winter, Adam. Nobody fed them."

She shivers.

"One day my little sister and I stole some scraps – eggshells, some mouldy bread, a bar of soap, some candles, anything we could scrounge that we thought they could use. We crept up to the wire away from the guard tower. Two prisoners saw us and staggered towards us. They were just skin and bone, with staring eyes. *Schrecklich*. We… we were very frightened. Just pushed the stuff at them through the fence and ran. We were scared of being shot by the guards."

She takes a long pull of her beer.

"You know the worst thing, Adam?"

She shakes her head, her eyes screwed tightly closed.

"We looked back when we thought we were safe. They were *eating* the soap. And the candles. Eating them. When we got home, I was sick and sick until my stomach was empty."

I shake my head. Horrible, horrible.

An ill-timed roar of laughter fills the cafe from the corner where the men are playing cards. Glad of the distraction, we laugh too, and speak of other matters. The sausages are delicious, black market of course, and very nearly pre-war standard, according to Rose. She smiles across at me.

"Do you think we could have some of that delicious looking *Apfelstrudel?*"

As we watch, another dilapidated building crashes to the ground, and work is instantly begun on clearing away the rubble. The skyline has changed even while we have been sitting here, and the war has receded another step into the past.

"Tell me, Adam," she says. "Why have our countries had these terrible wars with each other? Do you think they will do us some drinkable coffee? This place is amazing."

She is licking cream off her fingers in a most unladylike fashion and frowning as if each question demands the same serious attention.

"Probably because we are so similar. Cousins," I say, motioning to the waiter for coffee and reaching for my cigarettes. "Family feuds are the worst."

The air in the cafe is blue with smoke, but it is beginning to clear as the men leave to go back to work.

"Let's hope that this time it really was the war to end all wars," I say. "We can all be friends again. Perhaps I should take a German wife home to England, as a representative of a new beginning for Europe! What do you think?"

"What?"

I have spoken without thinking. Rose has put her cake down and is staring at me.

"Have I said something wrong? What?"

"Oh, did I miss something? Was there a wedding proposal in there?" she says, nostrils flaring. Not a good sign, I have learnt.

"Or was my acceptance taken for granted? For if that is how you go about such things in your country, then our two nations are in fact very different!"

"Look," I say, backtracking hastily. "No, that wasn't a proposal. I was just thinking aloud. I do want to marry you, of course I do. But I know we've got an awful lot to decide before we can think about that."

"Oh, do enlighten me?"

She plants her elbow on the table, and supports her head on her hand, contemplating me as if I have broken into an unfamiliar foreign tongue.

I begin to stammer.

"Well, what am I going to do for a living, for a start? And where are we going to live now?"

"Well, what's the answer to that one?"

She is really angry. I have put my foot in it properly. All I can think to do is to plough on.

"Well, without actually sacking me, old Foxy dropped some pretty good hints about me going back home to England. But when I said I wasn't sure about that, he suggested he might find me a job in the new commission that's being set up to start our two governments working together again. It's only in its infancy at the moment, but it's got to happen."

I hesitate. In for a penny.... I take a long pull at my coffee. It isn't at all bad. "Trouble is, it looks likely to be based in Berlin. And I'd have to sign a three year contract. How do you feel about moving there? I know you've often said you don't like Berlin, but..."

Rose reaches for a cigarette. Some of the tension seems to have gone out of her. She pensively blows a long smoke ring, staring across at the docks with unseeing eyes.

"No, well, I don't care for it much, nor for Berliners," she says. "But from what I hear, there's nothing much of the place left anyway. Everything's got to be rebuilt from scratch. Like here."

She gestures at the bleak dockland outside the window.

"So, yes, one bombsite is probably no worse than another. And it would mean a fresh start. For both of us. No, I can't pretend I want to live in Berlin. On the other hand…"

A crane moves slowly across my line of vision, its head pecking like a scrawny chicken looking for grain in the dirt. Everywhere is the clatter of activity, and signs of spring are tentatively appearing, even in this battered landscape.

"What is it, darling?" I ask gently, leaning across the table and taking her delicate hand in my rough one. She squeezes it a moment, then pulls hers away.

"Berlin's one thing. At least it's Germany. But I don't think I could face living in England, if you chose that option. I… I just don't like the sound of it."

"What do you mean? It's topping where I live. You'd love it, and everybody there. And they'd all love you!"

"Would they, Adam? Would they really?"

"Of course they would. Who wouldn't love you? You'd be the star attraction in Chipping-on-the-Fosse!"

"You must be joking! I couldn't even say it!"

She has perked up. Her mood has changed again. I try not to make my relief too obvious.

"Anyway, let's start with Berlin, shall we? At least we can agree how to pronounce that. Maybe we should give it a go. And another good bit of news – the British Army of Occupation have finally officially scrapped those ridiculous anti-frat laws. I've been meaning to tell you all day. They've finally made it official." I smile at her. "Just think of it. It's actually legal now for me to be seen kissing a German girl!"

She sticks her tongue out at me.

"Have you a particular girl in mind?" she enquires saucily.

"Well," I say, looking round, "as you're the only female in the place, I guess I'll have to make do with you!"

As we kiss across the table like sex starved teenagers, I imagine all the other customers on their feet behind me, cheering us on as heralds of a new, fairer world, where nationality doesn't matter, and peace reigns.

But when we come up for air and look around, no-one has even noticed. The place is nearly empty. We smile a little shamefacedly at each other, pay the bill, tip the old waiter, and go back into the noisy, hectic, frantic, competitive, angry world that awaits us.

§

Next day Frau Teck is in the hall as I come through the front door. She is wiping her skinny hands anxiously on her apron. She reminds me more than ever of a shrew, bright brown eyes in a pointed face, whiskers twitching, always making little worried movements as if about to flee some imminent danger. Surviving in this house all through the terrible strain of war will have had this effect on her. I scrape my boots on the doormat and open my mouth to speak, but she is too quick for me.

"*Herr Kapitän*! It is the Doktor! You should go up

and see him." She bites her lip. "I think he is very bad."

"That's all right, Frau Teck," I say, putting my hand on her shoulder.

"He has been asking to see you! He is very weak. I have taken him some soup, but…"

She shrugs, her face screwed up with concern.

"All right. I'll go at once."

Ernst is lying back with his eyes shut, but he opens them when he hears me come in. His old veined hands are gripping the coverlet. His eyes are bright, and his voice is very weak. His forehead is lined with the pain which has become constant in these last few months. An untouched bowl of chicken soup sits on the little table beside him. I don't think he is ready to die yet, but the end cannot be long delayed.

I take his hand and bend nearer.

"Adam…"

"Is there something I can do, Ernst?"

"No," he whispers. "But I must tell you something, before I… before…"

I have a sudden thought.

"Do you want a priest? Are you a Catholic?"

He half smiles. 'I am – was – a Catholic once. But no, I don't want a priest. But I must tell someone…"

I sit down carefully on the bed and prepare for a long stay. After a tiring day at the office and another fractious meeting with Foxy, I am ready for a meal, a drink, and a pipe. At least as regards to van Reen, there has been no more talk about proceedings against me for losing a prisoner.

Ernst twists on the bed. "I have been a very bad man. You know that."

"It's about that monster, isn't it?" I sigh. "You

have his life on your conscience. You have told me many times."

"Yes, yes, that's it," he says. But he is looking away, and twisting his hands together outside the sheets.

"Yes, that is it."

"You weren't to know how he would turn out, Ernst," I say soothingly. We have been through this so often. "It's over. It has happened. You might have ended his life earlier, yes. But a hundred other people could say that. Perhaps thousands of others, and far more culpable than you. The men who worked for him, carried out his orders…"

But it is as if he hasn't heard me.

After a while he speaks again. The atmosphere in the little room is hot and unhealthily stuffy. I have heard that some cancers have an acrid stench all of their own, and I am very conscious of that now. I long to open a window, but hesitate.

"There is something else. You see, Adam, during a war, one does many things – many things…"

He stops and chokes. His eyes are now tight shut. "Worse things even than not ending… his life when I had a chance. Horrible things… They are not all in my diaries."

Tears are running silently down his cheeks now, and his breathing is coming more quickly.

"I don't want to hear this, Ernst. I really don't. You don't need to tell me."

There is a long pause, and then the old doctor tries to sit up against his pillows. I help him, making him as comfortable as I can. He licks his dry lips. He seems a little stronger.

"Is there still some of that whisky over there?" he

asks, nodding towards the side table. "Help yourself to a glass. It is perhaps better than nothing."

I get up and do as instructed, enquiring with a gesture if he wants a glass too. He shakes his head, his eyes staring fixedly ahead. I lean forward. Clearly he is going to speak, whether I want to listen or not.

"What sort of things, Ernst?" I ask softly. "What do you want to tell me?"

"Yes, Adam, I must speak. You see, I have lied to you. I told you I was working in military hospitals through this war, as I did in the last. Oh, I did for a while. But they transferred me soon afterwards to a different area of medicine – *Sonderlage*, they called it. Special duties. They made it very clear that if I refused, Ilse would go to a concentration camp. It was not only Jews, you know…it was very easy for the Gestapo to add a name to a list. No questions asked. And once she was there…" He shuddered.

"They said my talents were wasted. I was to attach myself to a man named… Ah, I see you have already guessed his name. It was not for more than three months altogether, but that was long enough…"

I am struck dumb. This information goes through me like an electric shock, and I feel nauseous. I take a deep breath to steady myself. This is a subject I know all too much about from some of the people I have interviewed.

"Go on."

"I see you do know who I am speaking of. Then you will not need me to tell you the sort of work I was asked to engage in. The experiments, if that is what you can call them. On old people. Young people. Men and women, oh, yes, and on children too. All without anaesthetic… Dear Jesus, forgive me.

For I cannot forgive myself. Could not then, cannot now."

He chokes and can't go on.

"In the camps?"

"Yes. In Märchenholz, very near my home. In the very caves I used to love as a young man. I became something of an expert, you see, a specialist in certain aspects. Oh yes, we learnt many things. Things that could not have been proved except on living patients... Things that in a sane world would be used to save lives. My only tiny consolation – and believe me, it is very tiny – is that perhaps one day our research may be used for good. But, *ach*..."

He cannot go on, and huge gasping sobs rack his body.

I let go of his hand now, and go to stare out of the window. My heart is racing, and I wonder if I am actually going to be sick. The body and the mind work very closely together, the body wanting to expel something repugnant that the mind has discovered. This kind, wise old man, my friend, has done these things, things so terrible that the mind can only glance over them and move swiftly on for fear of collapsing into insanity. The cries for mercy he must have ignored, the human agony he must have closed his mind to. Suddenly my teeth are clenched and I am filled with hatred for him. I want to throttle him, to give him a taste of just a fraction of the pain he has inflicted on others.

I am always conscious of my difficulties with my feelings about the other Germans that I meet every day, the decent ordinary people. Who knows what atrocities the porter carrying your bag, the office clerk stamping your papers, the woman serving your coffee, the butcher cutting your steak with such accuracy, may have had a part in? What dreadful things have they seen or committed, during the long years of war?

My nails are digging impotently into the palms of my hands. For a terrible moment I stare into an abyss, so much aware of what may lie deep inside myself, Jung's 'murderer within.'

For what seems like ages I stare down at the dark street, where the occasional pedestrian disappears into the shadows. It is still cold, and the faces are pinched and drawn. A cat jumps suddenly down from a wall, knocking over a pile of empty cans, and I can dimly hear the clatter even from up here. Then I steady myself and turn back to the bedside. My teeth are gritted.

"If you think for one moment, Ernst…" I begin. But I stop when I see the despair in his face, and can't go on. He is very near death now.

In the end I go out of the room, closing the door behind me.

# 23

*Hamburg, 1947*

"Are all these people really art lovers?" scoffs Rose.

She daintily squeezes her shapely behind, into a narrow seat in one corner, casually clearing someone's coat off the chair beside her to make a place for me.

"I don't think so. Mind where you put your feet, darling – the floor's wet."

The noise level is rising steadily now, so that you can hardly hear the muttered curses of the waiters as they force their way through the excited chatter and animated laughter of the customers, carrying trays of hot coffee, small glasses of amber coloured liquor, and plates of *ersatz Sachertorten*.

"Ooh, may I have two of those please!" cries Rose. "And two large brandies with coffee! How perfectly gorgeous!"

A waiter catches her eye at once, smiles and nods. I personally wear a magic shroud that makes me invisible to waiters, but they always spot Rose within seconds. She only has to raise an elegant eyebrow and glance around, to gain instant attention. The technique works even with waitresses, though I notice that the less attractive ones are slower to serve her.

"The cream will be artificial, the chocolate bitter, the apricot a mere smear from a jam pot." I drop effortlessly into my languid man-of-the world pose, all too obviously in order to conceal my discomfort at my surroundings.

But she sensibly pretends not to hear me. She ducks her head to accept a light for her cigarette from a bearded youth in a paint-spattered smock at the next table, looking up at him as she does so. The smears of paint and the slightly torn garment look a little too contrived for my taste, but I give the boy the benefit of the doubt. Artistic licence, shall we say.

"I am Marco," he introduces himself, smiling, but she doesn't reciprocate, merely blowing a smoke ring and settling herself back in her chair. Above us there looms a huge canvas of a naked couple lying side by side by a sylvan pool. The brushstrokes are bold and the colours vivid. The painting is partly obscured from our view by the thick haze of cigarette smoke in the room. It blurs the faces of the uncaring woodland lovers, who appear to have their minds on other things. Perhaps they are all too well aware of the prospect of being frozen for eternity in a state of post coital *tristesse*, like Keats' Grecian lovers.

A saxophone wails in the background, and a girl with a white face, green hair, orange lipstick, sooty mascara and bare feet sways gently to the music, her eyes glazed and her gaze fixed. Even from here I can see that her arms are covered in tiny puncture marks. The waiters navigate around her, like ships round a hazardous rock.

"The food in Oxford is absolutely frightful."

A reedy voice is holding forth over the hubbub, in accented English. "My dear, I nearly starved to death at college. One actually had to go outside in the morning to the lavatories. The only decent thing about the whole place was the port after dinner. Oh, then of course, I forget – there were the breakfasts."

A full-lipped boy in a dark green silk shirt is sitting beside an older man. He is absorbed alternately in examining his nails and staring across the room. A bored expression is rigidly fixed on his face, which would be rather beautiful if it were not so sulky.

His companion drones on.

"Something called a full English. Fried pork and eggs. My dear, you can't imagine! And do you know the really ridiculous thing? It is absolutely delicious!"

The boy murmurs something suddenly and gets to his feet. He surveys the crowd for a moment, and then picks his way slowly towards the back of the room, occasionally raising a lissom hand as he does so. His trousers are perfectly moulded across his buttocks, which sway slightly as he cruises the room. His patron watches his slow progress while drawing on a Balkan Sobranie with a thin, heavily be-ringed hand, screwing up his lined face against the smoke. His face is expressionless.

I sit back and light my own cheaper cigarette, surveying the scene around me. The place is crowded, and through the haze of smoke I recognize one or two faces that I know. My illicit food supplier Gustav is at one of the busy tables, and judging by the laughter is something of a raconteur when at his leisure. I catch his eye and raise a hand in greeting, but he quickly looks away, embarrassed or too discreet to be associated with me.

The Café des Artistes has been open for less than a month, but has been an overnight success. Before the war the building was apparently a large hardware store, and is miraculously unscathed by the bombing, although the shops on either side have lost their roofs and much of their structure. These too are slowly being repaired, and the little street is coming back into life. Businesses are beginning to operate again. It is one of the first areas to struggle back to life after the almost total annihilation of this part of the city. There was once a well renowned art college in the neighbourhood, and the new café acts as a focus for the very few students and established painters who have survived, or the remnants of them.

Oil paintings, watercolours, acrylics, and charcoal drawings jostle for position on the dark walls, which are so crowded with pictures that it seems there can be no room for more. Yet Rose's young neighbour is clambering onto a chair, threatening to overturn his companions' drinks as he clumsily pushes other paintings aside to make space for one of his own. In thick oils, in an inappropriate ormolu frame, a portrait of a dark girl in a white blouse in front of a brightly stylised rural landscape stares angrily back over her shoulder at us. She holds a small red flower she has apparently just picked. It is an arresting image.

Marco has finally found a nail to hang the painting on, by the simple expedient of shoving some others up together in lopsided fashion. He leans back to admire his handiwork, teetering slightly with one foot on the table and putting his hand onto Rose's bare shoulder for support. She is staring up at the painting.

We in our little group all clap and cry "Bravo!", but Rose says nothing. She has a faraway look in her eye, recalling perhaps some distant memory. Then Marco clambers down as the waiter arrives with our drinks and cakes, and the mood is broken. The young man is flushed with excitement, or drink, or both. He takes a long swig of wine.

"There you are!" he roars. "The first public hanging of a Hübken oil! What do you say to that, *Fräulein*? History has been made, and you are here to see it!"

Rose has regained her composure and is busy tucking into a Sachertorte. The cream is going all over her mouth, but she brushes it off with an elegant backward sweep of her hand, licking her fingers one by one as she considers her reply. The table is waiting.

"I think," she says carefully, "that I have seen enough public hangings for one lifetime."

There is a shocked silence, then they laugh awkwardly. This is not really funny, judging by the expressions on some of the faces. Rose sees this, and the disappointment in the young man's face too, and continues quickly.

"But, Marco! I like your painting! It has colour, youth, hope – and a story to tell. You have talent! Here's to your art, Herr Hübken! And a successful future!"

There is a roar of applause from our table, and chatter begins again.

The old man has given up waiting for the boy to return, and his gaze has fallen on our noisy little group. He sees me looking at him and bows his head smilingly towards me. I bow back, more or less out of politeness, and after a moment he courteously beckons me over. I glance at Rose, but she is in animated conversation with one of the others, so I get up, my chair scraping on the wooden floor, and pick my way across the café.

The man half rises stiffly to his feet, but I refuse the proffered chair, absurdly conscious of my bruised nose and the grimy plaster of Paris on my forearm. I realise now that I know who he is, and he confirms it at once.

"De Souza, dear boy. Julius de Souza, at your service."

He smiles and languidly extends a pale hand. I mumble my name. "A pleasure to meet you. And how delightful that we are now permitted to speak agreeably to each other as friends again, and not as enemies! Oh, my dear, what a bore all that was!"

He spreads his hands, admiring his manicure, and adjusts his cuffs.

"I am, dare I confess it now, an Anglophile – an admission that would have had me shot as a traitor until very recently! As you very well know, of course, Captain?"

"Please call me Adam, sir."

"And you must call me Julius. Are you by any chance an art lover? If so, you will be in a minority in this gathering, I fear… but never mind, they mean well, bless their licentious little hearts."

He looks about him with loathing. I shake his hand again, but his thoughts are elsewhere.

"Excuse me, sir. I must see if my friend is all right."

"The very pretty girl over there? Oh, she'll be well looked after, I can assure you. You must bring her over and introduce her to me. I could use a clever attractive girl in this lunatic asylum. And an intelligent handsome young man like you too."

"Another time perhaps."

He holds my hand for a moment too long, and I detect a liberal application of eau de Cologne. I extract myself with a stiff smile and move away. There was a man in my college at University all too like him.

"I see you have the M.C., captain. Awarded for conspicuous gallantry, I think."

This is acutely embarrassing and never a subject I want to dwell on. In fact I have had quite enough of this man, and the atmosphere of the place. I try to catch Rose's attention, indicating that I am ready to go. There are few parts of my anatomy that are not giving me pain in one degree or another. But I don't think I'm going to get much sympathy tonight.

Rose simply blows farewell kisses to me and turns back to her new companions, as the little band strike up a fresh waltz. I watch her on the floor with Marco, the two a perfect fusion of fluid rhythm and sensuality. Then I quietly fetch my raincoat and limp out into the dark. The summer evening has turned unexpectedly chilly. Sometimes I feel very old, I reflect, turning up my collar and heading for home.

# 24

*Hamburg, 1947*

"Dr Mann is worse. I fear he is near the end."

Frau Teck seems calm as she delivers her message to me, although her hands are wringing together under her pinafore. She is about to say more. Then suddenly her composure breaks and she rushes abruptly into her sanctuary.

I hesitate, then go up the winding wooden stairs to his room.

I have no idea what to say to him, but I can't not go and see him, or at the very least check his medications. Perhaps he will even tell me something that will mitigate his crimes in my eyes. Until then I strive to put them out of my mind and treat him as before.

"Hello, Ernst," I say, pushing open the bedroom door and walking towards the window to draw the curtains. But there is no response, and I see at once that something has changed. Ernst is propped up against the pillows, his eyes staring ahead out of a contorted face. But that face has altered colour, and is as yellow and waxy as a mummy's. The thin chest is no longer rising and falling. When I bend over the bed, I can see that he has stopped breathing. There is no point even in taking his pulse.

The old man is dead.

After a long moment I close his eyelids, pull the cover up to his neck, and straighten up. The tide of emotion is slowly sinking back inside me.

"It is all over now, Ernst," I say, staring down on him. "Goodbye, old man."

His torment about whether he could have saved the world from Hitler is over. I shake my head. What a dreadful burden to take to the grave. I go slowly downstairs to break the news to Frau Teck.

I knock on her door, and after a minute she peeps her head around it. She has a duster in her hand. She sees immediately from my face what I am going to tell her. "He is gone," she says flatly.

"I'm afraid so. We should inform the authorities. Do you know…"

She interrupts me. She looks more shaken than I expected. "Please do come in, *Herr Kapitän*. Will you join me in some refreshments? Er – would you excuse me just a moment?"

She puts a hanky up to her face and rushes into the kitchen.

This is a departure from the norm. In nearly two years I have never been invited past her living room door. I stand there awkwardly on the threshold until she returns and ushers me in, beckoning me to an armchair. The room is over furnished, with mostly dark, elaborate fittings, heavy curtains, an antique clock dominating one wall.

In one corner a small draped table holds a cluster

of framed photographs. I get up stiffly to peer at them, perhaps to find a subject for us to talk about. Many of them show a much younger Frau Teck with a large man with a military bearing, handsome in his youth. Some of the later photographs show him in a black uniform which I do not recognize, some with other men similarly attired. I notice a blank space on the wall behind the table where a large picture has been hanging, judging from the hook and the slightly faded wallpaper.

"You recognize me still when I was young?"

Frau Teck has appeared with a large silver tray, on which sit beautiful Meissen china crockery, a teapot with a knitted cosy on it, and a plate of sugared biscuits. Even in very hard times it seems that conventions must be satisfied, at whatever cost. I am honoured indeed, and say so.

"Yes, you were very attractive, *Frau Teck*," I continue, as no doubt I am expected to do. It is not strictly true, though the young woman in some of the photographs has a shy, almost coquettish expression on her face which might be thought beguiling. But in one or two the timidity she reveals as she stands beside her much taller husband looks to me something more like fear. She follows my eyes.

"Yes, Manfred and I made a good-looking couple, once. He was killed in the winter of 1943, you know. I never heard the details. No, nothing at all." She shakes her head and busies herself with the tea things.

"What arm of the service was he in?" I ask politely.

This flusters her.

"Ach, I don't really remember. I never understood all that military stuff. He was very highly thought of, I know that. General Schutzmann sent me a very nice letter saying how much his devoted service was appreciated."

The name Schutzmann rings a bell. Wasn't he...? But my attention has strayed a little, as I have now spotted where something has been pushed behind a bookcase, presumably hastily. I can only see a little of it. I decide to change the subject.

"How long have you known Dr Mann?" I ask. The biscuits are delicious, and no doubt carefully preserved for such an occasion. "Was he an old friend?"

"*Ach, ja.* We knew him when he was working here in medicine. I don't know what he did during the war – he never spoke of it. Then we lost touch with him. When his wife died I happened to meet him again. The Herr Doktor was old and alone then, with nowhere to live, and I offered him the attic room. He took it gladly. I think he had lost everything in the bombing, like so many people."

Her eyes fill with tears.

"I shall miss him so much. He was such a kind man, and did so much good for people. He would never have harmed a fly."

She brushes a tear from her eye and lifts the teapot. We talk of other things, and when we have finished I rise to leave. While she bustles off into the kitchen again with the tray, I take a quick step towards the picture and pull it out from its hiding place. It only takes a second or two. It is enough time to reveal a formal posed photograph of Hitler shaking hands with her husband, and this time I can see his uniform clearly with all its insignia. *Obersturmbannführer* Teck had been a much decorated officer in the S.S., Hitler's private bodyguard. The cold blue eyes in his broad Prussian face stare challengingly back at me from the picture.

"What do you English know of us?" it sneers. "Who do you think you are, to sit in judgement on us?"

Who indeed. Frau Teck can put the picture back in pride of place on her wall once I had gone, and gaze at it as much as she cares to.

§

*Hamburg, 1947*

I have arranged to meet Pinkie after he finishes work. I am trying to get him to socialise more, and I also want to have a chat with him out of the office. I am restless. My role at work is now an uneasy one. Several of my cases have been delegated elsewhere, and I am beginning to feel like a back number. In fact my whole army career is hanging by a thread. I have the sensation of being caught up in a cataract and swept blindly onwards regardless of my will.

Foxy has said no more about the job in Berlin, and I suspect the moment has passed. But my father's former law practice has kept a partnership open for me, and there are days when the idea of returning to England sounds tempting. And if being a country solicitor seems too humdrum, I could always read for the Bar. This is another subject on which I would value Pinkie's advice.

It is a warm autumn evening, pleasant for a brisk walk. The little bar round the corner from where we work is a nondescript establishment but convenient and reasonably private. These places are beginning to over spring up now that access to alcohol and food is improving with the aid of American investment.

This is a part of the city that was particularly devastated in the firestorm of bombing, hardly one building without its terrible wounds. But even here most of the rubble has been carted away by the ever industrious *Trümmerfrauen*, and the street pattern, almost undetectable only a few months ago, is beginning to reassert itself. The faces of the citizens have lost that yellow tinge that lingered long after the bombing has ceased, and the memory of starving children begging for food has faded along with the lingering smell of death.

When I get to the bar, to my surprise I see that Rose is here. She is with Pinkie and two other people, chatting away animatedly at a table in the restaurant section. Whitewash roughly covers the worst of the damage to the walls and some attempt has been made at decoration. Rose's infectious laugh rings out at something Pinkie has said, and his face is flushed with pleasure.

They barely greet me as I join them, and after a minute I go to the bar to get myself a drink. The proprietor, a gloomy looking man with one leg, waves me impatiently back to the table for me to wait until he has time to attend to me.

I stare around me. Conversation ceases.

"Didn't expect to see you here. Well, you two seem to be having a good time," I say, easing myself into a chair as carefully as possible, and trying not to wince as pain shoots through my back and leg. "Hello, darling. What's new?"

There is a silence. Rose doesn't reply. It has

become obvious that now she has left the Lion House, she no longer has a use for a white knight on a charger, especially one as knock-kneed as me. It is as easy as that. Our recent assignations have been far less frequent, and noticeably strained.

Pinkie starts to tell me office gossip and tensions. A recent arrival from England, a lawyer I haven't met, has taken over a great deal of my workload, and I want to know more about this.

"Look, Pinkie, what exactly is this man Hetherington's brief? I haven't even been consulted properly. Have I still got a job, or not?"

Pinkie is ill at ease answering my questions, and seems reluctant to commit himself.

"Well, um, there's a bit of a row going on about whether it's our section's job to…"

"Yes, but who exactly will be…"

"Apparently there are some revised guidelines from London on…"

"*Ach,* for God's sake." Rose cuts in impatiently. It looks as if she is on at least her second large glass of wine, and an ashtray is filling up rapidly in front of her. "Never mind all this rubbish about court cases and prosecutions and trials. And who does what and who to. I too have news. But I have found a proper job! In catering! What do you think about that?"

I drag myself back to her concerns with an effort.

"That's really good news! Where?"

"Where do you think, darling? At the Café des Artistes, of course. Where all the best people hang out."

"Oh. Right."

I am taken aback. "Bit of a wild setup, isn't it? You're going to be working for that old queen?"

The club is rapidly getting itself a reputation as a house of ill repute, with bedrooms available for casual sex, the gender of the parties involved being irrelevant. It is also a place to buy stolen goods, deal on the black market or buy drugs, and is now officially out of bounds to British troops.

Rose shrieks with laughter, and thrusts her face near mine. She is much drunker than I thought she was. "Ooh, a wild setup, is it? Oh dearie me! Whatever would your mother think?"

"I just said…"

"You must be missing all the girls at Max's. Had the time of your life, didn't you? Didn't worry about my feelings, did you? We were meant to be in love, weren't we?"

I am indignant. "You said you didn't mind! Men are polygamous, you always said. 'Have as many other women as you want, as long as you come back to me' – remember? 'I'm not the jealous wife type.' Yes?"

She stares at me open mouthed. "My God, you really are so naïve. Don't you understand women at all?" She shakes her head.

There is a long silence. Pinkie is examining the posters on the walls as if they have some deep fascination for him. After a while I clear my throat. Rose has calmed down a little.

"So you've got a new job?".

"Yes, Julian has made me his head hostess or something. I'm working on a better job title, but that will do for now. I'm going to be in charge of hiring and firing, cabaret bookings, and entertainment. A very generous salary, and so many side benefits, you really can't imagine!"

"What sort of side benefits?" I ask, smiling.

Actually I can imagine all too well.

"Ooh, wouldn't you like to know?

She giggles, spilling some red wine down her perfect cleavage. I reach forward clumsily with a handkerchief to mop up the wine before it stains her dress, but she brushes away my hand impatiently.

"Get off! Stop pawing me. I've had enough of you. You're just a namby-pamby little English boy, that's all. And you damn nearly got me killed in that tunnel."

I feel myself flush, and stuff the handkerchief back in my pocket. I can feel my temper rising, but decide I'm going to ignore what she's said. There'll be plenty of time to think about it later, I know that.

"I'm just trying to help, you know that. I'm worried about you working there. You don't know what you're getting yourself into at a place like that. You've just got out of one nightmare scenario, and now you're getting into another."

"You just disapprove of me in general, that's all."

She smears the spilt wine off her skin with the back of her hand, and then licks it off, staring up at me short-sightedly, frowning as if trying to remember where she's seen me before.

"Like you do about everything about me. I'm having fun now, darling, for the first time in my life, I think. Really good fun. It's my turn now."

"Well, I'm glad to hear it," I say, tipping back my drink in an effort to get as merry as she is as quickly as possible. "I've been wondering where you've been lately. Hardly see you at all these days."

She seizes the bottle from me and slops the last of the wine into her glass.

"No, well, you're always so busy with your boring

old work, aren't you, darling. Defending all those poor sweet men who were only obeying orders and had no idea of what horrid things everybody else was doing to the Jews and the gypsies and the Russian prisoners of war... Do you think that miserable bugger could bring us some more wine? It's slipping down well tonight, don't you think?"

"What I think is that you've had enough, sweetheart. Why don't I take you somewhere nice where we can get something to eat? Perhaps Pinkie would like to come with us? We haven't been yet to that..."

"No!" she yells so loudly that people turn round to see what the noise is. "We're staying here! Why are you always so boring? Has nobody ever told you how boring you are, with your English accent and your silly leg and your..."

Pinkie has risen to his feet, embarrassed beyond bearing. He has been sitting back staring at the table, reluctant to interfere, but can clearly take this no longer.

"Look, Adam," he says, reaching for his jacket. "I'll see you tomorrow at the office if you want to drop in. We need to go over those depositions again and..."

"Hey! Rose! Hello!"

Some young people have just come in the door, and they flock enthusiastically over to our table. One of them is the young man Marco, the artist. She clasps them to her bosom, one by one, covering each face with wet kisses. I am omitted from any introduction, and join Pinkie as he prepares to leave.

"Sorry about this," he mutters. "I did try to stop her ordering another bottle. Must dash."

"Not your fault, Pinkie. I know what's she's like these days when she gets going. There's no stopping her. Or if there is, I don't know how to do it. Truth is, she's changed so much I hardly know her. Or I have."

I look back at the table. There are now six people at it, and more drinks are arriving. The noise level has increased, and my shoulder is giving me hell. I try to catch Rose's eye to indicate that I'm leaving, but she is deep in some conversation that inspires hoots of merriment.

"I'll come with you," I say to Pinkie. "Somehow I don't think I'm going to be missed."

We slip out into the summer night like guilty absconders. Although I have met them all at one time or another, no-one at the table has acknowledged my presence in any way or notices our departure. I glance at my companion, then stop in my tracks.

"Pinkie, old chap," I say. "Do you really need that napkin tucked into your collar? And are you intending to take that stein home with you? It doesn't actually belong to you, you know."

Pinkie starts guiltily and looks down at the empty beer glass clutched in his hand.

"Oh crikey," he says, tearing off the napkin. "Hang on! I'll be back in a mo. I just…"

I grin to myself as he ducks back into the bright lights of the bar. A minute later he is back. I take one last look at Rose, but her back is towards me. We walk briskly on past the black silhouettes of the townscape.

The buildings we pass are eyeless still, many without roofs. A light breeze hunts through the gaps where houses and shops once stood, but here and there are patches of light behind the windows, and the occasional snatch of music or conversation. People are out on the streets, enjoying the warm evening.

Pinkie is talking earnestly about something, but I scarcely listen. A cold conviction is growing in my heart, and I have the curious sensation of being detached from the scene and merely looking down on it all.

The scrap of driftwood in the river of Time that bears my name is being swept by chance eddies into a new place, whether into shallows or torrents, I cannot tell, and I am powerless to influence it. One phase of my life has come to an end, and it is time to move on.

*Chipping-on-the-Fosse*

At last Adam heard the key turn in the bungalow door. His carer had arrived. She was taking off her light raincoat, hanging it on a hook in the hall and muttering something about the heat.

"Good morning, Judge. And how are we today?" she said, bustling in. She tutted at the litter of papers by his desk where he had been doing some correspondence on the computer the previous evening.

Thankfully she didn't expect a long answer. She had little use for small talk. Adam wondered sometimes how Erica came to be a carer (there was a new name for that function now, but he had forgotten what it was) as she was not by nature *simpatica*. She was a woman of sixty odd, brisk and efficient, and polite enough, but with a hardness about her that made it difficult to warm to her.

He looked at Erica now as she went about her business. His polite enquiries about her life had had little success, but he did know that she was brought up by foster parents. Once she had dropped a tantalizing hint that her birth mother was of aristocratic lineage. He knew that such comforting illusions are not uncommon among people uncertain of their true parentage.

Sometimes, when her work was finished, he could persuade her to sit down and have a cup of tea and a chat. He suspected that she carefully calibrated conversation time into her already substantial fee bill, but his pension had left him very comfortably off and it was of little concern.

She was not his ideal choice of a companion, but he was very lonely without human contact all day. It was over fifteen years since his dear wife Margaret had succumbed to her cruel illness, and very sadly there were no children to comfort his old age.

Now Erica had finished putting away the clean dishes. She took off her apron and folded it neatly away, then accepted his offer to join him in a cup of tea and clicked the kettle on. The raised bump on her forehead, with its faint blue shadow, was very noticeable in the bright sunlight when she sat down. It was apparently the result of a childhood accident, never mentioned.

They spoke as they sometimes did of his time in Germany, a period to which he returned to more and more in his mind as he became less active.

"You have spoken before of your lady friend?" she said. "I think she was called Rose?"

"Yes, Rose." He smiled. "That's right. Clever of you to remember. She has been in my mind a lot lately..."

"Did you ever see her again, Judge?"

He looked away.

"No, never," he said eventually. "We went back to the city once, on holiday. Several years ago now. My wife knew I wanted to see it all again – the haunts of my youth. But so much had changed. A busy, vibrant city, completely rebuilt, with hardly a hint of its terrible past. You would not believe the transformation."

Erica nodded.

"You did not find what became of her?"

"She simply vanished into the massive confusion of post war Europe. We never even really said goodbye." He shook his head. "Have you any idea how many people died in the years after the war? Millions. Mass migrations, genocide, disease, starvation, the chaos of the new boundaries, the repopulation of lands. The armistice might have been signed, but…"

There was a long silence.

"You haven't been back to Germany more recently? Perhaps looking for this lady?"

"No, not since my dear Margaret died," Adam said, "No. I used to think that perhaps one day I might go. But there was little point. And sadly, going abroad isn't really an option for me nowadays."

He relaxed a little then, and they spoke of the difficulties and irritations of travelling in the modern world of over-zealous security precautions. Finally Erica rose to leave, on her way to her next client.

"*Wait!* Don't go, please."

He put an arthritic hand on her arm to detain her. His mind was made up.

She stopped and looked quizzically at him.

"You have something to ask me, Judge?"

"Yes. Will you get my painkillers?" he said, the words coming out slowly. "*These fragments I have shored against my ruins?* You may know the quotation? The pills are my insurance policy. But now – this damned back. Every day I am little more bowed, and so I just can't reach them. I've tried and I've tried. No use."

Now his eyes were tightly shut. She walked over to the bathroom.

"Where are they? Up here? You've never let me look."

She opened the door of the medicine cabinet on the wall, and frowned.

"There seem to be a lot of them. You've been saving up sleeping tablets as well?"

"Erica, I want to take them now. But I need your help."

She stood with the bottle in her hand, looking down on him, her eyebrows lifted in enquiry. She did not show any surprise.

"All of them? Are you quite sure?"

"Yes, I'm quite sure." He groaned and opened his eyes. "What do you think? I'm in constant pain, my back, my knee, my eyes, even my teeth... they all hurt. I'm nearly deaf. I can't see to read for long. I can't even hear the television properly, far less make sense of it. I take no pleasure from my food any more. I dribble. A glass of wine tastes like cough mixture. The only thing I can look forward to is everything getting worse."

*Sans teeth, sans eyes, sans taste, sans everything....*

Erica was staring at him. Her face was expressionless.

Your family? Friends?"

"I have no real family, as you know, only cousins. And very few old friends left alive. All gone now. Only the memories are left. And they will die with me."

He stared with unseeing eyes out of the window to where the midges were dancing in the sunlight above the sunflowers. Two young girls on horseback clip-clopped down the lane at the end of the garden, one laughing at something the other had said. They looked over the hedge and waved to him as usual as they passed, but today he made no response.

Erica shrugged.

"I understand," she said. "I hear the same thoughts from many of my patients at the end. I am sympathetic, you know. In fact, I am known to be very sympathetic... in the right circumstances."

There was a silence.

"Ah yes, of course," said Adam with a start. "I nearly forgot." He gestured towards his desk. "There is an envelope addressed to my lawyer there. Another to my cousin. And one for you. I want you to be able to take a good holiday, you understand? They say the Black Forest can be really very beautiful at this time of the year."

Erica relaxed, the glimmer of a smile on her hard face. Adam had said the right thing.

"I usually check such things in advance," she said. "But with you I shall not trouble. You have always been generous to me, Judge. Yes, perhaps the Black Forest. I have always been drawn to Germany. I don't really know why."

She paused and gestured towards her large handbag.

"Now, I can do a great deal better for you than your bottle of pills. They'll give you a very bad stomach ache, and may take much longer to work than you imagine. You could be in a great deal of pain, and we don't want that, do we?"

Her smile reached her mouth, but not somehow her eyes.

"The injection I shall give you gradually dulls the senses, and is certain. Better, I think?"

Adam could only nod. He was clearly in the hands of an expert. Erica put the bottle of painkillers into her handbag, and brought out a syringe. She loaded it carefully from a small phial of liquid.

"The doctor will invariably ascribe the cause of death to heart failure, without any need for a post mortem."

Adam looked up. Erica was advancing towards him, the syringe in her hand. She was looking directly at him. Her eyes were unblinking, and the blue shadow on her forehead very prominent in the sunlight. He knew now with certainty. Perhaps in his subconscious he had known before, but had pushed the thought away. *The shadow of Hitler.* Well, what did it matter now?

"Yes."

She took his arm and found a vein. Her hand was impersonal and there was no sympathy in her manner. He was just another tick in her case load.

Adam looked away, as he always did. He'd never liked injections. The sun was gilding the heads of the hollyhocks. It was going to be a very hot day.

"Are you ready, Judge?"

"Yes."

The roses would need pruning, and the buddleia too, but someone else would attend to that. It was not a big garden, and quite easy for a fit person to manage.

"There. That's done. Do you want to lie down?"

Erica held the syringe up and wiped it carefully before putting it away in her bag.

"No," Adam said. He looked into her eyes in vain for any sign of sympathy, and turned away. It was hard to speak. "I like looking out of the window."

"As you wish. Goodbye, Judge."

She checked her bag, put her coat over her arm, swept the room with her gaze in a final check, and frowned at the sunlight. Then she left without a backward glance, the door clicking closed behind her.

Somewhere on the windows the bee was still furiously beating its wings. Adam rose to move towards the sound, but he knew there was nothing he could do for the creature. His breathing was getting faster, and he sat back down heavily.

Now his sense of time blurred. The decades fell away.

Somewhere was the smell of ashes, oddly

mixed with perfume. He was struggling to remember what it reminded him of. The smell grew steadily stronger with the buzzing of the bee.

Rose was in the room with him now. The young Rose, laughing with him in the herb garden, with its broken walls and statues, the empty street of eyeless ruined buildings towering behind. Her long brown hair was tumbling down her back, and the sunlight was bringing out the blue of her eyes and of the silk dress that showed off her figure so well.

"Come on, Adam! Let's celebrate being young!"

She was reaching her hand out to him and smiling, her head on one side in the way he recalled so well. Edith Piaf was singing, and he breathed the intoxicating French perfume Rose wore on special occasions. She leant forward and touched her soft lips to his, but his mouth was so dry he couldn't swallow. A buzzing was in his ears and his heart was thumping wildly. He wanted to kiss her and take her hand. He wanted to speak.

"Rose! Rose!"

But now she was fading from his sight and from his grasp, and a black fog was rising, and his balance was going, and he was gliding, gliding away alone, down, down, into a blue horizon, infinitely far away.

*The author retired to the Cotswolds in 2010, after running a well-known retail business in North Wales and Chester for many years. Richard read English and Italian at Liverpool University, and wrote weekly columns for Men's Wear magazine and the Liverpool Daily Post. He has three children.*

While it is fresh in your mind, an online review of this book would be much appreciated.

*Richard's next novel will be called* **In the Shadow of Shakespeare.**